T0267518

Praise for *Skater Boy*

"He was a punk (with a secret soft center). *Skater Boy* is a perceptive, vividly emotional, complicated love story, told with candor and compassion. Can I make it any more obvious that you should drop everything and read it?"

—**Becky Albertalli,** *New York Times* **bestselling author of** *Simon vs. the Homo Sapiens Agenda*

"A poignant unraveling of the binds spun by toxic masculinity. *Skater Boy* kept me rooting for the disaster boy to find his way."

—**Xiran Jay Zhao,** *New York Times* **bestselling author of** *Iron Widow*

"A picture-perfect coming-of-age novel that will skate away with your heart."

—**Eric Geron,** *New York Times* **bestselling author of** *A Tale of Two Princes*

"*Skater Boy* drew me in from the very first page and was absolutely unputdownable! Not only does Nerada turn stereotypes on their head in his brilliantly nuanced debut, but he does it while writing something universally relatable and utterly charming. Wes Mackenzie puts the *oo* in swoony!"

—**Lynn Painter,** *New York Times* **bestselling author of** *Better Than the Movies*

"Nerada offers a nuanced and realistic glimpse into the pressure and the chaos and the growing pains of being a teenager, and what can happen when you open up and share your full, true self. A brilliant debut."

—**Rachael Lippincott,** *New York Times* **bestselling author of** *She Gets the Girl*

"*Skater Boy* is the beautifully written, poignant story of Wes, an angry, lonely boy struggling to find his place in the world. Anthony Nerada deftly handles Wes's character arc as he learns to love himself. An impressive debut."
—**Liz Lawson**, *New York Times* **bestselling author of**
The Agathas* and *The Lucky Ones

"In his witty and vulnerable debut, Nerada reminds us that labels are pointless, love is for everyone and that it is a truth universally known that everybody LOVES a 'bad boy' with a skateboard and a heart of gold. Honest, authentic and charming, *Skater Boy* skillfully highlights that queer kids can't be put into a box! A voice to watch!"
—**Amber McBride, National Book Award finalist and author of *Me (Moth)***

"Wes Mackenzie is one of the most authentic and refreshingly angry main characters I've read in a long time, and I ate up every word of his journey. *Skater Boy* is spectacularly queer and witty, and I have no doubt Anthony Nerada's debut will become a beloved addition to bookshelves everywhere."
—**Robbie Couch**, *New York Times* **bestselling author of *If I See You Again Tomorrow***

"Anthony Nerada shows, with the perfect mix of punks, bros, and ballerinos, that you can't judge a book by its cover, and that sometimes we have to go through the roughest points of our lives to discover truths about ourselves. *Skater Boy* had my heart from the jump!"
—**Jason June**, *New York Times* **bestselling author**

"I have a soft spot for angry gays, and *Skater Boy* delivers one of YA's all-time angriest! Wes is perfectly imperfect: defensive, emotional, and no, he does not have college figured out yet, thank you. Anthony Nerada is a fresh new voice adding to the much-needed growing wave of ill-behaved queer protagonists. I love love LOVED this one!"

—Adam Sass, award-winning author of *The 99 Boyfriends of Micah Summers* and *Your Lonely Nights Are Over*

"A fun, fiery love story for the misunderstood, *Skater Boy* is the nostalgic, opposites-attract gay romance we deserve! A confectionary pop smash that takes inspiration from its namesake, Nerada has crafted a power ballad of a coming out story for the mainstream punk rocker in all of us."

—Steven Salvatore, critically acclaimed author of *And They Lived . . .*

"*Skater Boy* is like a shaken up bottle of teen angst and first love. While examining masculinity and peer pressure, Anthony Nerada captures those complicated feelings of self-discovery and finding your place while providing endless swoons and laughs."

—Robby Weber, author of *I Like Me Better*

SKATER BOY

ANTHONY NERADA

SOHO
TEEN

Published in the United States by Soho Teen
an imprint of Soho Press, Inc.
227 W 17th Street
New York, NY 10011

Library of Congress Cataloging-in-Publication Data

Names: Nerada, Anthony, author.
Title: Skater boy / Anthony Nerada.
Description: New York, NY : Soho Teen, 2024.
Identifiers: LCCN 2023025098

ISBN 978-1-64129-534-5
eISBN 978-1-64129-535-2

Subjects: CYAC: Gay people—Fiction. | Interpersonal relations—Fiction. |
Self-actualization—Fiction. | LCGFT: Romance fiction. | Novels.
Classification: LCC PZ7.1.N46 Sk 2024 | DDC [Fic]—dc23
LC record available at https://lccn.loc.gov/2023025098

Interior design: Janine Agro

Printed in the United States of America

10 9 8 7 6 5 4 3 2 1

To every queer person who has ever changed the pronouns of their favorite song so they could live out a happily ever after— I see you. I hear you. So, sing your damn heart out. 🤟

And to Tim, for being the better half of the greatest love story I'll ever tell.

DEAR READER,

I want you to imagine you're ten years old again. It's 2000-something, you're in the back seat of your family's car, and your favorite song comes on the radio. It's an all-encompassing feeling, the way the hairs on your arms rise, the car suddenly transforming into a sold-out arena. But despite all that joy, you sing a little quieter than your siblings, secretly changing the pronouns to the lyrics you know by heart, so that you can capture in words a world where you are free to be yourself. I couldn't have known then what I was doing, but I'd like to think my debut novel, *Skater Boy*, was born in that moment—amidst carving out a space for myself where I, too, could live a happily ever after through song.

When I first came out in 2013, I thought it was my duty—my obligation—to embody what I perceived to be the defining pillars of the LGBTQIA+ community. And while I did grow to love and appreciate shows like *Will & Grace* and popstars like Lady Gaga, I lost sight of who I was. Writing *Skater Boy* gave me permission to return to myself. It reminded me that there is no one way of being gay. That we can love Broadway *and* My Chemical Romance. That we can paint our nails *and* rock out to Metallica.

At first, I set out to write a light-hearted romantic comedy that loosely paid tribute to a classic pop-punk anthem. But when its main character, Wesley "Big Mac" Mackenzie, revealed his true colors to me, I knew there was so much more to tell. Wes's story—of pushing back on the labels ascribed to him, of navigating through what it means to be out and proud, and of stomping down how he really feels in order to uphold his image—is one experienced by many queer kids, but rarely told. In fact, the only emotion cis teenage boys are encouraged to express is anger. Because anger makes you a "man." A "fighter." Any other emotions only serve to "emasculate" you. It's a slap in the face really, to yearn to express yourself, then be punished when that expression isn't the right one.

In Wes, I wanted to write a character who unapologetically shows his emotions. Who never questions who he is. And while he may come out within these pages, I never wanted that to be the focus. In my eyes, what makes Wes special is the fact that it's not just his sexuality that's holding him back, but the internal conflict of being gay while also being labeled a punk (something he never truly felt he was). In telling Wes's story, in giving a voice to a character who normally doesn't get to be in the spotlight, I want readers to understand that no matter who they are, or what they're interested in, their lives are valid, and they have every right to be here. I wrote *Skater Boy* as much for myself as I did for the queer kids on the outskirts of what society defines as being "acceptably gay"; the ones who are angry and hurt and filled with emotions they can't quite put a name to.

To that closeted kid in the back of his family's car, I want you to know that this one's for you. Your voice deserves to be heard.

Anthony Nerada

1.

GOD SAVE THE AMERICAN IDIOT

I hate people.

They're fake and pretentious, they make assumptions about everything, and no matter how hard they try, eventually, they always let you down. And let's be real, I couldn't care less if they like me back. But when I grab the kid by the collar of his Captain America T-shirt and pin him to the lockers, the pang in my chest is almost enough to make me question how I ended up here.

Almost.

"Hand it over," I growl into his ear, patting his pockets with my free hand.

What can I say? The kid had it coming. He'd been peering out from behind a dumpster when I first spotted him. I was bent at the knee, keying the side of Principal Cohen's car during third period, when the shutter on his phone went off. I'd been caught red-handed. Kids like that, we don't run in the same circles. They have a habit of turning me in. Lucky for me, though, I knew to wait for him outside the principal's office.

The kid never asked why I did it. If he had, I would have told him that I overheard Principal Cohen calling me a lowlife this morning. But I doubt he'd care. Telling the truth won't change anything. It never has.

"Please, I-I don't have the picture anymore, I swear. Tony got to me first and made me delete it." His eyes dart around the hall, searching for help.

It's not that I don't believe him—that does sound like something Big Cheese would do—but I can't just let him go. Stonebridge High's social hierarchy typecast me as a punk the second I moved to town. Whether I like it or not, I have an image to uphold.

I'm not going to lie. Aside from the occasional suspension, being Stonebridge's resident bad guy does have its perks. Not only can I not remember the last time I paid for my own lunch, but no one has ever tried to stop me from skateboarding down the halls between classes. Unless you count last semester, when I traded a joint with the hall monitor in exchange for her silence. You'd think punks would be hot commodities in this age of My Chemical Romance revivals, but we're not. No one wants to mess with the angry redhead in the black leather jacket and faded skate shoes. Except for this kid, apparently.

I shove him harder into the wall, bundling his shirt between my knuckles.

At first, the kid tries to fight back with a weak punch to my arm and a kick above my right knee. But he gives up fast, knowing he doesn't stand a chance. He has no idea that if he'd only kicked a little harder, I would've buckled over in pain. My kneecap is my Achilles' heel, made of more trauma than bone.

I make him empty out his pockets. I would never actually hurt the kid, but the fear in his eyes tells me he doesn't know that.

"You're kidding, right?"

I glance over my shoulder. Mr. Hamilton, the guidance counselor, is in the doorway to his office, his white Nikes glowing under the hallway's fluorescent lights. If he hadn't spoken, I would've missed him entirely—his beige collared shirt and brown corduroy pants blend in seamlessly with the school's walls.

He crosses his arms. "Are you really going to beat someone up on your way to our appointment?"

Confused, I say, "Our what?"

What does Mr. Hamilton think? That I'd actually remembered—let alone planned on attending—the counseling session Principal Cohen sentenced me with for tagging the gymnasium last week? If it weren't for my best friends, Tony and Brad, I wouldn't even be in this position. Sure, I was technically the one who bought the spray cans, but if Tony didn't talk his way out of every situation and Brad wasn't so damn fast, I wouldn't have been the only one to get caught. Besides, why bother going through the motions when Mr. Hamilton knows as well as I do that my future was decided for me a long time ago?

Mr. Hamilton moves his hands to his hips, and I throw my arms up in mock surrender, letting the kid slide to the floor.

I'm not like Tony and Brad. I know when to stand my ground and when to give up. I've been around for seventeen years, long enough to interpret the whole hands-on-hips charade as a telltale sign that if I don't smarten up, I'll be forced to spend lunch as the official garbage picker-upper for the rest of the semester. Just like junior year.

I reach for my skateboard as the kid collects his textbooks on his hands and knees and hurries out of sight.

Mr. Hamilton looks at me through horn-rimmed glasses, smiling like we're the best of friends, which is ironic considering he doesn't give a damn about me. I'm just another name on the list of delinquents he needs to cross off by the end of the school year.

Sighing, I push past him and take a seat, dropping my board in front of me. Mr. Hamilton's office is the size of a porta-potty with outdated wooden lacquered walls and barely enough room for the filing cabinet in the corner. Next to his desktop computer is a small, barred window that—while there to keep us safe—reminds me I'm serving time.

To make matters worse, Mr. Hamilton always smells like a cloud of body spray. He's probably convinced it makes him relatable.

"I won't sugarcoat this, Mr. Mackenzie," he says, swiveling in his chair. "Your grades are horrendous . . ." His voice trails off as he looks down the bridge of his nose at me, acting as if I should be surprised. Appalled, even.

I'm not, though. Not really. I've skipped more classes than I've attended this semester.

I don't know.

School's stupid.

Why would I intentionally sit through a teacher rambling on for hours when I can find any answer on Google in less than ten minutes, all while never leaving the comfort of my own bed? Even if you so much as glance at your phone in class or get distracted and sneak a picture of the season's first snowfall, it's taken away for the rest of the day. Total BS. And when said teacher announces to the whole class that you'll never amount to anything, it doesn't matter how much effort you put in when all you'll ever get are Cs and a "needs improvement" evaluation.

It's not like school prepares you for real life either. It didn't teach me how to change a tire on the side of the interstate in the middle of the night. Or how to sock away a few extra dollars each month for a rainy day. Ma taught me all that and more. Seriously, when would I ever need to know what the length of a triangle is? That's what rulers are for.

Mr. Hamilton leers at me.

Right about now, it'd be smart to say something like, "I hear your concern, sir, but I'm failing to understand the importance of the underlying issue."

Grown-ups love that. That flowery language shit.

But I don't.

"What's your point?" I shrug, fixating on the stray chin hair he missed shaving this morning.

"My point, Mr. Mackenzie, is that if you don't get your act together, you're not going to graduate."

He keeps using my last name like it's a threat, as if addressing me by my dad's name will scare me into submission. Joke's on him, though, because I barely knew the guy.

Still, my stomach twists in a knot.

I know I should show concern regarding my impending doom. I should be polite and address my elder with respect. That's what we're taught to do, anyway.

Instead, I say, "Are you shitting me?"

"*Language*, Mr. Mackenzie."

If you haven't already guessed, words and I don't get along. At least, not when it comes to talking to people. When I want to be funny, I get the tone all wrong, and people think I'm mocking them. When I want to sound sophisticated, I come across temperamental with a complete lack of self-awareness.

It's even worse with Authority Figures™.

Growing up, teachers used to think I had something called oppositional defiant disorder, but that wasn't it. I just can't find the right words to get my point across, which makes me angry, which makes me lash out, which makes me angry because I've lashed out. On top of everything, while adults were always so quick with a diagnosis—thinking they could medicate me into obedience—no one ever asked why I was so angry in the first place. Because what does a child know, right?

I'm not a victim or anything like that, but it's a vicious cycle.

To stay calm, I pull my black beanie further down my forehead and count in multiples of three in my head. It's something I've done since I was a kid.

Three times one is three.

Three times two is six.

Three times three is nine.

"If I were you, I'd take winter break to seriously consider what your next steps are going to be. The deadline for college applications is sooner than you think."

I twist the hairs on my left eyebrow, much like a villain would do to his mustache in a campy B-rated action movie. Except I'm not plotting Mr. Hamilton's demise. At least, not yet.

I've been told a million times I won't graduate at the rate I'm going. It's not exactly Breaking News at this point. But the thought of repeating senior year without Big Cheese and Bud—of watching them walk across the stage without me—makes me want to skateboard out of here and never look back. Or, at the very least, smoke a joint.

"What can I do?" I ask, deflating in my seat.

I regret it immediately.

Even a "lowlife" like me can see Mr. Hamilton's eyes gleam, like he's waited his entire career for this exact moment. I'm pissed I'm the one that gave it to him.

"Well, for starters, I'd pick up a textbook now and then."

It's meant to be funny—he actually pauses for my reaction—but I'm not willing to give him the satisfaction of a fake laugh. Not on the merits of a weak dad joke.

I tap my foot against the underside of my skateboard. Though all I want to do is make some quick retort, I know this man can prevent me from graduating. And since graduating is the only way I can put this hellhole behind me, I have to choose my battles.

When I don't respond, Mr. Hamilton opens a drawer to his right and slams a pile of college brochures—wrapped in red ribbon—onto the desk. Like he's Santa Claus and Christmas has come early.

"I wouldn't worry about any of these ones," he scoffs, taking most of the pile away with unnecessary flourish. "Given your track record, you don't stand a chance."

I crack a smile and feel the corner of my mouth lifting with pride. My rap sheet of detentions is longer than any of my academic achievements. The guys and I beat Austin McNally's '06 record last year.

After Mr. Hamilton's finished sorting through the pile, only three brochures remain: one for a community college in the next county over and two with such terrible stock images I don't even bother committing their names to memory.

"I don't want to go to college," I huff, flipping my skate-board up between my knees. "I just want to graduate."

I'm familiar with the look Mr. Hamilton gives me next. I've seen it from adults my whole life. Though the order can be, and usually is, interchangeable, it's always the same thing: lips pursed, arms crossed, followed by some snarky remark about "not wanting to believe that."

"I hope you don't mean that," Mr. Hamilton says, folding his arms.

It's like fucking clockwork.

His eyebrows are about to spark, that's how close they are. "Do you have any *passions*, Mr. Mackenzie?"

I pause, biting the inside of my lip.

This question always gets me. When we're kids, adults love to ask us what we want to be when we grow up, which is basically what Mr. Hamilton is asking now.

I was seven the first time I had to answer that. It was Career Day at school, and Malcolm Weaver's dad came to talk to the class about being a police officer. But I didn't want to listen. I already knew what that entailed. Ma and I had just moved to Valentine, Ohio to escape the officer that, up until recently, I called my dad. And this one was no different; he walked deliberately between the desks, his boots thudding over the linoleum like they carried the life sentences of his arrests. I felt his breath on the back of my neck as he spoke, felt my knees trembling against my seat.

When it was my turn to speak, I'd said I wanted to be Percy Jackson because Percy Jackson was *the man* growing up.

Sure, I got a few laughs from the room, but Officer Weaver wasn't amused. He rapped his knuckles along my desk and asked again, slower this time, like I hadn't comprehended the question.

That shut me up real quick.

I learned right then and there that I wasn't allowed to be the Riptide-wielding, badass demigod I wanted to be most in life. Because the truth is, when adults ask that question, they don't really want to know what you have to say.

I cross my legs, pretending to ponder my answer. "Ma says I'd make a good lawyer with all the arguing I do."

Mr. Hamilton's hollow laugh fills the air with the scent of stale coffee breath. "Sorry, kiddo, but you'll never be a lawyer. Not with these grades."

Did I mention I hate this man?

He pulls out a copy of my most recent report card, holding it between two fingers like it's covered in the Black Plague. Even from across the desk, I can see it's riddled with Ds. "Math seems to be your best bet. How about accounting?"

The first thought that comes to mind is Ma's mind-numbing fiancé, Tad, who popped the question last week at Red Lobster after one too many margaritas and a heated discussion about amortizations.

"I'd rather watch paint dry for the rest of my life," I deadpan, thinking of all the tax conversations I've suffered through in the last three years.

My phone buzzes inside my pocket, so I dig it out and find a text from Tony.

Where the hell are you?

When I look up, Mr. Hamilton is glaring at me.

"Sorry," I say, though I'm not sure if I'm apologizing for having my phone out or for insinuating his career suggestion was quite possibly the worst outcome known to mankind. I guess it works for both.

"Wesley." Mr. Hamilton gets up and sits on the edge of his desk as if to reason with me. "Can I call you Wes?" Without waiting for my reply, he continues, "I used to be you, Wes. The slacker, the"—Oh, *God*, not air quotes—"'punk.' The one whose only concern for the future was what beer he'd buy on the weekend with his fake ID."

Okay, that's not even a question. It's Budweiser. It's always Budweiser. Brad would kill me otherwise.

"But then I straightened out. I ditched my deadbeat friends, found the perfect girl, and got it together." He shakes my forearm at the end of his sentence, like doing so will cure me of my so-called punkness.

I side-eye him, wondering at what point touching my arm becomes unwelcome bodily contact. The answer is immediately.

"It's your turn now, son. I'm passing the torch." He grabs the college brochures and hands them to me like he's Emperor Palpatine tempting Luke Skywalker to join the Dark Side.

Just then, the bell rings, and I jump out of my seat because a)

I want to get as far away from this torch ceremony as humanly possible and b) it isn't something I hear on a regular basis since I'm always skipping class, so it legit startles me.

"Saved by the bell, it seems. Get to class, Wes, and if I catch you skipping again, so help me, I will drop-kick your ass."

"You can't talk to me like that," I say, throwing my skateboard to the ground. I relish the sound of its wheels screeching against the floor.

"I think I just did." Mr. Hamilton snaps his fingers, motioning for me to pick up my board. "Oh, and Mr. Mackenzie?"

I turn on my heels.

"Detention first thing Monday morning when you get back from winter break."

"What the hell? Why?"

"You don't honestly think I'd let you slam a kid into the lockers without consequence, do you?" He doesn't wait for my answer before closing the door behind him.

Speak of the Devil. I catch the kid from earlier snickering down the hall, having watched our entire exchange from afar.

"What are you looking at?" I bark, charging at him with my skateboard.

The kid jumps, dropping a black-and-white notebook, and races around the corner.

I watch him flee down the hall as Mr. Hamilton's words echo between my ears. *If you don't get your act together, you're not going to graduate.*

Groaning, I pick up the kid's notebook.

"What am I supposed to do with this?" I call after him.

The notebook's bursting at the seams, held together by an elastic band. It looks too important to throw away, so I shove it in my backpack and chuck the college brochures into the nearest trashcan.

There's something symbolic in the way the brochures fall

among the garbage—like I'm tossing away a future I could never live up to anyway—that makes me pause. The words "Community College" stick out from behind a crumpled piece of paper, as though begging me to reconsider. I glance around the hall to make sure no one's around before pulling out my phone and snapping a photo.

When the bell rings again, I contemplate heading to world history but decide against it. There's really no point since I didn't complete last night's homework and I'm not in the mood to explain why picking up a last-minute shift to help Ma pay rent was more important than some stupid assignment about the Great Depression.

Mr. Hamilton can go to hell anyway.

This whole situation is completely out of reach.

Graduation.

College.

Getting my shit together.

But above all else, the one thing next to impossible in his grand illusion of life is the girlfriend part.

The wooing of a woman.

The straightening up and straightening out.

Because despite the leather jacket and skateboard and disheveled bedhead, I'm as gay as they come.

Not that anyone would know.

2.

LIFESTYLES OF THE CLOSETED & CONFUSED

I hold in a deep breath as I burst outside, letting the school's side door slam behind me.

Being gay didn't happen overnight. And I'm not naïve enough to think it's a choice. There are enough bigots in the world to think that for me.

Realizing who I am happened gradually, over time.

The first step in my sexual awakening was Tom Hardy in *Venom*. It was Brad's eleventh birthday, and while Brad and Tony took turns pretending to be Eddie Brock and flinging each other around the room, I bawled my eyes out beneath my sleeping bag that night. I didn't understand why they made such a beautiful person transform into a monster when all he was trying to do was stop a power-hungry billionaire from taking over the world.

Screw Mr. Hamilton and his heteronormative equation for success. Does he honestly think that finding a woman will fix all my problems? That it'll somehow establish my worth? I hate that his natural default was to assume I'm straight.

And screw college applications for making me feel like I have to prove myself. To my teachers. To Mr. Hamilton. To an admissions board whose only concern is the money I'd contribute to their year-end bonuses. I don't need to put myself or Ma in debt for the rest of our lives because someone somewhere said that education is the key to a good life.

I can't believe that for a brief second, I actually considered telling Mr. Hamilton I enjoy photography. It started back in Louisiana when Ma gave me my first disposable camera. I used to love taking random photos of things like the wasp's nest next to the playground or my dad's face every time he screamed at the TV. Of course, that was before he took it away for distracting him from his baseball game. But I never got over the fact that when you take a picture, you can be anyone. A realist. A cynic. A visionary with a story to tell. No one judges the person behind the camera; they analyze the image for what it is. Art. And there's something freeing about that. But I know what Mr. Hamilton would've said. That I'd need to join the photography club to be taken seriously. That grainy pictures on my phone wouldn't increase my chances of getting into a good school (or improve my "attitude").

At least I don't have to deal with him for the next two weeks now that it's winter break. Headphones in, I blare "Carpe Diem Baby" by Metallica as I jump on my skateboard and careen through town. I take the long way home to clear my head, past the only 7-Eleven in Valentine and the abandoned elementary school me and the guys used to break into to blaze before the cops caught on.

When I make it to Main Street, my hands are so stiff from the cold I fumble with my keys.

Ma and I live in a two-bedroom apartment above Mr. Fong's Laundromat, which means the stench of wet clothes and bleach are permanently stuck in my nose. Mr. Fong has been our landlord for ten years, so we get the friends and family discount on laundry. In the summer, the air smells so strongly of detergent it masks the dumpster sitting in the alleyway below my bedroom window.

A man with ash-gray whiskers and a matching husky sits on the pavement next to the laundromat's entrance.

"Howdy, Ray," I say, handing him a packet of trail mix I snagged from a kid at lunch.

"Thank you kindly, Wes." Ray peels the package open and tosses a cashew to Roxie. The dog swallows it whole and stares up at me for more.

"That's all I've got today, Rox."

I jiggle open the lock on the building's gate and climb the narrow stairwell to our apartment. It isn't fancy by any means—Ma and I share a bathroom with a broken shower-head and mint green tiles, and you have to kick the fridge to stop it from sounding like a drunken lawn mower—but it's home. When we first moved in, Ma painted the walls yellow because it reminded her of Spain. Not that she's ever been; she was just inspired by some aesthetic board on Pinterest. A rust-colored La-Z-Boy that once belonged to apartment 2A sits in front of the family room TV next to the pink leather couch Ma found gently used on Facebook Marketplace.

As I throw my uniform on—black slacks and a T-shirt with a Dalíesque melting pizza slice on the front—I shrug off the worst of school and slip back into my comfort zone. Every Friday is the same routine: I get home after class, make a quick dinner out of whatever I can find, and head to work for my four o'clock shift at Vincenzo's Pizzeria.

I'm about to leave when Ma comes barging through the apartment door with an armful of what looks like branches. I have no idea how she fit them through the stairwell.

"Hey, Ma."

"Oh, hi, Stevia," she calls out as the door swings shut behind her. "Look what I found . . ."

I smile as she tells me about her day. Calling me "Stevia" is Ma's way of "going against the masses." She's never been a fan of "hi, honey" and "hi, sweetie" moms.

Ma has the same fiery red hair as me, tied in a loose pony-tail that rests over her left shoulder. It's always reminded me of burning embers in a dying fire. We both have a light spat-tering of freckles along our nose that stand out over our white skin. Where her eyes are blue, mine are hazel, a blend of honey amber and green. People have said that my eyes make me look approachable. That is, until they actually approach me.

Ma teeters on one foot now as she takes off her shoes, pre-ferring a comfortable pair of Crocs over anything fashionable. As she shimmies out of her winter coat, I notice a splatter of soup over the new blouse she bought on consignment last week.

Since moving to Valentine, Ma has spent her afternoons at a local shelter providing meals to displaced people deal-ing with substance abuse, all while working at the fabric store Quilts & Things. On top of that, she somehow finds time to host a *Golden Girls* drag show at the coffee shop down the street. Ma's been my role model my entire life, and she never even graduated high school. Mr. Hamilton can threaten me all he wants; he pales in comparison to her.

". . . I'm going to spray-paint them silver and cover them in glitter for the holidays!" Ma continues, snapping me back to the present. She crouches on the floor, emptying an old terra-cotta pot filled with random buttons and artfully stuffing the branches inside. "You know, 'all that glitters is not gold.'"

"Right," I say slowly, nodding my head. "How Shakespear-ean of you."

Ma smirks and in her best, but worst, British accent says,

"Yes, quite." She looks down at her watch, a plain, brown, no-name brand I bought her last Christmas, and frowns. "Don't tell me you skipped class again?"

I curse under my breath. I thought I'd wasted enough time before making my way home from school. "I didn't feel like going." I shrug, grabbing the remote from the coffee table and clenching it in a death grip.

"You know how much I hate it when you do that. Getting an education is important, Wes." Ma stops what she's doing to get a better look at me. "Do you want to talk about it?"

"Definitely not," I mutter as I flick mindlessly through the channels.

In my peripheral, I see Ma fold her arms. If I don't relent, she'll launch into one of her many lectures. Like the time she sat me down as a kid and walked me through the intricacies of teen pregnancy with a PowerPoint presentation she'd made the night before.

"Wesley," she whispers.

"There's not much to say," I sigh, remembering Principal Cohen's words. "No one at Stonebridge sees me as anything but a lowlife. 'Your grades are holding you back.' 'You're not taking life seriously.' 'You won't graduate if you keep this up.'"

The weight of my confession crushes me. I curl my toes inward to the point of aching.

"Well, like I've told you," Ma says, "if you applied yourself instead of—oh, I don't know—setting things on fire and arguing with your teachers, you might actually find you like school more than you thought."

"Maaaaaa," I drone, knocking the back of my head against the wall. "Can we not do this right now?"

"I'm just saying, what other people say about you doesn't matter! You are so much more than that."

Ma pulls me into a hug, though my arms stay at my sides.

I roll my eyes but eventually give in and wrap my hands around her. I bury my face into her hair, breathing in notes of patchouli and cinnamon. "Easy for you to say. You're my ma."

In my head, I tell myself that this is it. That I'm finally going to admit that I'm gay. It's the perfect chance to do so—we're already holding on to each other, so we can skip right over the "gushy accepting parent" speech and move on.

Truthfully, I've wanted to tell her for a while now.

I've just never found the courage to.

Besides, we don't normally talk about our feelings unless it's in a self-deprecating, flippant kind of way. Since it's only the two of us, we never bring up how we're really feeling in case we make it awkward and push the other away. And while I don't think me being gay would necessarily come as a shock—I mean, we spend more nights watching *The Golden Girls* than any straight guy would be comfortable admitting—something stops me. Because once it's out there, once I've acknowledged the truth, I can't take it back. Ma might be okay with gay people, but it's always different when it's your own kid.

And honestly, so what if I'm hiding a piece of myself from her? Ma's the only family I have. And I *like* what we have. It's familiar. Safe. Why would I risk even the slightest chance of ruining that? Especially now that Tad's proposal is looming over us like a dark gray cloud, waiting for the right moment to wash away everything we've built.

I sink into the La-Z-Boy as the *Golden Girls* theme song starts playing from the TV.

Like Dorothy Zbornak and Sophia Petrillo, Ma and I are a dynamic duo. It's all we've ever known. Or all we care to remember.

From what I do remember, my dad never truly loved us. Not in the way a dad should. Ma used to spend her mornings getting me ready for school while covering up the bruises he'd given her the night before. When I turned seven, she packed our bags, woke me up in the middle of the night, and drove until the sun set the following day.

Our journey ended in Valentine, fourteen hours north of Louisiana, because Ma liked the sound of it. "Valentine for my Valentine," she said.

As we passed the city-limit sign painted with baby cherubs and a crescent moon, she kissed me on the nose and promised everything would be okay. We spent the night freezing, courtesy of a busted heater, in a ratty motel off the interstate. The only good thing to come from that time was discovering my first leather jacket under the motel bed. For the next two years, I rarely took it off.

Back then, I used to have this fantasy where my dad would stumble into our apartment, a cloud of cigarette smoke clinging to his clothes, the way he always did. He'd hug me tight and promise to change, and we'd welcome him back with open arms. How messed up is that?

"Remember, we're going to the ballet tomorrow night with Tad and Hannah."

Dammit. For one blissful moment, I'd almost forgotten about Tad. I stick out my tongue, warranting one of Ma's affectionate punches.

"You love *The Nutcracker*." She nods her head facetiously like I'm supposed to agree, like I'm supposed to love the ballet when we both caught each other falling asleep during last year's production.

"Of course," I say, smacking my forehead, "because there's nothing I'd rather do on a Saturday night than take a nap in a theater full of rich snobs while a girl gets chased by a dancing mouse."

Ma punches me in the arm again and snorts.

I rub my bicep. "That one hurt."

"You'll get over it." She smiles, playing with the skin on her ring finger. "Speaking of Tad . . ."

"Nope. Not happening."

Ma's lips form a thin line. She's brought up the proposal every day since it's happened. I know she wants my approval before deciding, but I'm not ready to have that conversation yet. Or ever, for that matter. How do you tell your own mother that the person she chose to be with is literally the most boring man on the planet?

"Wesley," Ma drones.

"Tamara."

She clasps her hands in front of her. "We have to discuss this."

"I really don't think we do," I say, checking the time on my phone. "I gotta go." I stand up quickly, adjusting the bottom of my shirt and grabbing my skateboard from the hall.

I'm at the door when Ma whistles at me. I whip around to find her standing there, holding my red apron in her hand.

I kiss the top of her head and say, "Thank you for being a friend."

To some, it may only be the *Golden Girls* theme song, but it's come to symbolize our relationship. How even though we went to hell and back, we made it through together.

3.

TEENAGE DIRTBAGS

"Where were you fourth period?"

Tony slaps me on the back, leaving a flour handprint on my shirt.

"Probably wanking off the quarterback," Brad snorts as he enters the kitchen with his apron hanging loosely around his neck. He takes a swig from a blue water bottle before stroking it suggestively. Tony keels over with laughter.

They're always doing this. Making thinly veiled jokes. Though I don't think either of them suspects I'm gay, I clench my jaw every time I let them get away with it.

"Shut up, man." I kick at Brad's shin, then lower my head in shame. "Hamilton got me."

I've never been caught skipping class in all my years of school. Knowing the guys, I'll never live it down.

"Big Mac's lost his touch!" Tony says, throwing me into a headlock.

Tony "Big Cheese" Pecorino and I have been best friends since I got into my first fight at school. Shortly after moving to Valentine, some fifth grader thought it'd be funny to make a joke about Ma. Before he even had a chance to defend himself, I was tackling him to the ground, and a crowd was forming around us. Tony was the only one to notice that while my bruises may not have been visible like the other kid's, I was hurting too. He stuck by my side after that.

No matter where he is, Tony always wears AirPods and chooses to shout over the music blaring in his ears. He has olive skin, messy black curls, and the beginnings of a mustache he won't shut up about. He's also freakishly tall, which only makes being in his headlock worse. Tony's dream is to one day become a famous chef and turn Vincenzo's—his family's business—into a globally recognized name. Even if we're still struggling to crack "Valentine's Top Ten Spots to Eat" on Tripadvisor.

Over the years, Tony's family has been on the brink of bankruptcy more times than I can count. Tony doesn't let it get to him, but you can see it in the way the rest of his family walks; their chins lowered to their chests, their shoulders slumped to the point of being bad for their health. When the pandemic hit, Vincenzo's struggled to stay afloat. Tony blames all their misfortune on the firm, Sardinian cheese their name originates from, insisting his family invented it. When Brad and I try to correct him, that cheese doesn't work like that, he slaps us upside the head.

As for Brad, well, he's "Bud" for a reason.

Bradley Jacobsen came into our lives freshman year with a blond buzzcut, a backward baseball hat I've never seen him without, and an unhealthy obsession with the Cleveland Browns. Brad is built like a linebacker, though he's so quiet on his feet he can sneak up on anyone without them noticing. He's always pressuring Tony and me to take the two-hour drive up to the city to watch the Browns play—and when we do, Tony always ditches us for girls he picks up at the concession stand, and I'm left with Brad, who spends the entire fourth quarter yelling at the refs and arguing with the drunk guys in the bleachers behind us.

When we were fifteen, Brad's sister bootlegged a twenty-four-pack of Budweiser for us because that was what all the guys in her grade drank. He spent the entire night throwing up in the downstairs bathroom, thus earning his nickname.

"Did Big Mac get a spanking?" He teases me now, slapping the ball of pizza dough in front of him while Tony chokes on a mouthful of Dr Pepper.

"Give it to me, Big Mac," Tony mocks.

"Yeah, you want to see?" I start to pull down my waistband, cringing at the lengths I'll go to for an easy laugh. The guys shield their eyes.

Big Mac, that's me. As in, Wesley *Mac*kenzie.

In the spring of sophomore year, Ma and I were denied EBT and didn't have much money for food. I remember always being hungry. That was also around the time I started hitting up kids for their lunches. The granola bars from the nurse's station weren't cutting it anymore. On Wednesdays, I made a habit of stealing McDonald's from some kid at school. I'm not proud of what I did, but after a while, "Big Mac" stuck.

The three of us form The Tripod, a name we came up with back when one of Tony's brothers handed him down a beat-up telescope for Christmas. That winter, Tony made us watch the lunar eclipse, despite it being minus twenty out. Even though his obsession with space was short-lived—after some girls made fun of him, and he smashed the telescope into pieces—The Tripod remained. It's corny as hell, but that didn't stop us from going to the local tattoo parlor where one of Brad's cousins worked and getting three interlocking triangles tattooed on the backs of our right calves.

Tony assumes his position at the kitchen counter and smacks the printer on the wall as it pumps out the first orders of the night. I place my skull ring next to my phone on a shelf lined with half-empty salt and pepper shakers, and we form a factory line: Tony as the kneader of dough, I the swirler of sauce, and Brad the topper of toppings.

Most people would hate working on Friday night, but Vincenzo's Pizzeria has become my home away from home. I love Ma, I do, but when I'm at work with my friends, I get to step out of my life for a few hours. When we're up to our necks in orders, I don't have time to think about how much the gas bill is this month or how I need to get my grades up or risk having to take biology again next semester. When I'm in the zone, nothing matters except pumping out what we hope will be voted the best pizza in town someday. School never crosses my mind.

"Bud, the mushrooms!" Tony's dad pokes his head through the kitchen window. "You forgot the mushrooms!"

Vincenzo Pecorino is the typical Italian godfather if Vito Corleone were to quit the mafia and devote his life to pizza dough and tomato sauce. If he tilted his head any farther, his thick, black mustache would catch fire on the heater.

"Why are you busting my balls, Mr. P? I got it!" Brad huffs, grabbing the pizza and flinging some hastily chopped mushrooms on top. "Who orders raw mushrooms anyway?" He goes to hand the pizza back through the window when I reach out and stop him.

"Hold on a sec," I say, brushing my hands over my apron. I grab my phone from the shelf and open Instagram.

"Not this again," Bud groans.

Last summer, I took over posting on the pizzeria's Instagram page after Vincenzo noticed me always taking pictures of the food. I've only built up a few dozen followers since then, but it's given me a chance to flex my photography skills and, if anything, hammer out a good pizza pun every now and then.

"Dude, shut up and help me." I instruct Brad to lift one of the slices with a metal pizza server while I snap a close-up of the raw mushrooms. Satisfied with the image, I caption it with *Customizing orders on a knead-to-know basis* and click Share.

Vincenzo grabs the pizza from the window, swearing under his breath in Italian as he heads back into the restaurant.

"Boys, listen," Tony shouts over his music, pulling his phone out from his back pocket. "Crimson Sorrow is playing downtown at the Luxe tomorrow night. Should we test our luck?"

I try my hardest not to roll my eyes. Though he doesn't say it, I know what Tony is thinking. Because when is he ever not thinking it? He'll want to get wasted, pick up some chicks, and sneak in. It's the same old tired routine, weekend after weekend.

"I'm in!" Bud says.

They start air jamming out in their spots, Brad's hat flying off, Tony wiping his forehead with the back of his hand.

Crimson Sorrow's an indie metal band from Akron that we've been playing on repeat for months. While they're no Metallica, they're on their way to quickly becoming the next big thing to come out of Ohio.

When they turn to me to play bass, I continue swirling sauce on the dough in front of me without looking up. "Can't."

They both freeze. Brad raises his arms and opens his fists like he's dropped his drumsticks. Tony narrows his eyes. "What do you mean you *can't*?"

"I can't," I repeat, shrugging. "I've got a family thing."

Before they can argue, the printer spits out a series of orders like it's gagging on one of those endless rainbow tissues magicians pull from their sleeves. We take our positions in silence. Tony kneads the dough quicker, I tighten my sauce swirls, and

Brad flicks pepperoni faster than any knife-throwing assassin I've ever seen. We pump out pizza after pizza, making it a game by closing our eyes and passing off each order by intuition alone. We're completely in sync.

I wonder what Mr. Hamilton would think if he saw me now. Would he be impressed that I've found somewhere I truly belong? Or would he scoff if I said I'm perfectly content slinging pizzas for the rest of my life in the company of "deadbeats" like Tony and Brad?

The Tripod may annoy the hell out of me, but they're my best friends. My only friends.

So why can't I say it?

Why do my palms sweat at the thought of talking about my sexuality with the guys? If I could look them both in the eye and tell them the truth, tell them that nothing needs to change between us, maybe it wouldn't? Maybe I could finally start feeling okay about everything. But I've heard their comments. I've seen how they react when they're uncomfortable. They shut down and put up walls. Just like I do.

I can't imagine being the one who jeopardizes our friendship, the one that suddenly springs this on them after all this time. I'd lose their trust. And I'm afraid I'd lose them altogether.

"What's the deal, Big Mac?" Tony asks a few hours later as we divvy up closing duties for the night. My right knee seizes. Did I say something out loud without realizing it? "What could possibly be more important than Crimson Sorrow?" He lines a tray with fresh batches of dough for tomorrow and turns to face me, not noticing when I let go of my breath.

"Yeah," Bud adds, lifting himself up onto the counter I just finished sanitizing. He drinks from his water bottle, watching a recap of tonight's football game on his phone when he should be helping us close.

"Son of a—" I grunt, swatting at his hand with a damp

cloth. "We're going to *The Nutcracker* with Tad again. His boss's daughter is in it this year or something."

Tony and Brad wrinkle their noses at each other and burst out laughing. Tony races into the broom cabinet and, in the time it takes him to come back, has somehow fashioned a makeshift tutu out of a garbage bag and hoisted it around his waist. He arches his arms into the air and twirls around the kitchen.

"Save me, Nutcracker," Tony says, pretending to faint into Bud's arms.

"Assholes." I sucker punch them both in the thigh and head to the staff room to fetch my jacket.

We leave through the back, grabbing our skateboards and locking up behind us.

"Promise you'll save me a dance," Tony calls after me, batting his eyes.

I give him the finger and leave in the opposite direction. When I glance back and see them at the side of the road—the orange haze of a streetlamp illuminating them from above—they're still twirling around and stumbling in the snow, laughing.

And this is why under no circumstances will I ever tell them my secret.

4.

COMPLICATED AF

The next night, Ma and I are waiting on the curb outside the laundromat as Tad parallel parks his old, beat-up Mustang. I don't get why he tries to impress Ma. There aren't even any other cars parked out front, so he could've just pulled up.

After throwing the emergency brake on, Tad smiles at me through the window and pats the seat next to him, insisting I sit up front. I bulge my eyes out at Ma, trying to nonverbally communicate that that's the last thing I want to do right now, but she ignores me and climbs into the backseat.

I jimmy the handle—up twice, down once, and back and forth—before I'm able to open the door. Tad calls his Mustang vintage, but it's a POS. Some of the seats are even missing headrests, which means spending the entire car ride hunched over like we're some kind of gremlin entourage.

In the back, Tad's daughter, Hannah, bounces in her car seat like she's on her way to freaking Disney World. *The Nutcracker* is all she's been talking about for the last week. Hannah is five years old, with light brown skin from her late mother's side and even browner eyes. She's wearing her favorite pink tutu from after-school dance lessons. In a gentle voice, Ma tells her to sit still through the bobby pins tucked between her teeth as she pulls Hannah's hair into a ballet bun.

It's not that Tad and Ma wouldn't be good together. He has a stable, albeit boring, job. He showers Hannah with love and affection. And for some reason, he always makes Ma laugh. It's just . . . complicated. The first dad in my life didn't exactly work out for us. And it took Ma a really long time to trust men again. But we've come a long way since then. Sure, money is tight, and we may struggle sometimes, but we always make it work. So why fix what isn't broken?

Like me, Tad is white and wears a leather jacket for every occasion, which makes me reconsider my choice of armor every time we're forced to leave the house together. In his "heydays," as he likes to call them, Tad was the drummer in a rock band known as The Incisors. They got their name from one of the band member's dentistry textbooks and put on shows at weekend farmers markets and nightclubs across Idaho, where he grew up. His hair rests above his shoulders, and his voice is permanently raspy from singing at odd hours of the night. Despite having shaved this morning, Tad looks like a caveman who's just discovered fire.

"You smell like smoke," Hannah says to me, gasping like a fish out of water, as she sticks her head out the window for air. She doesn't know the difference yet between cigarettes and marijuana, and I won't be the one to educate her.

"You smell like a kid who's getting coal for Christmas." I reach behind my seat and tickle her. When she threatens to pee, I tickle her harder. Like I'd be the one cleaning up her mess.

I rest my forehead on the window, letting the glass meld

with my skin, in anticipation of what's to come. Tad's been in our lives for three years now, but he and I are still very much in the "getting to know you" phase. Though the ride to the theater isn't long, he somehow manages to squeeze in a game of Twenty Questions.

"How's school going?"

"Fine."

"Work busy?"

"Yup."

"Cold out, isn't it?"

"It's December, Tad."

I've made it pretty clear I want nothing to do with him—I sneak out of the apartment to hang with The Tripod whenever he's over, I pick up extra shifts on nights when I know he'll stop by after work—but the guy refuses to give up. Even now, he leans forward with every answer I give him, shimmying in his seat like this is all a fun game for him, like every day is another chance to peel back one of my layers. It reminds me so much of Mr. Hamilton I want to barf.

By the time we've reached the theater, I've had all I can take.

"Oh, look, we're here!" I shout a little too loudly as we turn into the parking lot.

There's a lineup of cars waiting for the parking attendant to point them over to a spot, but I jump out before Tad can grill me again. Ma glares at me from the backseat, but I pretend not to see her, busying myself by warming my hands with my breath. Hannah flings the door open once they've parked and bulldozes into my leg. I toss her over my shoulder like she's a rag doll and carry her to the entrance.

As I glance around the theater's courtyard, a sizeable lump forms in the back of my throat. Everyone's done up to the nines, in long, flowy dresses and suits we can't afford. The class separation is written on our clothes. Tad has a brown tweed blazer on under his jacket that he regularly wears to work, and Ma's got a lavender shawl draped over her arms so no one can see her dress is really a blouse and skirt. I set Hannah down, and she skips into the theater ahead of us, completely unaware of the elitism inherent in ballet.

I tug the hem of my white collared shirt down to hide the fact that I'm not wearing a belt.

"Hey, Wes."

I turn around at the sound of Tad's voice, a scowl already forming on my face.

He looks at me with a sheepish grin and hands me a ticket. "Can I offer you some advice?"

"If you must." I clench my fists inside my pockets, using the moment to hike up my pants.

Tad scratches behind his ear. "Let yourself have some fun tonight, okay? It's not about all this," he says, waving his hand dismissively at the people around us.

He must have noticed me surveying the crowd. I hate that I let my walls down enough for him to sneak in. Who does this guy think he is? Just because he proposed to Ma doesn't mean he knows what's best for me. The thought of calling him Dad sends chills up my spine.

"Sure, Tadpole, whatever you say." My nostrils flare as I snatch the ticket from his hands, then push past the line to go find our seats.

I'd never admit it to anyone, but Walter Prescott Theater is one of my favorite places in all of Valentine despite the class warfare. It's an exact replica of an old heritage building on Hollywood Boulevard in LA, complete with alabaster columns, ruby-red suede chairs that reek of better days, and a *Phantom of the Opera* chandelier that could very well fall on the audience at any moment. When Ma and I first arrived in town, they used to play old movie musicals every Sunday for a dollar. We were sometimes the only people in the theater, which was awesome because you can never fully enjoy *Les Misérables* until you've shouted "One Day More" at the top of your lungs. The memory makes me grin as I settle into my seat.

I can't exactly share my love of Broadway with Brad and Tony. Even if it's a TikTok video, any time I've tried to show them anything remotely musical-related, all Tony can do is comment on how hot the performer is, and Brad always loses interest after the first few notes. But that doesn't stop me from privately taking everything in now: the employees walking between the aisles with bags of peppermint bark and hot chocolate for sale, the gentle rhythm of music as the orchestra draws in guests from the lobby, the muffled hustle and bustle of dancers getting ready backstage.

Ma, Tad, and Hannah join me in our row. Ma gives me a stern warning with her eyes as she takes the seat next to me, then turns toward Hannah to show her pictures in the production's program.

I shift in my chair, trying to get comfortable while avoiding the elbow of the woman in a purple gown to my right. I wonder if she can tell I'm high.

"It's about to start," Tad says, squeezing Hannah's leg as he spots his boss in the reserved section at the front. His enthusiastic wave goes unnoticed.

The lights dim as snow begins to fall from the ceiling. It's just some dweeb shaking out a box of Styrofoam from the rafters, but the audience applauds anyway.

Easy crowd.

A bunch of children in white gossamer tutus start dancing around the stage. Because it's a local youth production, they most likely hired the help of the woodworking and art departments at a local school (maybe even Stonebridge) to get the scenes right. For all I know, Tony could have helped build the winter forest backdrop, since woodworking is the only class he actually likes.

While my love of Broadway knows no bounds, ballet is definitely not my thing. Ma will scold me if she catches me with my eyes closed, but I can't help it. My vision wavers after the lighting of the Christmas tree. I startle in my seat as the back of my head hits the top of my chair. I pull out my phone, dulling the light against my leg, and open a Snap from Tony blowing smoke circles into the camera as he and Brad head into the Crimson Sorrow show.

Without looking at me, Ma clears her throat, which is her not-so-subtle way of telling me to power down my phone.

"Look, Hannah, look. It's Emily!" Tad whispers.

I follow his line of sight to a teenage girl dancing on stage. She really is beautiful, with high cheekbones, golden hair, and fair white skin. Emily points her chin toward the upper balcony, the tiara on her head sparkling beneath the spotlight. As the music changes, she lifts herself up onto her tiptoes and prances around, tutu bouncing in time with her steps.

Hannah gasps, hiding her face in her dad's sleeve. "She's pretty."

Tad leans over and winks at me, which, gross. I sit back to shield myself from him, covering my ear when I feel it turn red. I turn to Ma instead, who's smiling, and wait until she sees me roll my eyes before mouthing, "All that glitters is not gold."

The music crescendos, and I return my attention to the stage in time to see the Nutcracker making his grand entrance.

Under the spotlights, I notice the way his red sergeant

coat contrasts the costumes of the surrounding ensemble and his own dark brown skin. There's a severity to his face, punctuated by the sharp outline of his jaw and the arch of his eyebrows as he concentrates on his next move.

Does he go to Stonebridge? I don't recognize him.

Is it sexist that I never knew guys could move like that? What do you even call a male ballerina? A ballerino? A male-rina? This guy moves around the stage with a fierce determination in his eyes, the likes of which I've only ever seen in athletes.

Is dancing a sport?

I have no clue, but watching him now makes me think it is. Suddenly, I'm not tired anymore. There's a precision to his step, a swiftness in the way he casts his arms out in front of him that's both calculated and effortless at the same time. I stealthily glance around the audience to see if anyone is laughing, but they're not. They're slack-jawed like me, following the elegant movement of his body. His feet graze the stage without ever really touching it.

The Nutcracker isn't just dancing; he's commanding the stage and everyone on it.

He leaps toward Emily, and unlike the rest of the dancers, he's wearing black ballet shoes. I follow the movement of his legs, holding my breath. My eyes gravitate toward his tights. I try not to. I really do try. But his costume moves with the beat of the music, accentuating everything in all the right places. I sink a little in my seat, shuffling my feet in the dark to adjust the crowding in my jeans.

As the orchestra swells, the Nutcracker's eyes flit over the audience, never staying on one person for more than a few seconds. Because they don't matter. You can tell he's dancing for the sake of the art itself. The thunderous applause that comes after? That's just a bonus.

Without thinking, I pull my phone out to take a picture of the scene, offsetting the image slightly so the Christmas tree on stage is in the background. The Nutcracker is midjump, suspended in the air like he's floating.

"No photos, please."

An usher in the aisle to Tad's left is waving a flashlight at me to put my phone away. I raise my hands to apologize. I'd been so transfixed on the Nutcracker's dancing I'd forgotten what I was doing. The rest of our row turns to glare at me.

Before I know it, the curtain falls for intermission, and even Ma looks surprised that I've managed to watch the entire first act. Tad takes Hannah to the restroom, and I reach over and snatch the program from Ma's hand. You know, totally nonchalant.

I have to rifle past several pages of ads but eventually, his headshot stares up at me.

Tristan Monroe.

The photo is in black-and-white, but Tristan's smile radiates off the page. His bio says he's a senior at Westgate Academy, a private Catholic school down the road from here.

"Quite beautiful, isn't she?" Ma nudges me out of my trance and points to Emily's picture, which is right above Tristan's.

"Oh, uh, yeah." I blush, pulling at my collar.

Ma giggles like a schoolgirl and wraps her arm through mine.

I look down at the program in my lap, suddenly unable to meet her eye. My shirt clings to my back as I read over Tristan's bio. He's apparently been dancing all his life and is the first Black man to lead the Sullivan-Richards Youth Dance Company. My breath hitches in my throat at Tristan being a "proud member of the LGBTQIA+ community."

I slam the program shut, acutely aware that someone might notice how long I've lingered on this particular page. At the end of the day, this is Ohio. White supremacists showed up at a drag queen story time just last year. By admitting he's part of the queer community in writing, Tristan's putting himself at risk.

But he doesn't care. He's proud of who he is.

And I can respect that, even if I could never put myself in his (ballet) shoes.

AFTER THE DANCERS take their final bows, we funnel into the lobby—right into a crowd hovering by the backstage door. It's funny how the arts do that. It's not like any of the dancers are famous or anything, but their friends and family gather with bouquets of flowers like we're waiting for Elphaba outside the Gershwin Theatre in New York City.

Tad finds his boss and waves us over to congratulate him on his daughter's success. He's an accountant like Tad, so he's exactly what you'd expect him to be (unremarkable in every way), except that a Lexus keychain dangles from his free hand.

"Dad!"

I freeze as Emily and Tristan come out from backstage, laughing and holding each other's hands. Emily still has her hair in a bun and her tiara on, though they've both changed into white singlets and sweatpants. Emily's dad hands her a bouquet of lilies and kisses her on the cheek.

"Bean, I'd like you to meet a colleague of mine."

I focus my attention on a dirt stain on the floor as Tad and Ma fawn over Emily's performance. Maybe if I stand really still, they won't notice me behind them.

Hannah hides behind Tad's leg, her thumb in her mouth, until Emily plucks a flower from her bouquet and hands it to her.

I pretend to check my phone as Hannah grabs hold of Emily's fingers and hangs on for dear life.

"Wes, *sweetheart*, say hello," Ma says through clenched teeth. She only ever refers to me as "sweetheart" when we're out in public, like the other parents would judge her for calling me Stevia.

"Right. Hi." I raise my hand, staring straight ahead, as Hannah lets go of Emily with a huff so we can shake.

"Hey, Wes. Thanks for coming to the show." Emily's eyes inspect my clothes, her forehead wrinkling. I'm suddenly aware of how baggy my pants must actually look.

"Thanks for having me," I reply, pulling away to wipe my palm along my thigh.

The hell?

Emily didn't invite me here. She didn't even know I existed two seconds ago.

"Isn't she beautiful? Wasn't she fantastic?" Ma asks, beaming. I'm pretty sure she's convinced herself a *Romeo and Juliet* love affair is unfolding right before her very eyes.

Let's hope I don't poison myself first.

"Yeah," I mumble. "You were great."

Emily looks over to Tristan, her eyebrows practically touching her hairline. "Thanks."

Ma purses her lips. She's not impressed. I wouldn't be either if I were her. I take in my surroundings, searching for an excuse to escape. I could pretend I need to go to the restroom, but the line's spilled out into the hall.

Thankfully, Emily's father finishes his conversation with Tad and pulls Emily away to introduce her to another family.

"I'll be right back." She grips Tristan's elbow as if to apologize for leaving him with a bunch of strangers.

"Hey," I manage to say, fixating on the lights overhead to avoid ogling over his tights again.

Tristan turns toward me now like he's just realized I've been standing here this whole time. His thick, black hair sits in tight coils on his head, glistening with sweat. A black cross dangles from his right ear. He must have put it in backstage, because he definitely wasn't wearing it earlier. As I watch his eyes take in my leather jacket and beat-up skate shoes, I notice his eyebrows are still greatly exaggerated by makeup. He's a few inches taller than me, and the tip of my nose lines up with his chin.

"Hi, I'm Trist—"

"Tristan, I know," I interrupt, surprising myself. I can feel my heart thumping in my chest, my throat suddenly dry.

He gives me a look, so I wave the program between us, and he rolls his eyes, smiling.

My knee starts shaking.

"Right," Tristan says, rubbing the back of his neck and extending out his hand. "What's your name?"

I stare down at his hand hanging in the open air. At the veins protruding beneath his skin, the onyx ring on his pinkie. His fingers are slender and bony, like I imagine a piano player's would be.

"Big Mac," I say, shoving my hand into my pocket. It's not that I don't want to shake his hand, but my fingers are dripping with sweat. I look away, mortified.

Tristan frowns and takes a step back, like I've broken some kind of social contract.

"Big what?" Tristan peers over at Emily, and from the corner of my eye, I see him tap his foot impatiently.

"Big Mac," I mumble. "Like the burger." Hearing my nickname coming out of my own mouth again makes me wince. While "Big Mac" might strike fear in the hearts of kids at Stonebridge, out here in the real world, it's the dumbest thing I've ever heard. It's so childish. So immature.

Judging by the way he shakes his head, Tristan agrees. Based on his figure, I bet he's never tasted a Big Mac (or even a burger) in his whole life.

"No," he says, scanning the lobby, probably looking for literally anyone to come and rescue him. "What's your real name?"

"Oh, uh . . ."

My throat tightens. I pick at the corner of my thumb in my pocket, pulling at the loose skin.

"Do you not know it?" he asks.

"Of course I know my own name," I say defensively. "I'm not an idiot."

I didn't mean for it to come out like that. I feel disoriented, still high from the joint I smoked earlier. The lobby's glass walls wobble and sway around me.

I want to tell Tristan that I could've watched him dance forever. That I'd never seen anything like it. But I don't. Because that's weird. And I don't want to be weird. I want to be the kind of guy Tristan wants to talk to. Not one he's doing everything in his power to get away from.

This is all going wrong.

I stumble backward and bump into Tad, who turns around.

"Chill, man, I never said you were," Tristan says, clasping his hands together and shrugging.

Tad squeezes my shoulder. Too tight. "Everything good here, Wes?"

"Yeah, Tadpole. We're fine," I hiss, shaking free from his hold. Tristan doesn't say anything.

Everything is happening too fast. I didn't mean to snap at Tad or not shake Tristan's hand. I've never been in a situation like this. With a boy who makes my heart both speed up and want to explode. A boy whose stare causes me to shrink into myself from embarrassment.

I clench my fists, feel my breath quicken. Ma steps toward

me, abandoning her conversation with one of the dancer's moms. She probably sensed a shift in the room's energy.

I close my eyes and inhale.

Three times one is three.

Three times two is—

"Your name's Wes?"

I open my eyes to see Emily standing next to Tristan, her arms folded over her chest. She's got a scowl on her face I can't place.

I nod my head.

"And you're from Stonebridge?"

I look between them, not sure what's happening. "Yeah . . ."

Emily stands on her tiptoes and whispers something into Tristan's ear. Whatever she says makes Tristan's eyes widen.

"Didn't you and your friends light a car on fire last summer?" he asks. I can't help but notice how he shuffles to the side, increasing the distance between us.

"I-I—" I stop myself. The way Emily and Tristan are watching me, it's like they're sizing me up over something they heard through the grapevine.

Word travels fast.

"Technically, yes," I admit, wondering how much they know. When they don't say anything, I continue. "My friend, Brad—his sister found out her boyfriend was cheating on her with her best friend, so we stole her phone and texted him to come over, and while they were fighting, my other friend, Tony, hotwired the dude's car, and we drove it out to the field behind the Lincoln Community Center and lit it on fire to teach him a lesson." I feel myself rambling, so I shut my mouth. But not before adding, "No one got hurt, though."

I return my attention to the stain on the floor. I can feel them judging me. Why did I say all that? I've never told anyone the truth. Not even the cops. I could've lied and said it was a rumor.

Or told them that Brad was the one who poured the gasoline, that Tony lit the match. But I doubt they'd believe me.

After a second that drags on for an eternity, Emily says, "Well, we've got to get going, but it was *so* nice meeting y'all."

Emily gets down on her knees to hug Hannah, who nearly strangles her in return.

"Nice talking to you, Wes," Tristan says politely. He turns to Emily and laughs at something she's said, probably related to my total lack of social skills. Emily pulls him away.

"Yeah, you too," I say to no one.

WHEN WE RETURN to Tad's Mustang, I yank the door open and barrel into the back before anyone forces me to sit up front again. I don't need another round of Twenty Questions right now.

I slouch down in the seat and throw my feet up on the window's ledge, taking up as much space as I can. My heart is racing. I saw the way Tristan and Emily looked at me. How wide Tristan's eyes went when Emily connected the dots about my identity. They judged me before even giving me a chance to explain. Good thing I didn't bring up my week in juvie. I don't even want to imagine how that would've turned out.

Hannah spreads her program across the middle seat, showing off all the autographs she collected. Tristan scribbled his name next to a quick sketch of a rose. I don't pay her much attention as she walks the car through her favorite scenes of the ballet because let's face it, it was all of them. Instead, I keep replaying the conversation Tristan and I had in my head.

Chill, man, I never said you were.

I rub my eyes with the back of my knuckles as we pull out of the parking lot, banging my head against the window. Tristan must think I'm a lowlife too. Between not shaking his hand and the torched car, I wouldn't be surprised if he ran in the opposite direction if we ever met again.

To make matters worse, Tad cranks the most overplayed Christmas song in the history of the universe to full blast (you know the one). The whole car sings along, which I guess is a good thing, since no one hears me scream into the back of Ma's seat.

I pull my phone out to a notification on my home screen.

"What? Whhhyyyy?" I groan, bolting upright.

Ma adjusts the rearview mirror, trying to catch my eye. "What is it, Stevia?" she shouts over the music. The front windshield's difficult to see through, fogged up from their singing.

At first, I don't swipe right. I keep rereading the notification, a tightness growing inside my chest. The time changes on the screen.

When I don't respond, Ma turns the dial down and asks again.

"That chick added me on Instagram," I whine, staring down at Emily's username in the dark.

I don't understand. Why would she do that? From our brief interaction, it was pretty obvious I'm the last person on the planet she'd ever associate with. I hear her and Tristan laughing in the back of my head, and I almost delete the app entirely. I can picture them making fun of my feed while drinking on a Friday night. I bet it would be with wine. They seem fancy like that.

"Emily's a lovely girl," Ma says, interrupting the mental spiral going on in my head. I remain silent as Ma and Tad start discussing the qualities that make Emily a good catch, which is both disturbing and kind of misogynistic coming from parents.

Tad glances back at me, inserting himself into my life like usual. "Maybe you need a little lady love in your life, Big Mac."

My whole body tenses. If I were driving, I'd have slammed on the brakes and pulled Tad from the car. I grip the side of the door, my fingernails piercing the imitation gray leather.

Everyone calls me by my nickname, they always have, but I have never, under *any* circumstances, let Tad get away with it. It sounds pathetic coming from him.

I know this.

Ma knows this.

So I'm not sure why he feels the need to challenge me now. I don't know when everyone suddenly became so enamored with my love life—or lack thereof—but it's seriously pissing me off. I can't stand all the little winks and comments about Emily. They're giving me major Mr. Hamilton vibes.

I can't become the prodigal straight stepson Tad seems to have created inside his head.

I glare at him through the rearview mirror.

"Don't say lady love, *Tadpole*, it's lame."

Ma whips around in her seat, her expression feral. "*Wesley*."

Tad places a hand on Ma's forearm, like I'm some kind of monster. "It's all right, Tammy."

Ma shakes her head. "No, it's not. Wesley, apologize. Now."

I let out a laugh, though there's an edge to it. I can't believe she's taking his side. Heat travels up my neck. "No. Not unless you tell your stupid *fiancé* to stop calling me by my nickname." I kick the back of Ma's chair like a petulant child. It wasn't even directed at her. I just felt an overwhelming desire to damage something of Tad's, and her chair was the best I could come up with in the moment.

Next thing I know, Ma's yelling at me about respect and what it means to act like an adult, but honestly, my head is spinning—my neck burning up now—that I tune her out completely after the first few minutes. If people stopped assuming my sexuality, I swear I'd actually tell the truth about everything so we could just avoid all this. I swear I would.

The car goes quiet. Not because we've run out of words to say, necessarily; I just think we've all lost the steam to carry on. It's been a long night.

I take the moment of silence to open my phone and unlock the notification from Emily. I scroll through her Instagram feed, passing photos of ballet shoes on park benches and screenshots of poems about the importance of kindness (which is rich, coming from her).

I lift my finger from the endless abyss of her profile, and that's when I see it. A throwback picture of Emily and Tristan from two summers ago. They're sitting at the edge of a pool midlaughter, somewhere in Tennessee. My thumb hesitates above the screen because deep down, I know nothing good can come from going down this path. Tristan's not going to suddenly reevaluate our first encounter with fresh eyes just because I've grown his Instagram following by one. Do I even want him knowing I'm looking at his page?

I click his username tag and wait for his profile to load.

His most recent image is a picture of him in a black hat and Ray-Bans in a scummy alley in downtown Cincinnati. The further I scroll, the more I realize his photos are all variations of the same thing; he's always smiling a perfect smile, always looking straight into the camera (and therefore, my soul), and there's always some deep quote in the caption like *To live is the rarest thing in the world. Most people exist, that is all.*

Normally, "Live. Laugh. Love." people make me puke, but instead of inducing nausea, Tristan's captions make my heart race. Between this and his bio in *The Nutcracker*'s program, it's like he's opening himself up for the whole world to see who he really is. And I don't know why, but that scares me more than anything that's happened tonight.

Tad stops the car in front of Mr. Fong's, and I catapult out without a word. Ma barks at me to say thank you, and I'm so distracted that I do (at least, I *think* I do) before climbing up the stairs to our apartment and locking myself in my room.

My heart flutters. Like, really flutters, like butterflies thrashing inside the confines of my aorta. I'd say it skipped a beat, but that would be one cliché too many, even if it is true.

I reopen Tristan's profile, and there, in six bold letters—below "Westgate Academy" and "Valentine, Ohio"—is the word SINGLE.

5.

I'M JUST A KID (WITH A CRUSH)

I rub my eyelids, feeling the heaviness behind them, as I down a spoonful of cereal. I didn't sleep at all last night. I lay in bed gaping up at the ceiling, agonizing over everything I'd done. Between the fight with Ma and the way I handled things with Tad and with Tristan and Emily, I royally screwed up.

Next to my breakfast, my finger hovers over the Follow button on Tristan's profile. Aside from his Instagram page, I discovered an old Facebook account, a YouTube channel filled with videos of him dancing, and an abandoned Twitter handle from 2022.

Obsessive? Maybe.

But I've never had a crush before. Not like this anyway. In retrospect, the last time I felt anything even remotely close to what I'm experiencing now, I was six years old and following the bigger kids around at daycare, hoping Donovan Blake would play with me. Of course, I didn't know what any of it meant back then—the clammy hands and shortness of breath, the way my skin tingled whenever he was around. And I have no idea what society deems appropriate now. But that's normal, right? To wonder what a complete stranger is doing every second of the day?

The Tripod's a lost cause when it comes to this sort of thing too. Tony doesn't exactly get crushes on girls; he's always moving on before he can catch any real feelings. And Brad? He's never shown interest in anyone. Most of the time, I don't even know where his head is at.

By the time the sun peeked through my blinds this morning, I'd memorized all of Tristan's favorite things. And though I cringe at the thought of listening to his favorite singer (some pop star named MARY I've never heard of), watching his latest TV obsession (a melodrama about rich kids living in a fictional town in Florida), or drinking his favorite Starbucks drink (peppermint mochas in the winter, PSLs in the fall), that's exactly what we're doing when I picture us together. Basic bitch and all.

Around noon, Emily slides into my DMs.

> Hey! Not sure if you can read this until you follow me (so follow me, obvs), but I was wondering if you wanted to hang out tomorrow night?

I hear Ma's excited shrill ringing in the back of my mind, the sound I imagine she'd make if I told her the news. I can already picture her bawling her eyes out at our hypothetical wedding.

Mental note: do *not* mention anything to her.

I click accept on the message request, though I have no idea why Emily's reached out. She wasn't exactly friendly last night, so why the sudden change of heart? Did her dad put her up to this? Was this *Tad's* doing? Because I swear to God, if it was him, after everything that's happened . . .

The last thing I need is to explain to Tad that the reason I'm not interested in his boss's daughter is because of the major boner I have for her best friend. My mouth goes dry at the thought.

Hey.

Yeah.

Alright.

I type each message separately, each a few minutes apart. While I don't think Emily could possibly be interested in me like that, I don't want her getting the wrong impression. Tony made that mistake once and found himself in a relationship before he even knew the girl's middle name.

Great! I'll be at the theater for rehearsals until 6. Meet there?

Emily ends the message with three dancing emojis, like I wouldn't understand what she's referring to when she says "rehearsal."

I shrug, putting my phone down to grab a water bottle from the fridge.

After two episodes of *The Golden Girls* with Ma, I realize a shrug isn't exactly an adequate response when messaging someone. I reply as I'm walking to the bathroom to brush my teeth.

Sure.

My phone pings almost immediately.

Is it okay if Tristan comes too?

My toothbrush (toothpaste, saliva, and all) falls out of my mouth and onto the carpet.

"Shit." I pick it up and automatically throw it back in my mouth, and a piece of Ma's hair hangs from my lip. I spit it out, or try to, then grab a towel to mop up the mess I've made.

"What's going on in there?" Ma shouts from the family room.

"Nothing!" I say, closing the door. I don't need her coming in and lecturing me at the sight of my dental hygiene debauchery.

I've got to play it cool.

Did Tristan ask to join us? No, that's stupid. Why would he do that?

I find a GIF of a man nodding and click Send. Except once I've seen that Emily's opened it, I realize he's moving his head at a speed that's too eager, like I can't wait to see Tristan.

I send a new one, this time of a cartoon turtle saying *Totally*.

Two separate GIFs in the span of a minute. So much for playing it cool.

Emily replies with a thumbs-up, and it's settled.

I'm hanging out with Tristan tomorrow.

Despite the sound of my heartbeat between my ears, I crack a smile at myself in the mirror.

"You've got this," I whisper, shaking out my bangs and flexing a muscle.

When I return to my room, I play the trust exercise with my bed and fall into its embrace.

"Hey, Alexa," I call out, lacing my fingers behind my head. "Play 'Unforgiven II.'"

An epic guitar solo pours out from the Bluetooth speaker

on my windowsill before James Hetfield's voice fills the room, singing about scarring black hearts and turning stones.

I fall asleep thinking of all the ways I can mess things up tomorrow.

WHEN MONDAY NIGHT rolls around, the temperature outside has dropped below freezing. The shop windows along Main Street are coated in frost.

Of course, I don't realize any of this until I'm already skateboarding to the theater in my leather jacket, camo cargo pants, and white Linkin Park band tee. Normally, I love the way the wind grazes my face when I'm riding, but tonight, my nose is leaking like a busted fire hydrant as I weave through Christmas carolers and Sally Ann greeters.

Right before I left, Emily shot me a message to say that the front entrance would be locked, so I boardslide down a railing to the back of the building, where some kid is guarding the door like he's a bouncer at the Luxe. I tell him I'm here to see Emily, and he flips through a guest list on his phone to confirm my name before leading me into the auditorium.

I take a seat in the second row, behind where Emily's dad sat last night. The lights are turned on high, so you can see paint chipping in places usually hidden in shadow. The chairs around me are tattered and worn. Some are even missing their lining. I guess the people who can actually afford to attend the ballet don't even bother pitching in a few extra dollars to fix Valentine's only cultural staple. Go figure.

I lay my skateboard on the ground, rolling it beneath my feet to settle my nerves. A worker in the rafters above fiddles with some wires on the chandelier. His legs dangle in the open space below.

On stage, Emily and Tristan are in their street clothes with the rest of the dancers. Emily's wearing a baby blue one-piece like she's stepped out of an eighties workout video. She's talking with the guy who plays Herr Drosselmeyer when she sees me in the audience and waves.

I wave back, cursing myself for how stupid I must look. Am I so desperate to make a good impression that I've resorted to acting like Tad? I run my palms over the armrests beside me.

Tristan peers over at me wearing a black muscle shirt and the same gray sweats as the other night. I guess I figured he'd at least say hi, but he doesn't wave or acknowledge me at all. Did I accidentally like one of his photos? Does he somehow know I've been checking out his social media all day? I try to shrug it off by taking out my phone and tapping at the screen like I'm texting someone, but I feel myself clam up.

I spent all night obsessing over his dancing videos, paying painfully close attention to the way he seemed to take up every scene, but I'm realizing now that I probably haven't even crossed his mind since we met. To Tristan, I'm a stranger; a nobody.

I sit in silence and watch as the ensemble goes over the next few scenes.

Turns out, the dancer who plays the Mouse King is also apparently a dictator in real life. He keeps flailing his hands and telling everyone they're doing it wrong. Even from afar, I can see Tristan's irritated. It's only noticeable for a second, though, before he puts on a smile again. Emily tries to lighten the mood by laughing it off and touching the guy on the arm. She glances over at me when she does it, and I drop my eyes to my lap.

When rehearsals end, everyone hugs goodbye like they'll never see each other again, even though tomorrow night is the Christmas Eve show.

Emily comes over and kneels in the front row. Tristan trails behind her and gives me a quiet hello. He takes a seat a few chairs down, slipping off his shoes and stuffing them into the gym bag flung over his shoulder.

Should I compliment them on their performance? It was only a rehearsal. Would it be weird if I did?

But Emily's the first to speak. "We were thinking of grabbing a bite to eat," she says, untying her laces. "Have you had dinner?"

I shake my head, and she claps. She does that a lot.

As we step out into the parking lot, a snap of wind forces its way past us. Tristan gasps, and I laugh, but I don't think he finds it funny. Why would he? We live in Ohio, where it's freezing cold half of the year.

"Why are you walking like that?"

I follow Tristan's gaze to my right leg. I'm surprised he's even noticed; I'm usually pretty good at hiding it.

"Pulled a muscle skateboarding," I say without missing a beat. It's the same answer I gave Tad the first time he asked. I was prodding my knee after chasing Hannah around their yard when he literally knocked on my leg and asked what was wrong. It's a lie, but whatever. I'm not ready to open that can of worms.

Tristan doesn't push either. I'm almost relieved until he says, "There's apparently this awesome restaurant down the street I just started following on Instagram," and turns in the general direction of Vincenzo's.

I freeze at the edge of the sidewalk, letting them continue to walk ahead without me.

Dear God, no.

Not there.

Anywhere but there.

"We're not supposed to eat carbs, but—"

Please don't say it.

Please don't say it.

"It's called Vincenzo's, ever been?"

Dammit.

While I'm flattered Tristan's followed the account I curate on a daily basis, I'm at a crossroads with what to do next. On the one hand, if I say yes, I'll also have to pretend like the food's disgusting or something to avoid eating there. Which I'm far too proud to do. But obviously, I can't be seen with ballet dancers. What if someone mentions it to Tony and Brad and I get outed in the process? Even worse, what if they're working? God only knows what Emily and Tristan would think of them after how they reacted to me yesterday. And if they knew where I worked, what would stop them from coming back another day and asking for me? But I also can't say that I haven't dined there because then they'll make me tag along, and I don't know how I'd convince them to go somewhere different when there's not much else in the way of restaurants nearby.

Tristan and Emily bob up and down in place, waiting for my response. Tristan stuffs his face in his jacket.

I have no choice. I lie again.

"Uh, no. I haven't." I exhale, watching my breath float away above us.

Tristan pulls out a set of car keys. "Perfect."

"Did you skateboard over?" Emily asks, tilting her chin at my board.

"Yeah," I say, tucking it under my arm.

"I would've pegged you as more of a DC fan." Tristan nods at the Spiderman sticker Hannah got me from a gumball machine.

My board's covered in stickers I've collected over the years. Mostly of band logos and skulls. And Betty White making a "rock on" sign with her hand. "I'm not convinced the Snyder Cut did any favors for the *Justice League*," I say easily.

They're both staring at me blankly, which makes me think neither of them has committed to the four hours and two minutes it takes to know what I'm talking about.

Ignoring me, Tristan double taps the fob in his hand and opens the trunk of the car next to us. He tosses his bag inside. "Do you mind throwing your board in here? And, uh, don't light anything on fire."

"Yeah—I mean, no. I won't. Not a problem." I blush, watching as he jumps into the front seat with a smirk.

I steal a glance at him through the tinted windows and wonder if he gets inside his own head like I do sometimes. I set my board down in the truck, eyeing the car in disbelief when I realize it's electric.

"Why the hell is a seventeen-year-old driving an electric car?" I mumble to myself.

Emily takes the passenger seat, and when I climb into the back behind him, Tristan's already halfway through listening to a loud instrumental track. I go to ask him what it is, but he throws the car in reverse so fast I clutch the back of his chair harder than I hope either of them notices.

WHEN WE ARRIVE at Vincenzo's, Tristan and Emily slam their doors and race to the entrance, bracing themselves against the cold. I linger in the car, sweating.

I peel my hand away from the inside handle, my knuckles pale white against the black leather interior. I rack my brain, trying to remember the guys' schedules. It's Monday, which we all happen to have off, but it's also Christmas Eve tomorrow. The restaurant's going to be busy. They could've picked up a shift without telling me.

I reach over the back seat to grab my skateboard from the trunk and get out of the car. As I step onto the sidewalk, I bend over and retie my already tied shoe so I can peek through the restaurant's blinds. As expected, the dining room is packed. Sheila, the assistant manager, runs past the window with an iPad. She never steps foot inside the kitchen, so she won't be an issue. I doubt she'd even recognize me.

The bell above the front door rings as we enter the lobby, and a squirrely looking hostess tells us it'll be a ten-minute wait. She must've just started this week.

Vincenzo's is modeled after an old train station, with green and red stained glass lampshades and exposed brick walls. There's a section in the back of the dining room designed like a train's caboose, and pictures of mob bosses line the walls to the restrooms. A chalkboard hangs from a wire over the kitchen window with Tony's weekly specials: a meatball marinara-inspired pizza and his spin on cacio e pepe.

We take up an entire wooden bench beside a family of four. While we wait, the dad offers Tristan an extra menu. It's one of those laminated ones plastered with pictures and Yelp reviews.

I let go of my breath. I'm never here on weeknights, and to my relief, neither is anyone else I know. But to be safe, I turn to Emily and Tristan and mimic having to pee.

"I'll be right back," I say, sliding off the bench.

I walk up to the front desk, pretending to inquire about the location of the restroom. "Could we get table 105?" I ask, subtly pointing to the floor plan in front of the hostess. Table 105 is a booth in the left corner of the restaurant. It's the only table in the entire dining room that can't see into the kitchen. On the off chance a celebrity ever comes to town, Vincenzo always offers up table 105 for privacy from the other diners. It's the perfect spot to hide.

"I'll do my best," the hostess says with a curt smile. For anyone who's never worked in a restaurant, that's code for "not a chance, buddy, but I'll say it to you so you'll go away." I get the game. I know the lingo.

I narrow my eyes and smile before heading to the restroom, though I don't actually have to go.

I poke my head into the kitchen. Cooper and Juan, middle-aged men with families of their own, are working away inside. They stand silently side by side, only speaking to clarify a new order that comes through the printer. When it's the two of them on the line, my role as sauce swirler is redundant. The kitchen's a complete 180 from the headbanging, metal music–playing mosh pit The Tripod prefers.

By the time I return to the lobby, the hostess is ready and leads us over to table 106.

Good enough.

Emily and Tristan slide into the moss-green leather booth without taking their eyes off their phones, confirming my suspicion they only invited me along because Tad must have said something to Emily's dad. Even though I'm glad Emily's not into me like that, I'll remember to punch Tad the next time I see him for forcing them to hang out with me.

I throw my skateboard under the table as the hostess hands us menus over the red and white checkered tablecloth and walks off.

"So what are we thinking?" Emily asks, rubbing her palms together.

"The Capone," Tristan announces, throwing down his laminated menu like it's final.

"Ignore him. He's just upset we didn't run through the

whole show tonight like we usually do on Mondays." Emily
gives Tristan the stink eye before turning to me. "What do
you think we should get, Wes?"

I hunch over the menu, acting like I don't already know
it by heart. "I'd say the Soprano. We use—they use day-old
sausage for the Capone."

Emily and Tristan stare at me.

"I read about it online when I was on the toilet," I say,
grimacing when I realize what I've said.

"Um, okay, nasty. The Soprano it is." Emily glances down,
probably wondering if I washed my hands. "Dr Pepper?"

We all nod.

"Hi, kids."

I look up and feel my eyes bulge out of their sockets. Our
server, Tracy, appears from behind the wall with a handful
of straws (paper, of course, because of the turtles). She's an
elderly woman with thick highlighter-pink reading glasses
and a blue tint to her short-cropped hair, and she's worked
for Mr. Pecorino since the restaurant opened in 2003. She
flips open her notepad when she notices me sitting there,
fiddling with my hands beneath the table.

"What can I do for you today?" she asks, addressing only
me. I wobble my head at her as discreetly as possible, trying
to telepathically explain the situation. Thankfully, Emily and
Tristan have returned their attention to their phones.

Tracy arches a penciled-in brow at me.

"We'll get one large Soprano and three Dr Peppers." Before
she can ask any questions, I collect the menus, banging their
ends on the table to line them up. "Thank you, *ma'am*."

Tracy's forehead turns into one big mass of wrinkles. I
never talk like that, and she knows it.

"Coming right up, *young man*." She smirks, tucking the
menus under her arm.

I relax as she goes to greet the table next to us, though my hands are shaking.

Tristan and Emily don't seem to notice. But Emily must sense me staring, because she looks up from her phone and places it screen-down at the center of the table. Tristan does the same, stacking his on top of Emily's front to back.

"What's happening right now?" I ask, blinking.

Tristan gives me a funny look and points at my phone on the table, motioning for me to copy them. I do as I'm told, grabbing mine and slowly putting it over Tristan's. Are they messing with me? Our phones look like the Leaning Tower of iPhones.

"It's just something we do." Emily laughs. "Whoever checks their phone first has to pay for dinner."

"Okay. . ." I say, hiding the fact that, for a second, my heart leaps from being included in their weird little friendship ritual. I doubt they'd care much for The Tripod's wet willy routine to determine who's designated driver when we go to concerts in the city.

"So, Wes, what's SOB like?" Emily asks.

SOB is Valentine's nickname for Stonebridge because it's the run-down version of Westgate Academy. And because people at Westgate never seem to venture to our side of town, Emily's probably asking because she genuinely doesn't know. Still, I hate it when people call it that.

"It's nothing special." I shrug. "There's a gym and a music room. And a bunch of classes that all look the same. I think there's a library somewhere." I furrow my eyebrows, trying to picture the school's layout. "If we're lucky, the cafeteria sometimes serves Sloppy Joes."

Tristan scrapes a fork over the napkin in front of him. "Does it have a dance studio?"

I scoff. "We could never afford something like that."

"Oh."

Emily shifts in her seat. Tristan collects the shreds of torn napkin he's made into a pile. If it weren't for the loud Italian music playing in the restaurant, we'd be sitting in awkward silence.

Emily searches the dining room for Tracy and our Dr Peppers, but it's futile, so she asks, "What colleges have you applied to?"

I tense. Why are people our age so concerned with what school they get into? Is there really that much of a difference between them?

"I haven't," I reply, carefully controlling the tone of my voice.

They exchange a glance.

"You haven't applied anywhere?" Tristan asks.

It's my turn to shift in my seat. "No."

"But it's December." Emily frowns. "Aren't applications due soon?" She looks to Tristan for backup, but all he does is shrug.

I open and close my mouth. I can't tell them I'll never be able to afford college. And I'm not exactly a model student, so scholarships are out of the question. "I've been busy," I lie. I have to act uninterested, because if I'm uninterested, they won't pry. If I don't appear disappointed that I don't have a chance in hell, maybe they'll buy it enough for me to change the subject. "It hasn't been a priority."

Emily leans over the table, clapping her hands together like I'm in kindergarten and she's my teacher. "Your future isn't a priority to you?"

Is she serious right now?

Tristan's smiling at me, but it's different than the one I drooled over last night. It's a Mr. Hamilton smile, full of pity. Or worse, judgment.

I want to defend myself, to tell them that I'm working on it, but that'd be my third lie tonight.

We can't all go to places like Westgate Academy. Some of us have to be more practical about our lives. And for someone like me, someone whose main priority is looking after his ma and making sure we don't get evicted, college is out of the question.

I open my mouth to say all that, to flip the table over and storm off in a huff, but the booth's light catches Tristan's eyes, and up this close, they're a rich, dark brown. Like the bark on my favorite hawthorn trees in Mariner's Park after a heavy rainfall.

"You have nice eyes," I blurt out.

Tristan recoils like I've smacked him from across the booth, but his features soften.

"Um, thanks." He thumbs his left ear, clearing his throat.

Suddenly, it's like a thousand degrees in here. I look around the dining room, searching for the asshole who cranked up the thermostat.

Seriously, where is Tracy with our drinks?

Am I blushing? Again? I touch my face, feeling the warmth of my cheek. God help me if my pasty skin betrays me now.

Emily coughs, trying to stifle a grin. "Well, you should join a club, at least. They look really good on college applications."

I let out a sharp laugh. "Yeah, right. Do I look like a mathlete?" I grab the hem of my leather jacket, as if to make a point.

I would never be caught dead joining a school club, not that they'd even want me. I'm pretty sure you have to attend class consistently in order to join one anyway.

"No, she's right," Tristan singsongs, grabbing Emily's hand like they're married and discussing the future with their child. "If your grades suck, having an extracurricular activity on your resume can make you more attractive as a candidate."

I know Tristan means to lecture me, but all I heard was "suck" and "attractive" and dammit, I shift in my seat again.

"What makes you think my grades suck?" I ask, folding my arms over my lap. I can feel myself getting defensive. I want to reach for my phone—to hide behind the safety of the screen—but I resist the urge, knowing that if I do, I'll be stuck with the bill.

Tristan raises his hands. "Sorry, I didn't mean anything by that."

The clock on the brick wall behind us reads 7:25 P.M. We've only been here for twenty minutes.

"I've got to use the restroom," I say, ignoring Tristan's apology and dipping out of the booth.

"Didn't you already go?" he asks.

"Small bladder."

Once inside, I splash water on my face and consider myself in the restroom mirror.

You have *nice eyes*? Why would I say that?

For one thing, Tristan's kind of a douche. How did I not notice this last night? And what's with the holding hands? Do gay guys do that? I've never had a girl best friend, so I wouldn't know.

With all that talk about college, I can't shake the feeling that maybe I was right about Tad all along. Maybe he *was* trying to set me up with Emily, but for an entirely different reason than I'd thought. Maybe he was thinking she'd be a good influence on me. That, like Mr. Hamilton thought, all I need is a girlfriend to kick me into gear. It's enough to make me want to punch the brick wall in front of me and leave out the back door.

I dry my hands on one of those old rolling cloth systems and make my way back to the booth. But before I get there, a voice behind me stops me in my tracks.

"Big Mac! What the hell are you doing here?"

No.

Tony nearly shouts in my ear as he jumps on my back and yeehaws like a cowboy.

I shake him off and elbow him in the stomach, looking back at the dining room to make sure neither Tristan nor Emily is heading this way. I want to tell Tony now's not a good time, but that would only make him suspicious.

"I—uh, came to pick up my check."

It's not a complete lie. I *do* have to pick up last week's wages. But I can't tell him the real reason I'm here. That I'm dining out with a girl and her ballet dancer best friend that I spent all last night stalking on the internet. Instead, I do the best thing I can think of—turn it around on him before he can ask a follow-up question. "What are you doing here?"

Tony takes an AirPod out of his ear. "Pops has me working overtime over the holidays. Says I got to pay my own way once I graduate. What a jackass." He takes off a rubber glove and shuffles the playlist on his phone. He must be working in the dish pit tonight, which is why I didn't see him earlier.

"Sucks, man," I snap, tapping my foot against the corner of the wall. We're inches away from the dining room, mere steps from Tristan seeing me from his seat. If I can get through this conversation, Tony will disappear into the dish pit, and I can slip back into the booth unnoticed.

He starts telling me how his night has been, but I'm peeking through the glass divider that separates the kitchen from the dining room tables. Tristan and Emily are sitting in the booth, diving into the pizza, which Tracy must have just dropped off.

"Look, man, I've got to head out."

"Okay, okay. Bud and I'll stop by Wednesday morning. And don't forget, we're crashing Stacy Evans's New Year's Eve party. She's gonna be so pissed!"

"Yeah, yeah, sure," I say, patting him on the shoulder.

The Tripod has spent Christmas morning together since we were fifteen. It started the year Bud's dad hit him for stealing one of his beers. We've made it a tradition ever since, with Ma making her famous Christmas morning wife-saver casserole. "It's funny because I'm divorced," she says every year, presenting the dish on the table and waiting for us to laugh.

I spin on my heels and turn to leave.

"Big Mac?"

"Yeah?" I say through clenched teeth.

"Your check?" He points down at my empty hands.

"Right." I walk past the restrooms and type the passcode into the office door. I stick my tongue out at the camera hanging in the corner and grab the envelope from the cubby with my name on it.

"See ya later, Big Cheese," I say, slapping Tony across the face with my envelope as I head to the entrance.

I'm about to turn the corner and slide back into the booth when my ears perk up at the mention of my name.

"Wes is gay, Ems," Tristan mumbles, putting down his pizza slice. "Anyone could see that if they knew what to look for."

My step wavers, and I cling to the brick wall, feeling the blood rush to my head.

Time screeches to a halt around me.

A woman passes me in the hall on her way to the restroom,

and I think she asks if I'm okay, but the thoughts inside my head are so loud I can't even make out what she says.

How does Tristan know I'm gay? Am I that obvious?

I force myself to stand up straight so my shoulders are square with the wall. I put my hand over my heart to try and steady myself.

No one has ever said my name in the same breath as the word "gay" before. Was that a laugh when he told Emily the truth? Just hearing the association, the conviction in Tristan's voice when he said it, makes my legs nearly give out from under me. If he could make the connection so easily after only knowing me for a day, who's to say other people haven't already too?

I shove my hands deep inside my pockets to hide even the slightest tilt in my wrist that could signal what I am to others.

Emily lets out a dramatic sigh. "Thank God, because I did not know how I was going to tell my dad I'm not interested. I usually go for bad boys, but . . . Wait, you're not into him, are you?"

Tristan snorts, coughing on what I assume is our late Dr Peppers. "Nooo way. That's a project I am *definitely* too busy to take on right now." His voice goes high then, like a kid who's sucked back too much helium.

Instinctively, I reach for my skateboard, knowing full well it's back at the table. I need to get out of here before I do or say something I'll regret.

As I round the corner, they're laughing among themselves.

"Hey Wes," Emily chirps midslurp.

I lean over the table to examine the sausage-to-pepperoni ratio on the pizza, avoiding having to look at either of them.

"I've actually got to run," I say, grabbing my phone. "Guess

I'm paying." My voice breaks as I pull forty bucks from my jacket and throw it on the table.

"Wait, Wes, hold up!"

I grab my skateboard and don't stop to listen to what Tristan is shouting at me. I don't even turn around.

I head straight to the door, shoveling a fistful of mints from the hostess stand into my pocket, even though you're only supposed to take one.

I chuck my skateboard to the ground as the bell chimes behind me.

Tristan calls out my name, but I fly down the street, wiping my nose with my sleeve.

6.

MISERY HAS NO BUSINESS HERE

Ma and I have spent the past three Christmas Eve mornings out in the rain, our socks soaked and slipping down our ankles.

All for a stupid tree.

And it's not like we'll even set up the tree in our own family room. It's for Tad and Hannah's house as some kind of leftover tradition from Tad's childhood growing up on a potato farm in Idaho.

Hannah's all for it, though, putting on a Santa hat and screaming Christmas carols the whole ride over. Ma's right there with her, her voice jumbled behind an oversized red scarf as we blast the heater.

I'm sitting in the back of Tad's Mustang. Arms crossed. Head low. Still recovering from last night.

No matter how loud I blare the music from my headphones, Tristan's words ring through my ears.

Wes is gay, Ems. Anyone could see that if they knew what to look for.

What had I done to convince him? I try recalling everything

I said—from the car ride over to Vincenzo's to walking out on them—but my mind comes back blank. And I hate that.

I drum my fingers along my knee, counting down the hours until I can be alone.

I don't get the point of this, of getting a tree the morning before Christmas. Ma puts ours up the day after Thanksgiving, which is just as ridiculous, but at least we get to enjoy it for a few weeks.

"It's so it stays fresh," Tad had explained from the driver's seat, like he did every year.

I don't buy it, not even for a second. I think it has more to do with the fact that Valentine becomes a wasteland over Christmas. We're not religious, so church is out of the question, but we may live in the only city left in America that still closes for the holidays. Except for a handful of restaurants along Ocean Boulevard, theaters, malls, even the damn rec center shuts down.

Like Christianity's the only religion that matters.

We drive through the countryside, snaking our way along the Ohio River, past barren trees and cornfields covered in untouched snow. I fog up the window with my breath, drawing little arrows with my finger.

As of this morning, Emily's left me fourteen DMs. She keeps badgering me to tell her what happened last night, but I don't know her well enough to know if she's genuinely concerned for my well-being or if she's just dying for gossip. Something tells me it's the latter.

And Tristan's the real reason I left. Why can't he be the one reaching out?

In the grand scheme of things, I know them talking privately about me in the booth isn't a big deal, but it still feels like I've been outed. In my head, I run through all the scenarios where this can somehow come back to bite me. Emily's dad could overhear her talking on the phone and bring it up with Tad at work. Tristan might have cousins I don't know about who go to Stonebridge. I've seen firsthand how fast rumors spread.

After twenty more minutes, Tad turns into the Christmas tree farm. Frozen pebbles crunch beneath the tires as we park.

I grab the extra pair of gardening gloves Ma shoved into the console earlier and sigh. Tad's already given me a pep talk about how it's a rite of passage for the men in his family to cut down the tree. He's trying extra hard to be all buddy-buddy today, never once bringing up Emily. I'm not sure what Ma's told him about last night; how I came home earlier than expected, how I barricaded myself in my room until she went to bed.

Tad grabs a fine-tooth saw and hands me a tarp from the trunk as we head into the man-made forest, filled with evenly spaced rows of Douglas firs and white pines. The birch mulch path we walk on is spray-painted red and white to imitate a giant candy cane. We hike along the curved part, which Tad explains is the warble.

Except for the owners, we're the only people for miles, surrounded by a valley of stumps like it's a Christmas morning massacre. All the good trees are long gone, so we spend the next few hours raking through the island of misfit toys while Tad tries to justify all the bald spots on the ones going for 50 percent off their original asking price.

Ma and Tad take off in one direction to look through the measly trees that are left while Hannah and I head to the gift shop to grab hot chocolate. They call it "sibling bonding time," but I caught them making out behind a noble fir last year. They tried passing it off like they were inspecting the branches, but I definitely saw tongue.

A lady dressed as Mrs. Claus passes me a tray with four

piping hot cups and a handful of mini candy canes. You're supposed to dip them in the hot chocolate, but I never do. It gives the drink a weird, plasticky peppermint taste. Hannah's the only one that likes the flavor, so I peel off the wrappers and stuff all the candy canes into her cup.

It's so cold outside we can find Ma and Tad in the back of the lot from their breath alone, which pillows in tiny clouds above the tree line.

I've got to hand it to them. They've actually managed to find a decent tree.

But there's a reason the one they've chosen was left behind. It's pretty wispy looking, with a thinned-out back and an underside that's already browning. It's like the tree knows how pathetic it is too because its needles are downturned in a frown. Tad's kind of a sap like that (pun intended). He always makes a case for the forgotten ones.

"Stevia, help your stepdad," Ma says flippantly, grabbing the tray of hot chocolate from my hands.

I give her a pointed look.

Tad sticks his head out from under the tree and ends up kicking over his hot chocolate. The liquid creeps over the earth, steam rising as it makes contact with the dirt.

By the time he hands me the saw, Tad's already managed to cut through to the middle of the stump.

I get down on my knees, groaning when I accidentally kneel into a puddle. I crawl underneath the tree, grabbing a branch for support, and a pile of snow rains down on my arm.

This is hands down the worst part of the holidays.

I'm not a guy's guy by any means. The Tripod and I don't rough it out in the woods. We don't even do physical activity, unless you count skateboarding or the occasional impromptu wrestling match. Being down on the ground like this, with dirt sneaking its way into the lining of my underwear, is exactly why.

Tad reaches into the tree to keep it steady as I saw away at the trunk. A bead of sweat runs down my forehead and into my eye. I can't get into a groove for the life of me.

"Hey, Wes?" Tad asks, tapping my leg with the toe of his boot.

I knew it. Emily told her dad, didn't she? Tad was just waiting until we were alone to spring this on me.

My grip on the saw's handle tightens as I prepare for impact.

"I'm, uh, sorry about the other day."

His apology catches me so off guard I stop sawing midcut. I shake a fallen twig from my hair, not knowing where to look.

"What for?" I grumble, cutting into the tree again. The bark crackles under the blade as I pick up the pace.

Tad shifts hands to give his right arm a break. "I shouldn't have pressured you into pursuing Emily like that," he admits, gazing back down at me. He says "pursuing" like we're in the fifties and I'm trying to court her.

I bite my lip. "Did Ma put you up to this?"

Tad laughs, his voice echoing in the empty field surrounding us. "No, she didn't. It was actually Hannah who made me realize my mistake."

Hidden beneath the foliage, I peek over at Ma dancing in the rain and notice Hannah watching us.

"Huh," I say, meeting her eye.

Tad lets out a breath. "Yeah, she's pretty intuitive for a five-year-old. Gets that from Amira."

The mention of Tad's first wife is so sudden I think I've imagined it. He never talks about her, at least not when he's around me. All I know is she died when Hannah was a baby. It's weird thinking about what people's lives were like before you entered them, how scared Tad must have felt becoming a single parent overnight. It's almost like you forget people exist at all outside your interactions with them.

"I'm sorry again, Wes," Tad says, smoothing down his jacket. "But I don't take back what I said. I do think you could use a little love in your life."

I pause, noticing the subtle way he's left out the word "lady." What did Hannah tell him? Can five-year-olds have gaydar? Maybe I should apologize for the way I acted too—*maybe*— but I don't even know what I'd say. I still think Tad's a loser, but the way he owned up to his actions? How even though he wasn't really in the wrong, he took the high road and said it to me first? I've never known a male Authority Figure™ to do that.

I go to open my mouth, but I've taken too long to respond, and the moment passes.

"Anyway, I'm freezing my ass off up here." Tad stomps his boots in the mud, letting out a quick *brrr*. "Ten bucks you can't finish this in two minutes." He glances down at me and smirks.

"You're on." I laugh, grabbing the saw's handle and frantically picking up where I left off. After dropping forty bucks on the dinner I didn't eat last night, I could really use the money.

When Ma and I make it home—after paying for the tree and tying it to the top of Tad's Mustang—I sneak away into my room, not bothering to turn on the lights, and reach for the newly acquired ten-dollar bill in my pocket.

Thumbing its edge, I gather the nerve to reopen Instagram and follow Tristan.

7.

ANOTHER STUPID CHRISTMAS SONG

When it comes to Christmas morning, Ma and I have it down to an art.

We aren't big on the holidays, but every twenty-fifth of December, we get up early, don animal onesies, and spend the day in front of the TV for our annual Christmas movie marathon. And yes, *Die Hard* falls into said category.

Ma's in the kitchen now defrosting her wife-saver casserole, while I'm in the family room trying my best not to read into the fact that Tristan hasn't followed me back yet.

Around eleven, Big Cheese and Bud come through the front door. Dressed as a dragon in his Cleveland Browns letterman jacket, Brad's carrying a backpack over his shoulder, and Tony has this ginormous bag of Old Tyme candies.

I waddle over to give them both a hug, but my penguin feet are too large, so I end up stepping on Tony's foot.

"Remember, Mama Mac," Tony says, wagging his blue shark fin, as Ma gathers us around the Christmas tree for our annual selfie.

"Yeah, yeah." Ma's dressed as a unicorn with an iridescent horn and a metallic rainbow mane. "Posting on social media is strictly prohibited."

Tony nods, going off about street cred and the importance of maintaining his image. While I'd argue posting the picture can only up his game—that of the hundreds of girls who have fawned over his bad boy image in the past, most of them would probably kill to see his softer side—Tony would never agree.

We're halfway through the opening number in *White Christmas* when my phone vibrates.

I click on an Instagram notification, my heart swelling at the thought of seeing the words "pas.de.tristan started following you," but it's only a friend suggestion for some random theatre kid.

I hug a pillow to my chest.

People at Stonebridge may think I'm a lowlife, but I never thought I'd feel compelled to prove to someone that I'm worthy of their time, even if my bad reputation preceded me. Tristan was so nonchalant about his disinterest in me. If I did or said something different at the table, would it have made a difference? I wasn't exactly nice to him either, but he hasn't even given me a chance.

Brad tilts his head at me when I groan, but I pass his curiosity off with a shrug.

On screen, Vera-Ellen and Danny Kaye start performing their dance number to "The Best Things Happen While You're Dancing." Why we still watch the damn scene is anyone's guess. Brad ruined it for all of us when he made a drinking game out of how many times Vera-Ellen breaks the fourth wall and looks directly into the camera. When Ma gets up to dish out the casserole, Brad reaches into his backpack and pours salted caramel Baileys into our cups.

"Merry Christmas, boys," Ma says, returning to the family room with an envelope in her hands.

Slowly, I peel back the seal and pull out three tickets to Metallica's Cincinnati stop on their North American tour next April.

"No *freaking* way!"

Before I can comprehend what she's done, Tony and Brad are up from the couch and herding Ma into a hug. They dance around the room, bouncing around and laughing. Tony's head is inches from the ceiling.

"Don't be such a prude, Big Mac. Show your Ma some love!"

I flip the tickets over to read the fine print. Gifts haven't usually been something we can afford, and these must have set Ma back a few hundred dollars at least. Especially with Ticketmaster's price gouging. There's no way she could've done this on her own.

"But how?" I ask, shaking my head.

Ma dismisses my question with a wave of her hand, stopping to catch a breath from all the jumping. "I've been saving for a while and wanted to treat my boys."

I bite my tongue. She'd do anything for Tony and Brad, they're basically her surrogate sons. But still. "Are you sure about this? I can pick up some shifts at work next week to repay you."

"Oh, Wesley, for goodness' sake." Ma gives me a hug. "Yes, I'm sure. Tad knows a guy at the ticket center. Quit worrying."

She brushes my cheek. I hadn't realized I was crying.

Tad did this? Why would he put in all that effort after everything I've done?

"Thanks, Ma," I whisper into her frizzy hair.

The Tripod pulls Ma and I into a group hug, and suddenly, we're laughing and wiping our eyes. For a moment, the rest of the afternoon feels so full of possibility. Like a damn Christmas miracle.

The sun is setting by the time I sneak into the kitchen to check Instagram again. I run my fingers through my unkempt hair and peer down at the screen.

Still nothing.

Tristan must have seen the notification that I'd followed him by now. It would have alerted him the second he opened the app.

I don't have time to sulk over what that could mean because Tony appears in the doorway then and glances over my shoulder. I hide my phone behind my back, hoping he didn't catch a glimpse at Tristan's profile.

"Dude, what's your deal? You've been acting so weird lately."

He must mean our encounter at Vincenzo's on Monday, which I was hoping he'd forgotten. So much for Christmas miracles.

"What? No, I haven't. It's nothing. I'm fine. Fuck off." I swat at him.

Tony narrows his eyes. He must see right through my lie, but he lets out a curt *hmph* and heads back to the family room with his third plate of food.

When I know it's safe, I reopen Instagram. I contemplate unfollowing Tristan right then and there. I don't even know why I'd want him to follow me back. We fumbled our way through two encounters now, each one ending up worse than the last. But I don't click the button. Maybe it's his bright smile or how his brown eyes seem to pierce through the phone screen like he's standing across from me in real time that stops me.

Brad yells from the other room. "Big Mac, get your ass back in here."

I grab a water from the fridge and pocket my phone. It burns like fire against my thigh.

Upon my return to the couch, Tony's in the middle of

shoving casserole into his mouth. He sticks up his middle finger when he catches me staring. I don't tell him I wasn't actually paying attention to him—that I must have zoned out—I just flip him off in return.

"Now, I know we don't normally do the whole gift thing," Brad says, grabbing his backpack from the door and returning to the family room. "But here."

He tosses both Tony and I a wad of tissue paper and tells us to be careful.

"This is *lit*, man," Tony shouts, reaching over to fist pump Brad.

I ruffle through the last of the wrapping, and a can of Budweiser falls into my lap. Except it no longer resembles a beer at all because Brad has somehow managed to cut up several cans and warped the aluminum to create a hamburger. There are strands of lettuce sticking out from the sides, a floppy tomato slice, and a beef patty that's been hammered out to look texturized. The bun's made from the bottoms of two cans, sandwiching everything together.

I glance over at Tony's three-dimensional beer can cheese, equipped with holes. "These are amazing!"

I can't believe Brad, whose only concern in life is when the Browns are playing next, has taken the time to do something like this. I turn the burger over in my hands, examining how he meticulously twisted each piece with pliers, how long it must have taken him to do.

"It's nothing, really," he says, shrugging. "I did them during metal shop before winter break."

Ma comes in from the kitchen to see what all the fuss is about. "Oh, Bradley, how wonderful," she exclaims, her eyes lighting up when she sees what he's done.

"Don't think I forgot about you, Mama Mac!" Brad throws Ma another of his paper wads. He beckons her to take a seat on the couch's arm, and Ma unwraps a larger version of my burger—only hers has a pile of pull tabs strung together on top to symbolize her unruly red hair.

Ma lines up our little beer can family on the fireplace mantle as Tony queues up *Die Hard*. And although I try to stay present for the movie, all I think about is Tristan. He posted a video to his Instagram Story earlier of who I assume is his little brother popping a Christmas cracker at the dinner table, which means he's definitely seen that I've followed him and has chosen to ignore it. My jaw stiffens at the realization.

A part of me wants to shut myself off from the world and just message him already. It wouldn't be anything serious—a "Happy Holidays" or a "hey, man"—something simple to get the ball rolling. I won't, though. Obviously.

It's getting late by the time Tony and Brad say their goodbyes. At the bottom of the stairwell, a gust of wind sends snow swirling along the sidewalk. Icicles lining our building's gate shimmer in the neon glow of Mr. Fong's Laundromat sign.

Brad hovers at the door, asking if he can stay. He does this every year. And every year, Ma lectures him about the importance of spending time with family. Even though his dad's tried to sober up on and off since Brad was a kid, December is usually when he falls off the wagon.

I close the door behind them, sealing off the cold, and turn around. Ma's leaning on the back of the couch with her arms crossed. She's watching me intently, her eyebrows raised like she's expecting me to say the first word.

"What?" I ask, looking down like I've spilled something over my shirt.

Ma sucks air between her teeth, but I can't take her seriously while she's still in her unicorn onesie. "Do we need to have a talk about underage drinking again?"

My body tenses. We've gone through this before: when Ma's

driven me home in the middle of the night because I've had too much to drink; when she's picked up The Tripod from the police station after some guys provoked us in Mariner's Park.

I fight the urge to discretely check my breath. "I don't know what you mean."

Ma pushes off the couch with a huff and clicks her tongue. "I know what Baileys smells like, Wes." She sighs, walking over to the coffee table to clear our dirty plates. "But I was a teenager once too. And there's a very thin line between being a cool mom and an overbearing one. You know I prefer you boys drinking where I can keep an eye on you, but don't pull that crap on me again. You might be some tough guy at school, but don't you ever forget who raised you."

"I won't. I swear." I throw my hands up and make an X over my heart.

"You're lucky I care for those boys. One more drink and I wouldn't have let them leave."

We move into the kitchen then to deal with the leftovers and the tissue paper explosion. Ma pauses as she shovels casserole into a plastic Tupperware. "I'm worried about Brad."

I pause at the fridge. "What? Why?"

"He drank before he got here. I could smell beer on his breath," she admits, waving a spoon in the air. "Which is not something you drink before 11 A.M. on Christmas morning. Especially not as a seventeen-year-old."

"You think it's an issue?" I ask, wiping the counter down with a rag. Sure, Brad's dad is an alcoholic, but it never occurred to me that he might have a problem too.

Ma purses her lips. "I'm not sure, to be honest. But he seems on edge." She closes the container in front of her and grabs my chin. "Keep an eye on him, will you? And let me know if things get worse," she says, her eyes softening. "I'll give his mom a call in a few days to check in."

I bite my lip, nodding, when my phone vibrates again in my pocket. It's probably one of the guys messaging our group chat to say they've made it home.

From the notification on my lock screen, I open Instagram to find that Tristan's added two new videos to his Instagram Story, and my heart plummets.

I mumble an excuse to leave, rushing out of the kitchen and turning the lock on my bedroom door. I take a deep breath and sink to the ground.

Three times one is three.

Three times two is six.

I replay one of the videos. Tristan's camera is tilted toward the ceiling so all you can see is the angel topper on a white Christmas tree. In the background, a dozen voices sing off-key to "Santa Baby," underscored by roaring laughter and a conversation I can't quite make out. I bite my lip, stifling a smile, when my finger grazes the bottom of the screen, accidentally tapping the heart on Tristan's Story.

"Dammit!" I yelp, panicking as I bolt forward and untap the screen. Tristan's Story moves on to him and his cousins dancing to a viral TikTok routine. My right hand trembles. Was I fast enough? Will he even be notified that I liked it if I've already reversed my decision?

I bury my face in the crook of my elbow.

Why can't I ever leave things alone? Why did I have to go and like his video the second he posted it like some craven fan?

Three times three is nine.

What's the point in getting my hopes up only to risk being hurt at the hands of someone who's made it clear they want nothing to do with me?

As I lie awake that night, I pull up The Tripod's group chat and fire off a text. Because if anyone can make me feel better, it's the two of them.

Skate park.

Tomorrow.

Be there.

I add a row of dynamite emojis just so we're on the same page.

8.

KING OF ENDLESS CATASTROPHES

When we arrive at the skate park the next morning, there's not a soul in sight.

Tony empties two spray cans from the pockets of his puffy winter jacket and surveys the area. We follow him to a bright blue ramp—the park attendants must have painted it recently—and hang our feet over the edge.

I can already feel myself starting to relax.

The Tripod's been coming to this skate park since we were kids. It's a few blocks down from the Walter Prescott Theater, tucked behind Valentine's city library.

This is where I'm supposed to be. With the guys. Hanging out. Without a care in the world. Not crushing on someone who won't give me the time of day.

I light a joint, and it dangles from my lip as I take pictures of Brad doing varial double heelflips in the concrete bowl below us.

"See if you can stop right there," I mumble, pointing to a spot on the ground. If Brad nails the takeoff, I can get a shot of him midflip in the exact moment where the bottoms of his shoes and the top of his skateboard don't touch.

Brad nods, taking position across the bowl, and continues the story I interrupted. "Rick didn't even make it to the dinner table this year." He charges down the ramp, kicking his right foot to gain momentum. "It's okay, though, I let my niece draw on his face."

For a moment, Brad is suspended in the air.

Tony snorts, shaking the spray can in his hand, as I snap a picture of Bud landing firmly on his feet. He curses out loud, his skateboard coming out from under him. I look at the photo: Brad's crouched down with his hands balled into fists. He's shouting in the direction of his board off camera. With the right Instagram filter, I think I can bring out the intensity in his eyes.

We take turns skating around the park, filming each other doing nosegrinds and big spins so we can upload them to Reddit, where there's a whole community of skateboarders online. The Tripod's made a pact to visit all the major skate parks in the US after graduation.

"At least your family stayed away from politics," Tony huffs, stepping back to admire his work. He's drawn a pinup doll in a sailor's suit, riding a humpback whale. "Mine was so riled up by dinner, no one appreciated my spaghetti alle vongole."

Unable to contribute much to the conversation, seeing as how the only drama in my life recently has revolved around Tristan, I grab the spray can next to Tony's foot and get to work on a bulldog midbark I stole off some website.

My night was uneventful. Hannah and Tad came over, and we sweated over spicy green lentil curry and aloo gobi. After washing the dishes, we squished around the kitchen table and played one of the board games Tad brought over, which, if I'm being honest, is the only Christmas Day tradition I'd rather do without.

I'm about to sign my initials next to my contribution on the wall when I stop myself. What would Tristan think if he saw me tagging the park? Every time I've tried not to obsess over him, my mind wanders, and I'm right back where I started. I lower the can in my hand.

I left my phone in my room after the debacle with Tristan's Instagram Story. I didn't want to fixate on it any more than I already had.

Then, as if I'd conjured him from my thoughts, the bell above the Starbucks door across the street rings, and Tristan steps outside.

He walks down the sidewalk in a black tracksuit, his head bobbing along to unheard music coming from the oversized headphones on his ears.

I tell myself to ignore him. To forget about yesterday and whether he saw that I'd liked and unliked his post. But when I notice one of Tristan's ballet slippers drop out of the gym bag hanging from his shoulder and onto the ground, my feet are moving before I can stop them.

I fake a call from Ma asking me to come home.

Brad shouts after me, but I'm already past the park's gate and picking up speed on my board.

What am I even doing?

I glance back at the library, seeing the edge of the skate park through its window, and weigh my options. I could turn around now and pretend this never happened. I could make some lame excuse about Ma not needing me after all and spend the rest of the afternoon with The Tripod before heading to work.

But Tristan continues on his way in the general direction of the theater, completely unaware he's dropped something. I assume he's heading to rehearsal, so I cross the street and grab his slipper by the laces without getting off my board.

I'll just pop into the theater quick, explain what happened, and return the slipper. This doesn't have to be awkward. He doesn't even have to thank me.

So why do I still find myself hoping he'll ask me to stick around? That if all else fails, he'll let me watch him dance again?

Eventually, Tristan walks around the side of the building and disappears through the back. I act fast, racing over and wedging my foot in the frame before the door has the chance to close behind him. The last thing I need is for that bouncer kid to return and notice I'm not on the guest list.

I pause for a second, waiting to see if Tristan will come back. When he doesn't, I slip inside, and darkness swallows me whole.

What the—I can't see a thing.

My eyes fight to adjust, but it's no use. It's pitch-black in here. Where is everyone?

Tucking my skateboard under my arm, I run my fingers along the wall, searching for either a light switch or a door handle to get out of here. From what I remember since being here last, I have to go down a long hallway and through another entrance before it opens up to the auditorium. Did the bouncer take me left or right?

I decide to go right, feeling good about my decision, until I stub my toe on the corner of something blocking the way.

"Ow!" I shriek, falling into the wall. I cover my mouth as my voice echoes into the abyss. My toe is throbbing.

Footsteps appear down the hall.

"Who's there?" Tristan calls out into the void.

"Uh," I say out loud without a pause before realizing what this must look like.

I'm in the dark. Alone. Having followed behind Tristan without him knowing.

I legit look like a certified stalker.

It's so quiet my ragged breath is the only thing I hear. I turn around to leave—I think—but I have no idea where I'm going and burst through door after door until the cement floor gives way to veneered wood. I've walked out onto the stage.

Someone flicks a switch, and the stage lights above me come alive. I cover my eyes, wiping the sweat from my forehead.

"Wes?"

I turn around and see Tristan standing there, clutching a pipe wrench like it's a baseball bat. I throw my hands up over my head, and my skateboard clatters to the floor with a bang.

"I-I swear I can explain," I stammer, fighting to catch a breath. Tristan lowers his arms. His eyes bulge out in alarm.

"What the hell, Wes? You nearly gave me a heart attack!" he shouts.

Papier-mâché trees surround us. We're in the middle of one of the first *Nutcracker* scenes, where snowflake children danced around Emily in the pinewood forest. A gigantic cardboard moon sits overhead.

"Sorry," I say between breaths. The heat coming from the stage lights above radiates down on my neck. "I saw you coming out of Starbucks, and then you dropped this, and I—" I hold the slipper out as a peace offering, failing to explain myself any further.

Tristan blinks. And blinks again. "And you thought it'd be a good idea to sneak up on me?" He huffs, shaking his head in disbelief. "What is wrong with you?"

I feel myself crumble under Tristan's scrutiny. My cheeks burn. "I wasn't thinking."

He clutches his chest. "Jesus, Wes, have you learned nothing from the news?" Tristan motions around himself, waving the wrench in the space between us.

I stare down at my feet. Across the stage, Tristan's laid out an unnecessary number of pencils beside a copy of *Paradise*

Lost. A notebook with a BLACK LIVES MATTER sticker on the cover sits on top of his bag.

I look back up and see the fear written plainly across Tristan's face. My voice catches in my throat. It's been less than twenty-four hours and I've already humiliated myself again. No—it's so much more than that. I unknowingly made Tristan feel unsafe. "I'm so sorry. I should go."

I grab my skateboard off the stage and maneuver past him. I can't imagine what ran through his head when he thought he was being followed. I'm used to people watching me out of the corner of their eyes, but this is not the same thing. Not at all.

Tristan's frown deepens. "No, wait. Stop," he whispers, grabbing my elbow and sighing. "Stay."

What is he doing? Tristan's eyes search my face. For what, I don't know.

"It's actually super creepy in here alone," he adds.

As if on cue, the theater groans in the cold. I thought maybe Tristan had been on his way to rehearsal, but I was wrong. We're the only ones in the building, illuminated by the vintage lights lining the stage.

The knot in my stomach untangles, and I force air back into my lungs. "I just—I don't know how to do *this*. Any of this, really."

I shift under Tristan's gaze. He doesn't ask what that could mean. I'm not even sure I know the answer. My toes curl in my shoes.

Tristan returns the wrench to a box next to the pulley system backstage and shrugs off his jacket. He's wearing a white long-sleeve shirt and takes his time rolling the sleeves to his elbows. I clear my throat when he notices me watching him and move to set my skateboard down next to his things. I take a seat on top of my board, rolling the wheels back and forth beneath me.

From up on stage, the rows of seats in the audience look like they go on forever. I try to pinpoint where we were sitting that night, but it's hard to tell in the dark.

"Is it bothering you again?" Tristan asks, breaking the silence.

"What?"

I look up and he's pointing at my leg. "You're limping."

I don't bother correcting him. While the doctors never found anything wrong with my knee, I'm technically *still* limping since the last time I saw him, and every day before that since I was seven. Nowadays, the pain fades in and out, and it's such a small thing—him noticing the gait in my walk—that I almost tell him the truth. I just wouldn't know where to start.

"How's the book?" I ask instead, reaching over and tapping the cover of *Paradise Lost* next to me. I wonder if he can hear my heart pounding in my chest.

Tristan rolls out his shoulders. "I have to read it for English. This is where I come to clear my head."

He bends at the waist, reaching to touch his toes. I try my best to look anywhere but at him, afraid I'll check him out again.

"You remind me a lot of him, y'know." He turns to glance at me, still in his bent position.

"Of who?"

Tristan raises his eyebrows as if to say "duh." "Lucifer."

"I remind you of the Devil?" I ask with a scoff.

He rolls his eyes. "Every story has its villain, Wes. It just depends on the one who's telling it. Lucifer may be God's antagonist, but what does that make God to Lucifer? It's all about perspective."

"Ohhh." I nod, wishing for once that I'd actually done the reading. I have no idea what he's talking about, but I don't want him knowing that. My chest tightens, and I feel like I should say something to impress him. But I can't even remember the last book I picked up for school, never mind for pleasure. I always feel stupid when I read. Like I can never quite decipher what the words written in front of me are saying.

Tristan sees me hesitate and chuckles to himself. "You should really read it sometime."

I turn the book over in my hands and see the PROPERTY OF WESTGATE ACADEMY label in the bottom corner next to a cross. I want to object like he hasn't seen right through me, but Tristan smiles and drops down next to me. He tucks his left leg under him.

"So you're like, *really* into skateboarding, aren't you?" he asks.

"Yeah," I say, leaning back. "I've pretty much been doing it since my ma bought me my first board when I was eight." I leave out the part about her finding it at a yard sale, afraid he'll judge me.

Tristan nods, biting his lower lip in concentration. He walks his fingers over the ground in front of him to stretch out his quad.

"Who's your favorite . . . boarder? Player? Sorry, I'm not up to speed on skateboarding lingo."

"Nyjah Huston, no doubt," I reply without skipping a beat. "Who?"

"Highest paid professional skateboarder in the world? Six-time world champion?"

Tristan scratches his chin. "I didn't know skateboarding was considered a sport."

"Is dancing?" I smile, making sure to catch his eye so he knows I'm joking. The last thing I want to do is upset him again, but as I wait for his reaction, Tristan lifts his head and laughs. He falls out of his stretch, and suddenly, we're laughing together. And it feels good to know I haven't completely ruined everything.

"How long have you been a dancer?" I ask when we finally settle down.

Tristan grabs a pencil and jots something in the margins of his notebook before getting back up on his feet. "Twelve years."

I tilt my head back, stunned. "You started dancing when you were five?"

I don't know what that kind of dedication feels like. Besides Vincenzo's Instagram page, I've never taken anything seriously in my life.

Tristan nods, unfazed, rotating his ankle in circles. "I've wanted to be a dancer for as long as I can remember. But my parents were afraid of how people would treat me, so they signed me up for basketball. I hated it so much. But Black guys play basketball, right?" He asks the question, but I think it's rhetorical because he continues without a pause. "One day, I got hit by the ball during a game and cried. My coach did *not* like that. He grabbed me by my jersey, pulled me off the court, and told me that real men don't cry."

"Brutal," I breathe.

"My parents could not have yanked me out of that game faster. After that, I quit the team and picked up dancing." Tristan pushes off the stage with his right foot, pirouetting in one swift motion. "And suddenly, I was the happiest version of myself. I practiced day in, day out, more than anyone I knew, because I wasn't going to let anyone take that away from me. I couldn't. Deep down, kids know who they are, and I was lucky to have the parents that I do. Who encouraged me to be myself. If they had kept me playing basketball, doing something I hated, who knows where I'd be today. I could've become someone else entirely. A musician, a stoner, a—"

"A punk?" I interrupt.

Tristan stops dancing. He squints like he's trying to see me better. Finally, he says, "I could have become someone who'd rather hide themselves because they're afraid of what other people might think if they knew the real them."

The tips of my ears turn red. I'm not entirely sure he was even directing the comment at me, but I look down at my leather jacket nonetheless. "This is the real me," I say, noticing the heat of the stage lights again on my neck.

"I think both of those things can be true. But I see you, Wes. The boy in the audience that night, the one who didn't think anyone was watching him, was not the same guy I met in the lobby after the show."

I raise my eyebrows. "You were watching me?"

Tristan laughs. "Don't let it get to your head. I only saw you when the lights came up as we took our final bow. No offense, but have you seen yourself? You're not exactly the ballet's target audience."

I don't reply, not knowing what to do with everything he's revealed. A part of me thinks this is all a joke, that he can't actually be serious. No one ever notices me except when I'm in trouble.

"You intrigue me, Wesley Mackenzie."

Tristan's words come out slow—deliberate—and he makes me sit with them. Leaving their meaning up for interpretation. He watches me closely, as if he can see the gears turning in my head. He's unlike anyone I've ever known.

I grab a pencil from Tristan's endless supply and tap it against his notebook to avoid his eyes. "Then why didn't you follow me back on Instagram?" My voice comes out in a hurry, softer than I had meant for it to.

Tristan stands up straight and clasps his wrist. "What?"

I open the notebook, flipping through until I find a blank page. I feel so petty for bringing it up. Like Instagram is the worst of my problems. Tristan told me his life story, and all I can think about is social media? What is wrong with me?

"I followed you on Christmas Eve and you never followed me back," I admit, drawing little circles on the page.

Tristan puffs out his lower lip, blowing out a breath. "I turned off my notifications years ago because they were ruining my focus during rehearsals. Here." He looks around the stage and charges over to his bag. He makes sure I'm watching before getting out his phone and unlocking the screen. After a few seconds of scrolling, he says, "Done."

I feel like I should thank him, and I open my mouth to do so, when a phone rings.

Tristan looks down at his hand, his eyebrows squishing together. He whips his head around, following the sound to the edge of the stage.

"A Mr. Pecorino is calling," he says, reaching down and waving my phone in the air.

I stand up, patting my jeans, and flinch at the sound of Tony's last name. When did my phone fall out of my pocket? My breath catches in my throat as I practically knock it out of his hand.

I let the call go to voicemail. The walls of the theater feel like they're coming down around me with the weight of my lies finally catching up to me.

"Ahem."

I turn around to see Tristan's hands on his hips.

"What?" I cough.

"Don't 'what' me." He scoffs. "Why was the owner of the pizza parlor calling you?"

"Because I ordered a pizza . . ." Though I look Tristan in the eye, my voice trails off into the empty rows of the theater. I stand my ground, puffing my chest out to appear more confident than I actually am.

Tristan doesn't buy it. He crosses his arms, arches his eyebrow.

"Okay, *fine*," I admit, reaching for the back of my neck. "Me and my friends work there."

Tristan ponders my response. "Ah," he breathes, dropping his hands to his sides, "that explains why you were acting so strange that night."

"Right." I can't share with Tristan the real reason I lied. That I didn't tell him and Emily the truth because I didn't want The Tripod seeing us together. That if they had, who knows what they would have said?

"Is that why you left?" Tristan asks, leaning closer. "Because of your friends?"

"Yes," I say a little too quickly, watching the way his shoulders slump when I do. I'm always so quick to lie, but right now, I don't want to. "Well, no, they weren't the only reason," I admit, scuffing my shoe along the stage. "I overheard you and Emily . . ."

"Oh," Tristan replies. At first, I'm not sure he gets it until the realization dawns on his face. "*Ohhh*. You heard us talking about you."

I nod, recalling how he drew out the "no" in "no way" when Emily asked if he was into me. How he said he didn't have time to take me on as a "project." I pinch my eyebrow. "Were you telling the truth?"

Tristan lets out a breath. "Wes, I—" He redirects. Tries again. "It's just that sometimes, Emily can be—"

"Judgmental?"

"I was going to say a bitch, but that works too."

I laugh, unlocking my phone to check the time. "Shit, I'm going to be late for work!"

I turn around, and Tristan's so close we're almost touching. I can feel his breath along the collar of my shirt. He smells like black coffee and sweat. I catch a whiff of his deodorant, of lemongrass and ocean breeze. If I leaned forward, our lips would touch. I realize I want them to.

"Where'd you get that picture?"

Before I can ask what he's talking about, Tristan reaches over and awakens my phone with a tap.

I look down at the screen, at the row of columns reaching toward a starry sky. I took it on Halloween night, outside Valentine's city hall. Brad's cousin had made us some fake IDs, and we tried to sneak into a local bar. We figured if we put a costume on like everyone else, we'd blend in with the crowd, but the bouncer kicked us out of the line before we even made it to the door. We spent the rest of the night wandering the city. The photo I took is in black-and-white. I bumped up the shadows so the ridges of each column were more pronounced. Sitting in the bottom right corner, sandwiched between two of the columns, is a homeless man sleeping. I thought it made for a startling contrast between the opulence of American architecture and the poverty riddling its streets.

"I took it."

Tristan grabs my phone and inspects the photo again like he doesn't believe me. I try taking it back, but he spins around on his tiptoes and prances around the stage. Literally.

"*You* took this?" He glances over at me. "It's beautiful."

I shrug again. "I'm always taking pictures. Of food I order at restaurants. At people walking in the streets. I actually run Vincenzo's Instagram page."

"You're really talented, Wes," Tristan says, looking up from my phone. "You should pursue photography. Even if you don't want to go to college." He says the last part with a wink, his face illuminated by the white light radiating off the screen.

"Well, you clearly don't know what you're talking about." There's a bitterness to my voice I wasn't expecting, a sharp edge

I didn't mean to add. I wasn't prepared for him to compliment me like that. For all I know, Tristan could be mocking me. I feel my shoulders rounding inward.

Compliments and I have never been friends. On the off-chance The Tripod ever says something nice, it's usually paired with a headlock or a swift punch to the arm. When I was in elementary school, I threw dirt at anyone who called me cute. I didn't like the attention.

Tristan takes a step back, almost like I've wounded him. But I didn't mean to. I didn't realize what I was saying before it was too late. So I do what any levelheaded teenager would do when they've misread a situation; I rip my phone out of his hand and take a picture instead of apologizing.

Tristan opens his mouth, but no words come out. He reaches for my phone again, but I jump backward, walking over to retrieve my board.

"Did you just take a picture of me?" Tristan asks, his voice lifting at the end.

I open my camera roll to see my latest work. "Yeah, I did. So what?" Based on his reaction and my general lack of reading the room, maybe taking a picture of someone you've basically just met isn't what any levelheaded teenager would do. "Is that okay?"

This time, I let him yank my phone out of my hand. Maybe I'm overthinking it, but I feel Tristan's fingers hesitate over mine. The hairs on my forearm stand to attention as he inspects the image.

"You're lucky I look cute," Tristan says, shoving my phone into my chest. Like Cupid's arrow straight to the heart.

He walks me through the backstage hall, this time flooded in light.

"You know, you didn't actually answer my question back there. About whether you were telling the truth or not," I say as he gestures for me to step outside.

I hear him laugh behind me. "Don't worry, I'll get to it eventually. And hey."

I turn around to see his face poking out the door.

"You better send me that photo before your shift," he says, slowly closing the door. "Because if you don't, I know where you work."

JUST BEFORE MIDNIGHT, when I'm winding down and getting ready for bed, my phone pings with a new notification from Instagram.

> In case you feel the need to tell me
> how nice my eyes are again.

My phone slips out of my fingers and crashes along the bathroom tiles.

I pick it back up and reread the screen to make sure I haven't made the whole thing up.

Below the message, Tristan's left a ten-digit number.

No.

What?

I must be hallucinating.

Tristan gave me his number. His actual phone number. I now have Tristan's personal number in my phone.

I can't breathe.

To make sure he didn't give me a fake, I send him a quick text, followed by the picture I took.

He replies a second later.

> Meet me at the theater tomorrow? I
> have an idea. 🐷

9.

DEAR PHOTOGRAPHER, COUNT ME OUT

Life has a weird way of showing up when you least expect it to. And I don't mean in an "everything happening for a reason" way either. That's some "tattoo on your arm when you're drunk" load of crap anyway.

It's living your life in a cycle of skateboarding, skipping classes, and pizza-making one moment, then showing up fifteen minutes early to an empty theater the next, all because you're trying to impress someone who, until a few days ago, didn't exist in your world at all.

Tristan meets me at the spot where we said goodbye yesterday and ties a bandana over my eyes.

"How do I know I can trust you?"

He takes a moment to consider the question before patting down the bandana to make sure I can't see anything. "You can't." He coughs.

I go to object that I never agreed to this, but he takes my hand and leads us inside. He squeezes my fingers to reassure me, his skin warm against mine.

I fumble my step.

Is this a date? I've never been on one before. How do you know when something is a date and not a casual hangout between two friends? Tristan did give me his number, but maybe his Wi-Fi is finicky. Instagram messaging isn't always reliable.

I didn't tell Ma where I was going this morning when I asked to borrow the car. It's not that she didn't care—she did ask—but if I told her what I was doing, she wouldn't have let me go without asking a million questions.

Silence falls between us as Tristan walks me through the hall, but it doesn't feel wrong. I don't feel the need to speak. Neither does he, because we remain like that until he coughs again.

"Are you getting sick?"

"Oh, no," Tristan replies when he catches a breath. "My throat gets super dry when I'm nervous."

My upper lip grazes the edge of the bandana. I can't help smiling wide. Maybe this *is* a date after all.

I reach out in front of me with my free hand, pretending to feel my way around. "Why are you nervous? You're not the one with the blindfold on."

"Touché."

Tristan texted me this morning to tell me to wear loose-fitted clothes, which was weird since I'm never not in loose-fitted clothes. I settled on an old pair of black sweats and a gray Henley. My hair was not cooperating after I stepped out of the shower, so I threw on a green beanie.

"You won't be needing this," he says, guiding me out of my leather jacket.

I pinch my eyebrow. My jacket is my comfort zone, what I use to shield myself from the rest of the world. Without it on, I feel naked. Exposed.

"Is this the part where you tell me what's happening? Or is someone about to jump out of the shadows and knock me out?"

Tristan doesn't answer. I hear him scurry off to my left, and a second later, he claps his hands.

"It is time," he announces, dropping his voice for effect.

I reach behind my head and let the bandana fall to the floor. It takes my eyes a moment to get accustomed to the light, but when they do, I see that part of the stage has transformed. In the corner, a white backdrop now covers *The Nutcracker*'s pinewood forest with a pair of umbrella reflectors hovering over it. Things I've read about—they help soften the glow of bright lights—but have never seen in person.

It's then that I realize I'm standing in the middle of a makeshift photo booth.

"What is all this?"

"Sorry, I . . . know it's a lot. I have a tendency to go overboard. But I thought it'd be fun to do a photo shoot." Tristan smiles and positions himself in front of the backdrop. He must have changed right next to me, because he's now standing across the stage in a black leotard with soft pink leg warmers. I knew I should've peeked when I had the chance.

Tristan turns out both of his legs, bending his knees and straightening them again.

"But why?" I ask.

I've never been put on the spot like this. My photography—if you can call it that, which you really can't—has always been something I did in my own time, spontaneously, when no one else was around. Aside from the few photos I've printed at Walmart and hung around my room—of the Ohio River at dusk, of Dublin's bizarre Cornhenge attraction, of The Tripod skateboarding through town—they usually just sit on my phone. No one has ever seen my work.

This was all a nice gesture, sure, but I can't perform under pressure. Everything feels too staged. Too manufactured. I grab the skin on my elbows.

Tristan notices me stalling and frowns. "I let you see my world. And after that amazing photo on your phone, I wanted—" He pauses, tracing the backdrop with his fingers. "I wanted to get a glimpse into yours."

I don't know what to say to that. No one's ever done anything like this for me. How long did it take him to set all this up? Like, the pair of reflectors hanging from the rafters? That's easily a two-person job. Did he have any help?

I shuffle my feet forward, eyeing the light stand a few meters away. I suddenly feel the need to sit down. "I've never used any of this equipment."

Tristan smiles again, coming over to grab my hand. "That's okay, they're all ready to go. I borrowed everything from the theater's storage room and spent the last two hours watching YouTube tutorials," he says, pulling me over to where he's propped open a stepping stool. He motions for me to take a seat.

"But I don't know how to take someone's portrait," I admit, feeling restless. I want to get up and go anywhere else but here. Maybe I should leave. Block Tristan on Instagram. Erase his number. That feels a hell of a lot easier than what he's asking me to do.

I fan my face. The heat emitting from the stage lights is burning my neck again. Why do they always have to be so damn hot?

"No worries. We can do motion shots then." Tristan grabs one of the light stands and moves it further away so he has room to dance. He kicks off the ground with one foot, extending his leg behind him, and lands on the other. "As long as you're okay with me being your muse?"

He throws me a joking wink, but my chest aches. How do I tell him that he's inspired me from the first moment he set foot on stage as the Nutcracker?

I shift on the stool, pulling my phone out from my back pocket. My breath comes out in a hurry, my face still impossibly warm. "I'm not sure about this."

Tristan pauses, his hands held together in the air above him. "There's no one here, Wes. Give it a try. You'd really be helping me out anyway. I need photos of myself dancing for my college application."

He waits for me to agree, which I do reluctantly, then runs backstage to turn on some music. I rub my palms over my sweatpants as an instrumental track pours out from the theater's sound system.

"So . . . what do you want me to take a picture of?" I call out, holding my phone up half-heartedly.

Tristan reappears and stretches his neck, rolling it from side to side. "Whatever you feel like."

I follow him with my phone as the lens captures his movement, and I let the music guide me. It starts off slow with the gentle caressing of piano keys. Tristan twirls around to warm up.

I take a few practice shots, swearing each time they turn out blurrier than the last, and trash the first ten pictures. "I suck at this."

"No, you don't," Tristan says. "Keep going."

I watch him take over the stage, extending past the corner where we're set up. He tiptoes around so elegantly I forget I'm watching Tristan and not the actual Nutcracker.

As the music grows louder—with a violin joining in on the chorus, followed by the echoes of a church choir—I place where I've heard it before. "This is the same song you were listening to in the car on our way to Vincenzo's."

Tristan looks over his shoulder midleap, smiling as he lands. "It's the one I'm auditioning with for St. Sebastian's in the new year. I've been practicing this routine for months."

"Wait, you've been doing this exact same dance the whole time? Aren't you sick of it?"

I can't imagine spending weeks, or even days, on end fixating on something like that. The thought makes my head spin.

Tristan taps his pointed right foot along the stage. "Emily says I'm a perfectionist, and maybe she's right, but I have to work ten times harder than any of my peers if I want an actual shot at a scholarship. I get super anxious unless I've put in at least two hours of rehearsal a day."

My mouth falls open. "Two *hours*? Like, on purpose? I'm lucky if I can focus on anything for more than two minutes."

I swerve around the stool then, and as I follow Tristan's footwork with my camera, I can feel my confidence growing. It isn't an obvious thing, but I hold my phone a little closer, my eyes scanning the stage ahead to figure out my next shot. I inspect the latest image, impressed that I've not only captured the lift of his leg without obscuring it, but also the emotion that flickers across Tristan's face. If I'm not mistaken, it looks like joy.

"How does it feel to break your record?" Tristan laughs.

I go to ask him what he means when he points at a clock behind the stage's red curtain. I could've sworn we just started, but according to the time on the wall, we've been at it for nearly an hour. I open my camera roll and scroll through hundreds of pictures of Tristan dancing as proof. How did that even happen?

"If that makes me the first person you've lasted more than two minutes with, I'm honored."

I throw my face into my hands to hide my blushing as Tristan pirouettes in tight circles around me.

"What's St. Sebastian's, anyway?" I ask through my fingers.

Tristan skids to a halt and collapses to the floor, slamming his fists in mock anger against the stage. "What's *St. Sebastian's*?" He gapes over at me. "Only the number one performing arts conservatory in New York City. You don't get out much, do you?"

I shrug my shoulders. "Apparently not."

Tristan wants me to be as excited as he is, I can tell by the way he's side-eyeing me, but I don't get it. It's only a school. And New York City is halfway across the country. Immediately, I think, *Where would that leave us?*

Not that there is an us.

"Focus," he says, pointing at my phone in my lap.

Tristan's moves are so graceful, like how I'd imagine a swan would glide across the lake in Central Park. He twists his face in pain to match the rise and fall of the song as he tumbles across the stage, his arms and legs conforming to the music.

I watch him through my phone when he falls to his knees and looks up at the chandelier hanging from the ceiling.

His brown eyes reflect the lighting from above as dust motes dance around him.

Click.

The song comes to an end, and he picks himself back up, grabbing a paper towel from a dispenser backstage and bringing it to his face.

"How'd you do?" he asks, making his way over.

I place my hand over his chest and take an exaggerated step back so he knows not to come any closer. "An artist never reveals his secrets."

Tristan tilts his head, adjusting a strap on his leotard. "So I'm a secret then?"

Though I scoff, it's the truth, isn't it? He's becoming a secret faster than I know what to do with. One I've already started to keep from everybody in my life.

I feel myself spiraling.

How long will I be able to do this before messing up? Before I lose The Tripod, or Ma, or even him? Or worse: all of them, all at once. It's enough to turn away, to hide the redness creeping up my neck.

"I. That's not what I meant—"

Tristan puts a hand on my shoulder. "Wes, I'm kidding."

I swallow hard.

Kidding.

Right.

Because this is our first time hanging out alone on purpose. There's no reason to be getting worked up like this. And yet . . .

I try not to let it get to me.

The weight of everything to come.

"How do you manage to act so cool all the time?" I ask, pocketing my phone. "Nothing ever seems to faze you."

Tristan arches an eyebrow, looking at me like I've said the stupidest thing possible. But I wish I could be as calm as him and not have to count in multiples of three to bring myself down from an outburst. Tristan seems so assured of himself. Even now, he's holding himself like he's striking a pose on a runaway.

"Believe me, under all this"—he circles his face—"I'm a mess. I just don't have the luxury of being anything but positive. At least, not in public."

Between the comment about working harder than his peers and what he's just said, I realize Tristan is opening up to me. He's allowing me in, little by little.

"Sorry, I didn't mean to bring it up."

Tristan has a faraway look on his face, like he's remembering something. "A mom almost called the cops on me last week because she thought I was causing a 'disturbance' in the parking lot at school. There's this one move in my audition piece I can't get right." He demonstrates what he means by flicking his left foot out to pivot but gives up. "I wasn't hurting anyone. I only lost my cool for one minute and hit a tree." Tristan sighs, his shoulders sagging.

I walk over so that we're standing side by side and bring the back of my hand to his. He loops his pinkie through mine, and I lose my breath. It feels so intimate. So trusting. All I want right now is to turn and hug him, but I don't know if he wants that. I don't want to ruin the moment. "If it makes you feel any better, I've had the cops called on me more times than I care to admit. I've usually deserved it, though."

Tristan pushes my hand away, letting out a laugh. "I bet."

And we stand like that, facing the empty audience.

I'm in no position to understand what he's gone through. I've never once had to stop myself from saying or doing anything because of the color of my skin. I've never been judged by something I can't, nor would ever want to, change about myself. I don't know what that feels like.

From the corner of my eye, Tristan wipes his nose. "Wait here," he says, walking away from the audience. "There's something I've always wanted to try."

I turn around, and he's at the opposite end of the stage, fixing his attention on the floor.

"What are you doing?"

Tristan shushes me and counts the number of panels between us out loud. When I think he's got what he's looking for, he claps his hands again.

"You ready?" he calls out, crouching down into a runner's starting position.

"Ready for what?" I look around frantically, hoping I missed something, but Tristan takes off, charging toward me like a bull to his matador.

When he's within reach, I throw my hands up, and he catapults himself into my arms. He forms a plank with his body as I lift him into the air and spin in my high-tops.

Tristan barks with glee, waving his arms in triumph as we lose it laughing and collapse to the floor. I fall back onto the stage, the wind escaping my lungs when Tristan drops on top of me.

"I can't believe we just did that!" he cheers, shoving me as he tries to stand.

I reach for his arm, pulling him back to the ground. I've never wanted to be closer to anyone in my life. Tristan looks me in the eye, his breath rippling over me as he gasps for air.

"Are you . . . ?" He doesn't finish. He shakes his head, that perfect grin of his forming along his face.

I know what he's asking without actually saying it. He already knows the answer, but it's something we have to get out of the way. To protect ourselves.

"Yeah, I am," I say, before quickly adding, "But don't tell anyone."

Tristan's gaze briefly falters. "I would never do that, Wes. You have my word."

I don't say anything more, and he doesn't press the issue.

I've never actually said the words out loud to another person. Sure, I've stared at myself in the mirror and said it when I was certain Ma wasn't home, but this feels different. Like if I shared my truth with him now, it would make it all the more final somehow. More real.

I like Tristan. There's no denying that. He makes me feel alive. And more importantly, after the stunt he pulled today with the photo shoot, he makes me feel seen.

Tristan smiles again, and in this moment, I know there's a possibility he might like me back. I can feel it in the way his palm rests gently on my chest. How his eyes never quite leave mine.

We're forced apart suddenly when a janitor enters the mezzanine and turns on a loud vacuum.

I stand first, using both hands to help him up.

Tristan checks his phone.

"Emily." He laughs when he sees me staring. "If I didn't know better, I'd think she were a lesbian."

"Why's that?"

"You know," Tristan says, rolling his eyes, "because there's that running joke about lesbians getting too attached too quickly? Meeting, moving in together, getting married before they know each other's last names—" He stops himself mid-sentence. "Actually, that's pretty offensive now that I think about it, so let's pretend I didn't say anything, okay?"

"I don't think she likes me that much," I admit, then mentally face-palm. Why did I have to bring that up? Maybe it's a gut reaction from what she said about me in the booth, but I have no reason to believe Emily actually feels that way.

Tristan heads across the stage to pack up his things. "No, she does." He grabs his bag off the floor and pauses before throwing it over his shoulder. "I just don't think she gets you."

"And you do?" I ask, racing over to help him tear down the backdrop.

Tristan looks right at me. "I'm trying to."

I let go of one of the corners of the backdrop and it shoots toward the ground, rolling into itself with a deafening clang. I wince, adjusting my beanie to avoid eye contact, as Tristan laughs.

No one's ever chosen to get to know me before. Especially not willingly. And I don't know what to make of that.

After gathering the rest of the equipment and shoving it into the theater's storage closet, we linger next to Tristan's car in the parking lot, stealing glances at each other when the other isn't looking.

"Thanks for today," I say, fidgeting with my skull ring. "Really."

"It was nothing. I actually needed that too. I've been under a lot of pressure lately," He replies, playing with the side-view mirror. He holds up a finger and turns to me. "But I do think you should reconsider joining your school's photography club. That is, if SOB even has one."

I smirk. "I'll think about it."

I look around the empty parking lot. Once I see that no one's around, I pull Tristan into a hug. His arms stick out at his sides, like he's not sure what to do outside of the darkness of the auditorium, before leaning in and laughing into my shoulder.

I hold on longer than I should.

At some point, we wish each other a happy New Year and say our goodbyes.

When I climb into Ma's car, it takes me a long time to come down from the high I'm feeling. It pulses beneath my skin, like sunshine wanting to return to the sky.

For a while, I just sit there, key in the ignition, running my hands along the steering wheel.

Wondering if it's possible to feel like this forever.

10.

AULD LANG(UISHING) SYNE

I get my answer three days later.

By the time Brad, Tony, and I climb the hill to Stacy Evans's New Year's Eve party, icicles have formed along the hem of our pants. We hip check each other into the mountains of snow piled along the street. Brad throws snowballs at passing cars with such accuracy that it squashes any suspicion I previously had that he'd already been drinking.

"Grab my foot!" Tony shouts as Brad hoists him over the wall of Stacy's gated community. We take turns carefully scaling the bricks so we don't drop the beer Tony's brother bootlegged for us.

Brad and I drag our boots through the snow. Stacy has a party every year, and every year, we aren't invited. I try telling Tony this isn't a good idea—that like usual, no one will want us there, and we'll end up getting thrown out—but he's unrelenting.

"What exactly is our plan? They're going to know we're coming," I say, pointing to the lamppost overhead where a security camera is following our every move.

"Don't worry about it, Big Mac," Tony says, punching my arm. "That's what the snow gear is for." He turns his back to the camera to demonstrate that we could be anyone under our baggy jackets.

Brad gives me the side-eye and shakes his head.

When I pull out my phone, Tristan's sent a selfie of him and Emily blowing on party horns. They're standing next to a wall done up with gold and silver streamers.

Having fun?

He replies instantly with a GIF of Betty White clinking a gigantic glass of wine with a friend. We bonded over *The Golden Girls* through text last night, taking turns to answer a BuzzFeed quiz determining which characters we were. To no surprise, Tristan got Rose while I ended up with Dorothy.

I send back a shivering selfie followed by a meme of Bea Arthur holding her hand up to her chin with the caption *I've had it up to here.*

Tristan reacts to the message with a thumbs-down, and I stifle a laugh.

Tony turns back to look at me, then kicks snow at my feet.

I've spent the last three days diverting any questions about my recent whereabouts. Between hanging out with Tristan and texting any moment we're apart, The Tripod's begun to notice my absence. Though we've seen each other at work, we usually spend all of winter break together, so it's enough of a red flag when I stopped being around. Honestly, the thought of hanging out with them while I'm keeping this huge secret makes me want to avoid them entirely. I try to be nonchalant about it by running over and sliding on a frozen puddle, but I can tell something's up by the way their eyes narrow every time I check my phone.

As we head further into the gated Shady Pines community, Brad hugs the beers to his chest. "Let's get this over with," he groans. Unless he's at a football game, Brad hates large crowds. He's been that way since his dad left him alone at the county fair to go day drinking. I don't blame him.

Music spills out into the night from Stacy's open front door. We push our way inside, and strobe lights dance through smoke-filled air like we've entered a nightclub downtown.

My feet stay rooted on the wet doormat.

The entire senior class is here tonight. And then some.

There must be at least a hundred people.

Peeling off my snow gear, I notice a cooler of White Claws sitting on a bench next to the door. The guys dismiss them for being "too girly" as they pass, but I reach down and grab a raspberry one, suddenly desperate for a drink.

I search the faces closest to me and freeze when my eye catches on the kid I cornered before winter break. He looks me up and down with alarm, muttering something I can't hear, and disappears through the basement door. Had I known he'd been invited, I would've brought his damn notebook with me.

But the run-in with him now makes me think. Tristan and Emily wouldn't be here too, would they? I just assumed when Tristan told me they were going to a party tonight, it was for one of his Westgate friends. But as I look around the room now, I'm not so sure. There's even a pretty good chance this is his neighborhood.

I'm on high alert as I poke my head around every corner. My heart is racing. I elbow past couples grinding in the family room, hunting for any sign of them.

Sliding the back door open, I scour the patio. "Do you mind?" I ask a kid smoking at the table. I don't wait for him to reply before grabbing the cigarette from his hand and taking a long, slow drag to quell my panic.

"Dude, what the hell?" he shouts, shoving me into the wall.

I mumble an apology, smoke escaping my lips, and step back inside.

Brad finds me at the door, his arms raised in the air. Beer spills from the overflowing cup in his hand. "Where'd you go?"

"I thought someone called my name." I know I told Ma I'd watch Brad's drinking, but I'm honestly too distracted for that right now. I don't meet his eye, afraid he'll see right through my weak lie. Like anyone at this party would be calling me.

Before he can answer, I do another lap around the house, and when I'm certain Tristan's not here, I realize Brad has followed me.

"We've got a situation," he says, nudging the crook of my elbow as he leads us back into the kitchen.

"I said go!"

Stacy yells into Tony's face, slurring her words. She hikes up the top of her silver dress. Her cheeks are bright red.

"Come on, Stace!" Tony pleads, though he laughs when he says it. On the way here, a part of me worried that Tony was always planning to cause a scene. That no matter what, we were always going to end the night with the football team tossing us out into the cold. "Nothing'll happen this time. Promise!"

Stacy flinches at what I assume to be the memory of sophomore year. I flinch too.

The guys and I were playing drunken football in the living room. I don't even know where the ball came from, to be honest. I remember Tony looking over his shoulder at Stacy, throwing her a kiss, and then proceeding to knock her grandma's urn off the mantle. Ashes filled the air like someone let off a smoke bomb.

"Fuck off, Tony!" Stacy warns, poking a manicured finger into his chest. "Grab your asshole friends and get out of here!"

I shove my hands in my pocket when Stacy glares over

at me, hatred spewing from her eyes. I haven't actually spoken to her since fifth grade when I stuck gum in one of her braids. To be fair, she did call me an idiot in front of the whole class for not knowing how to spell "metamorphosis." But I was eleven. Who knows how to spell "metamorphosis" when they're eleven?

Everyone in the kitchen goes quiet. Some even take out their phones to film. I can feel the judgment radiating off them as they sip their drinks, only barely pretending to make conversation with the person next to them.

I knew this was a bad idea.

Brad grabs someone's red cup from the counter and takes a swig. Where did his own drink go?

"I think we all just need to take a step back and breathe." Tony pinches his fingers together in front of him, pretending to meditate.

Stacy shoves him against the fridge. "If any of you start a fight," she says through her teeth, looking between us. "If you break anything, or set another car on fire, I'll call the cops." Stacy whips back to Tony then, her gaze turned to steel. "And if you so much as look at any of my friends, I'll chop off your balls."

Tony deflates as Stacy storms away in a huff. He grabs a drink from the guy next to him and downs it in one gulp.

"Come on," I say, reaching for his arm. "Let's bounce."

But Tony ducks out of the way. "We just got here, bro," he shouts over the music. "Stacy never makes it to midnight, anyway!" To drive his point home, Tony directs our attention to where Stacy's leaning over the dining table in the next room, her eyes fighting to stay open.

I have to squint to see her through the haze.

It's only been fifteen minutes and I've already had enough. My head hurts. I'm sore from standing at work earlier. And my search for Tristan left me mentally exhausted. "I'm getting the hell out of here."

I'm heading for the door when Brad steps in my path. "Please don't leave me, man," he says, passing a beer into my hand. "I'm begging you."

I run my finger over the cup's edge and sigh. If I head out now, I'd be breaking my promise to Ma to keep an eye on Brad. Even though I have no idea how I'd stop him if I did have to cut him off, I know I should stay.

"Fine," I grumble, taking a drink. "But I'm only doing this for you."

Brad presses his hands together in mock prayer and tilts his head over to the kitchen table where a group of stoned hipsters are setting up a game of flip cup. They seem less than amused when we walk over, but they move out of the way to let us join.

I give the crowd another once over before turning my attention to the game.

SOB's version of flip cup is the same as anyone's, except that the losing team has to chug beers from the mouth of a plastic flamingo that's been passed down through every senior class since 1991.

Brad and I have never lost a game, so we buddy up. And because we always win, Tony ends up losing, which makes him furious. When Brad calls him over to play, Tony dips into the living room and returns with the biggest football players he can find. We've tried telling him in the past that size doesn't matter, but he never listens.

Once we've counted down from ten, Brad squares off against a linebacker whose hands are way too large to even grasp the cup. From across the table, Tony barks at his teammate, shouting for him to move faster.

"One day we'll go easy on you," I say after flipping my cup over in two tries and winning the game for our team. I reach over to give Tony a handshake, but he swears under his breath and grabs the flamingo to chug back a beer.

"Good game," someone says behind me.

I whip around and standing there are the last two people I want to see.

Time stops as Tristan goes in for a hug. I want to wrap my arms around him in return, but my muscles tense beneath his touch.

I feel my lips move, but nothing comes out. For a second, I forget how to breathe.

I case the room over Tristan's shoulder and spot the gold and silver streamers hanging behind Stacy's couch. They're the same ones from his selfie earlier.

My words come out in a jumble. "Whatareyoudoinghere?"

"Everyone in town knows about Stacy's parties," Emily says, glancing up from her phone to wave at tonight's hostess. Stacy squeals, her hair flying around her as she twerks on the dance floor. "Hi, by the way."

All I manage is an unenthusiastic wave.

I lock eyes with Tristan.

I'm hyperaware of Brad beside me, pressing the hollow of his back into the window, but I don't move to introduce him. If I remain still and ignore the giant elephant in the room—that my worlds are colliding when I'm not ready for them to—maybe he'll go away.

But he doesn't.

Brad just stands there, fidgeting with the rim on his hat.

"Dude, why do girls take so long in the bathroom?" Tony pushes past the group of people congregating next to us and hands Brad another beer. "A man's got to go when a man's go to go!" When he notices Brad's fist at his side, the way I'm leaning back like I'm about to fall over, Tony glances over at Tristan and Emily.

I look between the four of them like I've pulled out my phone and immortalized the moment in a photograph. I see Tony's confusion, Brad's quiet anger. Because that's definitely what it is—anger.

A pit forms in my stomach.

Tristan watches me out of the corner of his eye like he's not sure what to do, and Emily's gaping at our clothes.

I pluck away at a button on my leather jacket. The Tripod's dressed like we always are—in baggy jeans and oversized hoodies. But scanning over Tristan's purple floral bomber jacket and skinny jeans and Emily's sheer midnight-blue party dress, I realize how dumb we must look to them.

I didn't even want to come here tonight. It's bad enough we weren't invited, but watching my friends size each other up, a visible divide between them, makes my blood boil.

Three times one is three.

I pass my beer between my hands, rubbing the condensation off along my hoodie. "Guys," I finally manage to choke out, "this is Tristan and Emily."

No one says anything.

The party carries on around us, but the music's so far away, like the speakers are submerged underwater.

Brad ends up breaking the silence. He points down at Tristan's hand. "Is that nail polish?"

Tony takes one look at Tristan's metallic-silver nails before heading to the kitchen to raid Stacy's pantry.

Tristan shoves his hands behind his back. "Yeah." He laughs awkwardly, rocking back on his heels. "I was going for Shea Couleé vibes, but I'm realizing now how wrong I was . . ." His voice trails off, his eyes following the current game of flip cup going on behind us. I suck in a stilted breath, instantly ashamed that he feels the need to hide himself from my friends.

"I don't get it," Brad replies blankly, just as Emily tells

Tristan how hot he looks. Brad holds back a laugh. "What the actual fu—"

"Don't," I interrupt, warning him with my eyes.

He chugs his beer. "Don't *what*?"

I'm not sure how to answer, so instead I hiss, "Slow down, Bud," grabbing the now empty bottle from his hand with too much force. Ma was right. Maybe his drinking *has* gotten out of control.

Brad wrinkles his nose. Then shoves me.

I feel the intensity behind his glare, see the muscles clench in his jaw. I've never stopped him from making fun of someone. Not once. His eyes drop to Tristan's chest, moving back and forth as he thinks.

I don't know what goes through Brad's mind then, but he doesn't like the conclusion he's arrived at. He turns his back to Tristan, stepping into the space between us.

"Can I talk to you for a second?" Brad huffs, then grabs me by the arm.

He leads me through the crowd and into Stacy's den. When we enter, a couple is making out on the computer desk.

"Leave," Brad demands.

The guy goes to object, but upon seeing Brad, he pulls his girlfriend from the room without another word.

Brad shuts the door behind them. I take a seat on the brown leather computer chair, spinning it around to face him.

"What was that?" Brad asks, fiddling with a paperweight on the desk.

"What was what?"

He refuses to look at me, his eyebrows connecting with the shadow of his hat. He tilts his chin up, squinting at a spot above my head. "Are you hanging out with those Westgate kids?"

I bite down hard, my teeth clattering together. I don't like the sudden change of tone in his voice. How he snarls at the end of his question. How his lip curls in revulsion.

"Does it matter?" I place my feet down on the floor, stopping the chair from swerving.

Brad considers me now, with the same intensity as earlier. "Yeah, it kind of does."

"Why?" I stand up, feeling beer as it thrashes inside my stomach from the sudden movement. I have to cover my mouth to stifle a wave of nausea.

Brad slams the paperweight down. "Because you disappear off the face of the earth and then these people show up, who we've never seen before, and they're acting like they're your best friends?"

I waver in my place from both the alcohol and the bluntness of Brad's words. The way he's standing now—leaning his weight against the desk, twirling his finger along the surface—I feel terrible.

But then, he keeps talking.

"And since when do you associate with people who wear *nail polish*?" He twirls his fingers around when he says it, like a puppet master with a marionette.

"Are you kidding me right now?" I cross the room, bumping Brad's chest with my own as I move into his space. Brad staggers backward, and I shove him into the bookshelf next to the window. "Why is that even important?"

Brad pushes off with a grunt and lunges at me, but I slam my hands into his chest again. He bares his teeth, momentarily stunned that I've hit him. But I could feel the anger surging within me the second he made fun of Tristan. Like the flick of a switch.

He left me no choice.

I hold my palms flat against him, pinning his shoulders down.

A memory flashes before my eyes.

I'm swinging from a set of monkey bars in Louisiana when I overhear my parents fighting on the park bench. Something about the other night, when Dad failed to come home. My dad's voice grows harsher, and tears start falling from Ma's eyes. She notices me watching them, and tells me not to worry, but I can't look away.

Something about our conversation now transports me back to that moment in the park, except I'm the one sitting on the bench, angry, while Brad's the one crying.

He's actually crying.

I let go of him, and his shoulders slump, like my hands were the only things holding him up. "Why are you so upset?"

I reach out to comfort him, even though that's not a thing we've ever done, but as soon as my hand makes contact with his arm, Brad grabs a handful of my hoodie and shakes me. I think he's about to storm off when he closes his eyes and pulls me back in—for a kiss.

On the mouth.

With his mouth.

His breath reeks of stale beer.

It's not like this is my first kiss. That happened during a game of Kick the Can when I was twelve. I always hid in this one spot, wedged between a dumpster and the back wall of a now defunct corner store. Tony's neighbor, Mohan, found me and bartered kisses in exchange for not making me "it." Though I didn't want to agree at first—because boys didn't kiss other boys—we met there every day after school, stealing quick pecks when we knew no one was watching. His family moved the following summer, and because Ma forbade me from having social media until I was in eighth grade, we lost touch.

This feels like that, but much, much worse. Like a transaction I never agreed to make.

I keep my lips shut, staring at him with wide-open eyes.

This is all wrong. Brad's my best friend. He's been a constant in my life for so long, I can't even remember what it was like before he moved to Valentine. But I can't process what's happening right now. It doesn't make any sense.

As he lets go of me, tears are streaming down his face. He exhales.

I've never seen him like this. His cheeks burn scarlet red as his eyes come back into focus. He doesn't wait for me to say anything before yanking open the door and hurrying down the hall.

I blink slowly.

I should go after him, make sure he's okay, but I don't move. I can't. My feet are stuck to the carpet, my heels backed into the wall. I watch through the den's window as he hurries out into the storm.

Three times one is three.

Three times two is six.

A football player, whose name I think is Chase, pokes his head in and sees me standing there, unmoving.

"You okay there, bud? The bathroom's down the hall if you're going to puke."

Bud.

I snap out of my trance, ending my count at thirty-three, and race to the door, not bothering to grab my shoes. I thump down the front stairs and onto the lawn, my socks instantly drenched.

The snow has started up again, obstructing everything in sight. I call Brad's name, my voice breaking over the roar of music inside, but it's no use.

He's long gone.

I pull my phone out and dial his number, but it goes straight to voicemail.

"Fuck."

I contemplate sending him a text, but I don't know what I'd say. That I'm sorry? That *he* should be sorry for forcing himself on me like that? That I don't get what just happened? My frozen finger hovers over our last conversation when the front door opens behind me.

"Big Mac, are you okay?" I turn around and Tony's on the steps, his arm wrapped around a junior. He looks at me like I've lost my mind. Maybe I have. I'm in a foot of snow without shoes on.

"I just needed some air." I wiggle my toes to make sure they haven't fallen off.

"Where's Brad?" he asks, suddenly sounding sober. He searches the driveway behind me.

"I have no idea," I answer, stifling the memory of Brad's tears.

No matter what I do, I can't tell Tony the truth. That Brad kissed me and ran off. I'd be outing him, and that's not something I'd ever do. Because where would that leave us?

"He's a big boy. He can handle himself," Tony mumbles, turning to head back inside.

"That's not what I'm afraid of."

I follow behind them and shake the snow from my sleeves. Stacy's passed out on a piano in the living room, one arm draped over the side.

The girl on Tony's arm laughs into his hair. "Come on, Big Cheese, I need another drink!" She's wearing a pink jacket and scarf like she's come straight out of the movie *Grease*.

Tony says something into her ear, and they disappear into the kitchen.

My head is throbbing.

I reach up and pinch my eyebrow, feeling more alone than ever.

11.

MY OWN WORST ENEMY (IS ME)

I didn't know Bud was gay.

Or bi.

Or even pan.

I pat down my pockets to make sure I haven't lost my phone and call Brad's mom. She's the only one who'll know what to do. After it rings for what feels like forever, I hang up and shoot her a message, choosing my words carefully.

> Can you let me know when Brad gets home?

> He left the party and isn't answering my texts.

> Thanks.

I grab another White Claw from the cooler and crack it open. The seltzer burns down my throat. I check my messages again just in case. There's only five minutes until the New Year.

When I walk back into the family room, everyone's huddled around the TV watching the countdown, completely ignorant to the fact that my whole world just became a million times more complicated. Not that they'd care.

Tonight sucks.

I try to find Tristan in the crowd to apologize for making a complete ass of myself. I should've defended him when Brad made fun of his nails. I actually thought they were pretty awesome.

I slide open the screen door to Stacy's patio and step outside. As I tip my face toward the sky, snowflakes attack me. I stick my tongue out, trying to catch one in my mouth. It's that time of the night where everything's still, like if you listen hard enough you could hear the trees talking.

I sink down onto the patio step, pulling my right knee close to my chest. It tends to seize up in the cold. I don't know how much time has passed when I hear, "There you are."

The door closes shut behind me. Without the sound of music bleeding into the backyard, I can hear Tristan's sharp intake of breath.

"Hey," I mumble, pawing at my knee like an itch I can't quite scratch.

He takes a seat next to me on the step and pulls at one of the rips in my jeans. "Hey."

"Shouldn't you be inside with everyone else?" I trace over the spot where his fingers grazed my thigh, feeling the leftover warmth though my skin is raised from the cold.

"Probably," Tristan says. "But no one in there is going to tell me how nice my eyes are."

"You're never going to let me live that down, are you?" I drop my head in my hands and laugh. But it's a weak laugh. Like my heart's not in it.

"Not a chance."

Tristan bumps his shoulder into mine, and I jokingly let myself fall over in the snow.

"Is everything all right?" he asks, wrapping his arm around me when I sit back up. My body goes rigid beneath his touch. "You seem far away."

I peer over at the house. The curtains are drawn on the sliding door so no one can see us, but I hate that I have to check before I can feel any ounce of comfort. Straight people never have to worry about stuff like that. "Tonight's been a weird night."

Tristan stares out into the yard, fixing his gaze on the play-set buried in white. "Do you want to talk about it?"

"Yes." I give him a tired grin. "But I'm not sure how."

Tristan doesn't need to know what Brad's done. Not yet, anyway. I'd have to explain how he kissed me, how I haven't done anything about the very real drinking problem I now know he has. I'm not even sure why he did it. Was it because he was drunk? Or does Brad actually have feelings for me? And if he does, has he always felt like this?

Tristan studies my face. When I don't speak, he shakes his head. "It's okay. You don't have to tell me."

"Sixty!"

"Fifty-nine!"

"Fifty-eight!"

We both turn toward the noise. I know we should be in there with the rest of the party—as they scramble to refill drinks, search for someone nearby to kiss—but I can't bring myself to get up. I don't want to be around anyone, faking enthusiasm, pretending to be happy, when everything around me is falling apart.

"So your friends are something else," Tristan says, looking back at me. "Don't take this the wrong way, but you're better off without them."

I avoid his eyes. Did he see Brad and me in the den? Does he know that Bud ran out of the party? I try picturing what he's said—my life without The Tripod—but my mind draws a blank. Like it can't even comprehend a future like that.

I don't have the energy to talk about this right now. To convince Tristan that even though the guys are rough around the edges, they mean well. Because I'm not even sure I believe that anymore.

I've never been in this position before, itching to be close to someone but too terrified to actually go through with it. I reach into my pocket for the dollar-store lighter I keep for emergencies and light a joint.

Tristan bats the air in front of him to fan away the smoke.

"Sorry." I jut my lower lip out so my breath travels sideways away from him.

"It's fine," Tristan replies. He's doing that thing where he's trying to act cool, indifferent, but he drops his arm away from me and shuffles his feet on the step. "It's just not good for my lungs."

I pound my chest with my fist. "It's probably not good for mine either," I admit.

Tristan eyes the joint in my hand. He reaches over and plucks it from my fingers, taking a deep inhale like his life depends on it.

"Whoa." I lean back on my elbows, laughing as he stomps his foot and wheezes. "Rebel."

"Ten!"

"Nine!"

"Eight!"

Tristan nudges me when he's cleared his lungs. "If it's any consolation, I'm happy you're here tonight."

"Me too," I say, trying to sound sincere when all I can see inside my head is Brad pulling me in and kissing me.

As the clock strikes midnight, I wipe my mouth with the back of my hand, dreading the thought of seeing Brad Monday morning at school.

The house erupts into cheers behind us. Pots bang. Horns honk. People fall drunkenly in love. Down the street, fireworks burst in the sky.

Tristan and I sit in silence, staring up at the falling snow. I take another drag, watching the smoke rise and dissipate above us.

His eyes explore my lips.

Does he want me to kiss him?

I want to.

I *really* do.

I want to grab him by the cuff of his sleeve, close the distance between us, as I breathe in his scent—the subtlety of his lemongrass and ocean breeze deodorant, the hint of aftershave on his neck. But I already had my first New Year's Eve kiss tonight.

It just wasn't with the person I imagined.

Tristan's knees knock together from the cold. Or maybe he's nervous?

"I can't believe it's January first." He whistles, drawing circles in the snow with his heel. "In six months, we'll have already graduated. It's wild to think of all the things we've accomplished since kindergarten."

I scrunch my nose. I know he means to be optimistic, that New Year's makes people reflect on their past, but other than escaping Louisiana with Ma and getting a job at Vincenzo's, I haven't done much of anything. I let myself think that maybe the New Year would be different, but after tonight . . .

"My life isn't that interesting."

Tristan turns to me then, contemplating my face.

"I'm serious," I continue, unable to contain the desperation in my voice. "Don't you ever feel like that? That anyone watching would be completely and utterly bored?"

I know Tristan doesn't know what that's like, but I ask anyway. The thought of crossing the stage at convocation, into the unknown, makes me squirm in my seat. That is, if I don't fail senior year.

"Sometimes." Tristan licks his lips, pondering the question. "I'm terrified of not getting into St. Sebastian's. I think that's why I've been pushing myself so hard lately. I don't know who I am without ballet." He eyes the smoldering embers at the tip of my joint and sighs. "But the next chapter in your life is for you to define, Wes. Whatever you were in high school, whatever mistakes you made, all that goes away."

"I don't know if I believe that," I whisper.

I can't ignore the pit of dread growing inside my stomach. What if I don't get my grades up in time to graduate? What if this doesn't work out between us? What if things are never the same with Bud? Even if I do magically make it to graduation, after high school, all I'll have is Vincenzo's.

Valentine was supposed to be a new start. But it's been ten years since we began our new lives here, and I've got nothing to show for it except a bunch of failing grades and a permanent record.

"I'm just so damn angry all the time, and I have no idea why." My heart lodges in my throat. Even now, I feel my fingernails digging into my palms, the sweat forming at my hairline. The word alone produces a visceral reaction in my body.

Tristan reaches over and pats my knuckles. "Have you ever talked to someone about it?"

Yes. I feel my shoulders collapse inward, feel the shortness in my breath. My elementary school principal referred me to a counselor after only a month in Valentine. We couldn't afford more than two sessions, and the school did jack shit to help.

Not that it mattered anyway. I couldn't even make it through the first thirty minutes before punching a hole through the counselor's wall and storming off.

"I'm talking to you, aren't I?" I laugh it off as a joke. As if my chest doesn't hurt when I say it.

The sliding door opens then, and Omar from my biology class sticks his head out. "Happy New Year, boys!"

He looks over at us and holds out his hand for a high five. This kid doesn't care that we're two guys huddled together in the snow. He doesn't even bat an eye.

I oblige, only because I want him to leave.

"Yeah, you too," Tristan replies, getting up to follow him inside.

In my pocket, my phone pings with a text from Brad's mom.

> He's home. Thanks for always looking out for him, Wes.
> Happy New Year.

I should be relieved, but my heart sinks as I reread the message. Because I didn't look out for Brad. I stood there and watched him leave. Did nothing as he disappeared into the night. What kind of friend does that?

I step inside after Tristan, letting the body heat from a hundred drunken teenagers take me over. Emily's on the couch making out with someone, and it's only when she comes up for air that I realize it's Tony. What happened to the junior he was with?

Tristan runs over and jumps on the cushion next to Emily. "So much for not drinking tonight!" he shouts, taking a pillow and pretending to suffocate her.

"I am stone-cold sober, bitch," she mumbles beneath his grasp. "I'm just a sucker for bad boys." She grabs Tony by the hood on his hoodie, and they pick up where they left off.

Tristan shrieks, catapulting off of the Emily-Tony-saliva mash-up like he's been electrocuted. He catches my eye and winks. "I guess I am too."

We spend the next half hour hunched over an abandoned game of Jenga on the floor before Tristan offers to drive me home. I puff out my cheeks, holding my breath, as we grab our snow gear from the hall closet and inch through the crowd.

"Did you mean what you said back there?" I stuff my hands into my pockets as we weave through the parked cars along the driveway. "About me being a bad boy?"

Tristan shrugs, pointing to my leather jacket like it's the only proof he needs.

I unzip the jacket and tuck it under my arm, and Tristan stares at me like I've fallen off the deep end.

"I never meant to be one, you know. It just sort of happened."

Climbing into the passenger seat of Tristan's car, I remember the first day of fourth grade. One of Ma's ex-boyfriends had introduced me to Metallica over the summer, a band my dad *hated*, and I spent the two months leading up to school growing out my hair like Kirk Hammett. I even carried a guitar from Toys "R" Us everywhere I went.

My teacher, Ms. Higginbottom, took one look at me before sending me to the principal's office. I didn't even do anything wrong, but I had to spend the rest of the afternoon under the watchful eye of the secretary while the rest of my class played outside.

That night, when I told her what happened, Ma let me dye my hair electric blue in retaliation. And from that moment on, I fell into the role of the troublemaker. I stopped listening in class. I let my grades slip. And I found out, through trial and error, what I could and couldn't get away with.

Between that and the incident with the fifth grader when I

first moved to town, kids learned to stay away from me, and in a way, I thrived from that. Like I'd found a purpose for all the anger I felt inside, all the pent-up rage from being forced to flee the only home I'd ever known, from losing the one other person in my life besides Ma—regardless of how terrible he ended up being.

Once Tony and Brad joined in, we checked off every stereotype of a punk: head thrashing, skateboard riding, pot smoking. Looking back at it now, I have to laugh. Did I honestly turn out the way that I did because a teacher didn't like my hairstyle when I was ten?

"I get that, Wes." Tristan says. "I know what it feels like to build up walls to protect yourself. But it's never too late to be a good person."

I ball my hands up in my lap, rubbing them against my jeans to stay warm. "I did some pretty messed-up things to a lot of people." My vision spots as I look over at him. It feels like the car's air is suffocating me.

"Why?"

I search for answers through the window over his shoulder, imagining all the people I've hurt or disappointed standing at the side of Stacy's driveway like drudged-up ghosts from my past. "Maybe I wanted attention. Or for someone to tell me what I always felt I've known in my heart: that I don't deserve to be loved."

I can tell I'm starting to choke up, but it feels good to say the words out loud, to have Tristan be the one hearing them. I look at him, see the worry on his face. "If I could go back and do it all over, I would."

"I know that, Wes," Tristan says, squeezing my arm. "Maybe you just lost your way."

I shake my head. "I've always been myself. I just pretended to be what others expected from me."

Tristan gives me a look—head tilted, mouth raised in the corner—like Ma does when I tell her a lie.

"Whatever." I sigh, rubbing my eyes. "Can we please stop talking about this?"

I can tell Tristan's not ready to let it go, but I click the Bluetooth icon on the car's touch screen and connect my phone.

"What's going on here?" Tristan asks, reaching to take back control of the dash. I slap his wrist away and sniff.

"We're starting the New Year off right."

Tristan pouts as we pull out of Stacy's driveway and head toward my apartment.

"I'd like to introduce you to someone near and dear to me."

I press play, and "Nothing Else Matters" comes on through the speakers. I crank the volume dial, opening up my phone's camera to capture the moment.

"Tristan, meet Metallica."

12.

ENEMA OF THE PHOTOGRAPHY CLUB

On the first day back from winter break, I spend the morning before class in detention. Mr. Hamilton makes me read an article about the link between higher education and violence reduction, and it's so obvious what he's trying to do, I hide my face in the crook of my elbow to prevent myself from smirking.

At lunch, Tony and I meet at the picnic tables in the courtyard behind the cafeteria. Beneath the stone, there are broken tiles littered across the ground, like someone once took a hammer to the courtyard and the administration just never bothered to fix it. We're at the back of Stonebridge, hidden behind a thick brick wall.

"Do you think he's okay?" I ask, lowering my voice so the drama kids in the corner don't overhear us. Brad didn't show up to class. He skips school more than any of us, so I shouldn't be surprised, but I have a sinking suspicion it's because of what happened on New Year's. I tried calling him, but I don't think we've ever spoken on the phone.

Though I'd do anything to forget what happened that night,

New Year's wasn't all bad. Tristan and I haven't stopped talking since he dropped me off. We've been texting all morning, swapping our favorite songs in the chat.

I still refuse to tell The Tripod about us—partially because I don't even know if The Tripod is still a thing, and partially because when my two worlds crashed into each other at the party, they nearly went up in flames.

My phone pings.

> Any luck?

I filled Tristan in about Brad missing class this morning. I didn't go into details about the kiss. I just mentioned I hadn't seen him today and that he'd left the party early because he was upset about something. I reply back with a Nope, and Tristan sends a teary-face emoji.

> He'll show up eventually. He can't just not go to school.

That earns a laugh. I can't help myself. If anyone could stop showing up to school, it'd be Brad. His mom is a nurse who's always working overtime, and his dad's got his nose deep in the bottle; I doubt either of them would notice if Brad even left his room.

Tony snaps to get my attention. He's glaring at my phone.

I tell Tristan I've got to run, and he sends back a GIF of someone blowing a kiss.

He's been doing that a lot lately, sending hearts, prodding me to share pictures I've taken with him. I usually reply with a skull emoji and an obscure photo of something stupid in the moment—like a particularly artful pile of mud—because I never know what to do when he openly flirts with me.

Tony puffs a cloud of smoke at me, extending his arm out of reach when I go to grab his joint. "He probably just slept in. You know how he is."

Brad hardly ever makes it to school before lunch, but it doesn't make me feel any better.

"He drank a lot on New Year's," I say, gauging Tony's reaction. Even if I ignore the kiss, I can't assume Tony knows anything about Brad's drinking problem. After all, it took Ma pointing it out for me to realize how out of hand it's gotten.

"So? Brad's hilarious when he's drunk," Tony replies blankly, staring off in the distance. I deflate against the picnic table. I don't know what I expected. I'd wanted to talk about Brad, but Tony always does this. Zones out anytime something difficult comes up.

The door to our left bangs open, and a group of football players step into the courtyard in teal-and-white letterman jackets. Tony makes eye contact with one of the cheerleaders and winks.

"Cassandra totally wants me."

"Dude, what about Emily?" I frown, shoving his knee. "Focus, Big Cheese. We can't just ignore this—"

Tony looks back at me and rolls his eyes. "The hell we can't. Bud would tell us if he had a problem, so *chill*," he snaps, leaping from the table and stamping his joint out on the ground. He turns his attention back to Cassandra.

"Jesus, Tony. Is that all you care about?" I call after him.

"Pretty much."

He leaves me alone at the picnic table before I can react. Would Brad really tell us the truth if he knew his drinking had gotten worse? He's spent his whole life around his dad; would he even notice a difference? I want to push Tony further, see if Brad's said anything about the party, but he's leaning on the wall, teasing his finger through one of Cassandra's pom-poms.

My phone buzzes again in my pocket.

> If you could live anywhere in the world, where would it be and why?

Tristan responds a second later, like he's already given his own answer some thought.

> If Russia wasn't so awful to gay people, I'd consider Moscow because of their world-renowned ballet company.

> But I'd have to go with Paris.

> Definitely Paris.

> I mean, look at this!

He sends an image of the Eiffel Tower, its frame lit up at night.

I smile, letting my mind wander. I can picture us together laying out on the stretch of grass in the photo, watching the lights twinkle from above. We'd get baguettes from a market and hide a bottle of champagne inside a brown bag, passing it between each other, and pretending to speak French. Was Tristan right? Would I be better off without The Tripod? The thought of it is enough to distract me from worrying about Brad as I turn the corner and head back into the building.

By the time I've made it halfway down the hall, I have no idea where I am. Paper music notes are stuck along the wall. A sign-up sheet for this year's production of *Into the Woods* hangs from a bulletin board. Someone's practicing vocal warm-ups in the distance, though it sounds more like they're gargling saltwater.

My step falters as Stacy Evans appears in the open door to my right. When she sees me standing alone in the hall, she frowns.

"Can we help you?" Even when posing a question, Stacy somehow manages to scold me. Behind her, the words "Photography Club" are written on the classroom's whiteboard. I'd forgotten she was the club's president.

Except for a darkroom in the back corner, the classroom is like any other in the school. Stapled to the wall are old *National Geographic* magazine covers and a large color wheel.

"I-I—" I stammer, looking over at the window. There's a prism dangling from a string that catches the light from outside, reflecting it back in slivers of rainbow.

My first impulse is to just laugh it off, to tell them I walked here by mistake. It's not like I actually meant to end up outside their door. But the memory of Tristan telling me to reconsider stops me.

You might actually enjoy it.

I think back to our photo shoot. How it made me realize how much I like taking pictures. I glance over at the nearest desk, at the Nikon camera sitting there. Like it's waiting for me.

Clearing my throat, I decide to go for it the same way Tristan did when he leaped into my arms that day. "Do you think maybe I could sit in on your meeting today?" I run my fingers through my hair, peering down at my shoes.

Stacy blinks. "Pardon?"

I know she heard me, but I speak up anyway. This time, I look right at her. "I want to join your club."

I pull out my phone and flip to my camera roll. "I take pictures all the time. I know it's not much, and you're all probably way more talented than me, but—"

"No."

I know I shouldn't let it get to me—I've been shut down my whole life by people like Stacy, people in charge—but my cheeks burn at being denied.

One of the other members, a girl with light brown skin and auburn hair that's shaved on one side, raises her hand. "Wait a minute, Stacy, give him a chance."

Stacy shakes her head like she's trying to flick a mosquito from her hair. "No way. This guy is an asshole."

"Aren't all the best photographers assholes?" The girl snorts, throwing her leg up and placing her black army boot on her desk. She has her eyebrow pierced with a Hello Kitty piercing, and her jean jacket is covered in anime and "the future is female" patches.

"No. Absolutely not," Stacy hisses. I'm afraid her head might actually snap clean off of her neck. "We all know how he's treated Skye."

The rest of the club turns their heads toward the back of the room where Skye Nguyen is sitting next to the kid I confronted before winter break—*Seriously, why does he keep popping up everywhere?*—captivated by a book on cameras.

It takes me a second to place Skye.

Until I do.

Back in sophomore year, to avoid bugging Ma for the money she didn't have, I built up an impressive schedule of students who would bring me lunch each day. Skye just happened to be my Wednesday appointment. The day I always had a Big Mac.

I haven't thought much about Skye since then.

"School policy is to let anyone in who expresses interest," the girl with the piercing says.

I glance from her to the guy next to Skye. They look identical. I've never had any classes with either of them, which makes me think they're super smart and in all the AP classes at the opposite end of the school.

"Him and his friends are total dicks!" someone shouts from the darkroom.

I raise a finger, leaning into the room. "He's also still here."

"Shut up, *Wes*," Stacy barks, banging a plastic gavel onto the teacher's desk like she's Judge Judy. "Skye, do you have anything to say about this?"

Skye glances up and our eyes meet from across the room.

I take a step back, my foot edging out into the hall. I've learned to numb myself to Authority Figures™ telling me I'm worthless, but this is different. I've never had to face my own actions from someone I've hurt before. These are entirely uncharted waters.

I try to force a nervous smile, but Skye's expression is unreadable.

"He can stay."

I let out a quiet breath, squeezing my shoulder blades together to stretch.

Stacy stares at Skye in disbelief. "Are you sure?"

Skye nods. "Everyone deserves to be part of something."

After a brief pause, Stacy grunts and turns her back to the class. "You get one shot, Mackenzie," she says, then scribbles a series of numbers onto the whiteboard.

"It's actually Big Mac—" I stop myself from talking when Stacy drags her marker down the board like a knife ripping through a bedsheet. "Never mind."

Heading to the back of the class, I pass the girl who spoke up for me earlier and mouth a quick "Thanks." She brings two fingers to her brow in a salute before whipping back around to face the front. I should probably learn her name.

Once I find a seat, I get a text from Tony asking where I went.

> Stopped at 7-Eleven for a drink.

I lie, annoyed that he's only now just realized I've left.

Tony replies with a Whatever, man and a purple message appears at the bottom of my screen saying that he's silenced his notifications. I stare down at my phone, a vein throbbing in my neck. What did he expect? That I'd wait around while he hit on Cassandra, freezing my ass off in the cold? If he won't talk to me about Brad, why should I bother telling him where I am?

I scroll over to my conversation with Tristan, realizing I never answered his question about where I'd want to live. I look around the room at the *National Geographic* covers, stopping on a picture of the Empire State Building. I've always loved taking pictures of architecture; the way the light reflects off the surface of buildings, how they tower over a city, seeming so out of reach.

> NYC would be cool.

Tristan reacts with a heart.

> NYC is THE perfect choice for you! Especially since I'll be there. 😊

"Don't forget, everyone. The PIC-tacular is only a month away," Stacy announces as she weaves through the desks. "I want every single one of you submitting an entry this year, so make sure it's of the caliber to make Regina Hale proud."

Regina Hale is the Annie Leibovitz of Valentine. She died like thirty years ago, but she's the only real success story to ever come out of Stonebridge, so the administration takes photography very seriously around here. There's even a plaque next to Principal Cohen's office dedicated in Regina's honor.

Stacy hovers next to my desk before reluctantly handing me a yellow flyer. She slaps the top of my hand when she catches me texting in my lap.

I stash my phone away and turn the flyer over.

It reads:

Though the cash prize does pique my interest, I shove the paper inside my backpack. Stonebridge High would never be proud of me. Not in a million years.

Today, the photography club is working on framing. How you can tell a story by the way you set up a shot. Seeing all the members interact with each other—the subtle closeness of their chairs, the way they lean over to help a friend navigate their camera's interface—makes me wonder how anyone different than them could ever fit in. I have no idea what they're talking about when they mention something called apertures, but they nod their heads, so I do too. Embarrassed, I flip through my iPhone's camera settings as everyone else around me fiddles with the touch screens on their Nikons and Canons—but at least they let me stay.

The bell rings to signal the end of lunch, and the club funnels out of the room. Stacy throws me a final scowl before disappearing through the door.

When we're the only two people left, I walk over to Skye and reach into my backpack to pull out the black-and-white notebook I've been carrying around since December. "Do you think you could give this to your friend?"

Skye takes the notebook from my hand and adds it to a stack of books next to me without a word.

I'm already turning around to leave when Skye asks, "Why exactly *are* you here?"

Panic rises in my throat again. "It might not make a lot of sense," I mumble, "and I'm not sure I understand it either, but I'm trying out this new thing where I'm not a total prick. I don't want people seeing me like that anymore."

I wait for Skye's response, knowing what I've said isn't enough.

Skye walks over to the back of the room to return a stray camera to the cabinet. "I get that."

"You do?"

"Uh, yeaaaaah," Skye says, nodding and blinking at the same time. "Before I came to Stonebridge, I went by another name. It can be hard for some people to get accustomed to. And using they/them pronouns adds a whole other level to it."

I hang my mouth open, confused by the sudden curveball they've thrown. Why is Skye being so open with me? Historically, I haven't exactly been friendly to them. "How's that going for you?"

Skye takes a minute to lock the cabinet. They're wearing a salmon-colored button-down with a Venus flytrap pattern, sleeves rolled past the elbow. Their black hair—longer on the top, short at the sides—is slicked back on their head. I can tell by the way they fiddle with their watch that they don't like attention. I notice the mole just below their left nostril. Almost like Marilyn Monroe.

"In this town?" Skye asks, nervously smiling. "Being nonbinary, I get misgendered daily. Most of the time, I'm pretty sure it's on purpose too. But I don't see myself as a 'him' or a 'her,' and I don't like conforming to what society says about gender."

"Oh," I say, nodding. It's probably better if I keep my mouth shut in case I say anything stupid or offensive. I have a tendency to do that.

"I contemplated not saying anything because I didn't want to give you another reason to make fun of me."

Skye giggles, snort and all, but I don't laugh with them. I pull back, my lips moving without saying anything. I'm not going to lie and pretend I'm Holier than Thou all of a sudden, but I've been a royal douche. I never realized Skye could be hiding part of who they were too, in order to protect themself from people like me. And I can't believe it's taken me this long to recognize that.

"I'm sorry I hurt you." I take Skye's hand, and they squirm, like they're not sure what to do. That makes two of us.

I notice their skull ring next to mine and smile. Maybe we're more alike than I realized.

Skye shrugs. "I know it was all in good fun."

I shake my head because I can't accept that.

Skye's so innocent, and not just because their phone case has a literal kitten on it. There's a softness in their eyes that, despite years of relentless hounding from Yours Truly, they never lost. I think my problem was that I never saw people for who they were. I never once took into consideration that there might be more to them than what I could see on the surface. Assuming they were one-dimensional made it easier to steal from them.

"Maybe for my friends and me, but not for you. I really am sorry."

Skye rubs their arm. "Thanks, Big Mac."

Hearing my nickname from the mouth of someone I've hurt makes my skin crawl. "Please call me Wes."

"Okay, *Wes*," Skye says, drawing out my actual name—probably for the first time ever. "I have a chemistry test I can't miss, so . . ."

"Right, sure," I say, stepping out of the way. "Have a good rest of your day."

"Um, thanks. You too."

I watch Skye scurry from the room.

This is going to be more difficult than I thought.

I knew joining the photography club would have its own set of challenges. I just never imagined it like this.

But I can at least try to change. Right? I can see where this goes while improving my photography skills at the same time. I can put more effort in with Tad, be more open with Ma and The Tripod. Figure out how the hell to navigate things with Bud.

I pull my phone out again, bypassing the lame photo I took of the window's rainbow prism as part of today's lesson, and message Tristan.

> You'll never guess how I spent my lunch today. 📷

He texts back instantly with a close-up selfie of his face and "Qué?" written on the screen across his nose.

I take a picture of the whiteboard and click Send.

My phone goes off in my hand, one ping after the other, as a flurry of messages appear. They're all the same thing; a million exclamation marks and star-eyed emojis.

I bite my lip to stop myself from smiling. I didn't think it would matter much coming from someone I only met two weeks ago, but seeing Tristan share in my excitement confirms what I already know to be true.

I send a single blue heart, not caring how it comes across.

13.

I'LL KEEP YOU MY FLIRTY LITTLE SECRET

Tristan and I meet behind 7-Eleven after school on Thursday. I figured if we're going to be spending all this time together, I might as well teach him a thing or two.

"You have got to be kidding me." Tristan gawks when I hand him the extra skateboard I dug out of storage this morning. I hid it in my locker all day to avoid any questions from The Tripod. Not that I saw either of them.

This whole thing between us is fucked up. We've gone from sixty to zero, best friends to complete strangers, in a matter of days. It's like they're blaming me for what happened. The first time I saw Brad at school since the party, he physically turned around and went in the opposite direction to avoid me.

Tristan takes a step backward over the curb and shakes his head. "Not happening."

"Don't worry, I'll go easy on you."

The sun is shining for the first time in weeks as we walk the three blocks to the skate park. It's warmer out today, so I'm wearing a plaid shirt beneath my jacket with gray pants cuffed up to show off my Vans.

I force Tristan to put on the helmet and kneepads I pull out from my backpack, and he does so willingly. He looks like a sexy Michelin Man, if you're into that sort of thing.

I take his hands, and Tristan steps onto the board, his knees wobbling like he's forgotten how to walk.

"Aren't you a dancer?" I tease.

"I'm used to solid ground, thank you very much."

We circle around the park so Tristan can get used to the motion. He holds on to my shoulders the whole time, flinching at every turn.

"You actually *like* doing this?" he asks, shifting his weight when he begins to tilt.

I shrug, and it causes him to temporarily lose balance. His fingers dig into my jacket, his grip tightening on my shoulders.

"We can't all have electric cars," I say with a smirk, feeling the crisp January air on my face before adding, "There's something about the wind blowing through your hair on a hot summer day while you cruise down the street, rocking out to music, without a care in the world. I forget myself sometimes."

When it's just me and my board, nothing else matters. Not school or the way everyone's eyes follow me as I'm sent to the principal's office, not my grades or graduation. When it's just me and my board, I feel like I can breathe.

"I'm the same way with dancing."

It's still wild to think we have anything remotely in common. I drop my chin to hide my blushing. "How do you feel?"

"Good, I guess," Tristan says, laughing when he accidentally lifts his foot and the skateboard thuds beneath him.

I help him step to the ground and run over to collect my own board.

"Now," I say, throwing it down with the tilt of my ankle,

"the trick with a basic ollie is to have your right foot straight just behind those front bolts there." I push Tristan's foot with the toe of my shoe. "You want to keep your shoulders square with the board and make sure to look straight ahead." I grab on to his shoulders again and position them over his feet, turning his chin to the left with my finger.

My voice catches in my throat, and I let my touch linger there on his skin. Tristan's in a thousand layers like he's getting ready to climb Mount Everest. He should be boiling under his enormous lavender scarf, black feather down jacket, and joggers, but his chin is cold to the touch. I wonder what he'd do if I just stood on my tiptoes and leaned in for a . . .

"With this foot on the t-t-tail," I stammer, motioning him to move his left foot, "I want you to bend your front knee and drop the back of the board to the ground like this. Now, *lift*."

Tristan does as I say, his eyes lighting up when he jumps into the air.

"Land with your knees somewhere in the middle of being bent and straight."

The motion has to be quick, but Tristan doesn't seem to comprehend what I've said in time, because his feet flail out from under him. He lands on his knees over the asphalt, watching miserably as the board rolls away.

"I'm terrible." Tristan checks his hands over for cuts, then lifts himself up with a pout.

"No, trust me, you aren't." I jog over to retrieve his runaway board. "You're better than I was when I started."

He arches a brow. "Weren't you, like, eight?"

"Minor details." I smirk.

Returning with the board, I gesture for Tristan to try again, and he looks at me with a sly grin. "Do you think you can show me? I'm more of a visual learner."

Nodding, I push off the ground, my skateboard's wheels

rumbling over the concrete. Testing my movement, I dip my knees and head toward Tristan. I circle around him, waggling my eyebrows, performing one ollie after the other. Tristan cheers me on, his eyes noting the way my feet move and lean slightly every time I set myself up for the trick.

He holds his tongue between his teeth in concentration when I make him get back up and try again. We go back and forth like that, taking turns, until he can land without stumbling.

"See, I knew you'd get the hang of it," I say, watching as he attempts to do another one.

I pull out my phone and sprawl out on the ground to capture the moment. Because apparently, I do that now.

Tristan's eyebrows knit together, deep lines forming along his forehead as he focuses on his shoes.

Click.

"I can't believe I'm actually doing it!" he squeals, forgetting for a moment to act cool.

I laugh and jump back on my board to follow him, and we ride around the skate park's bowl, doing laps around each other until it gets dark. We skate past familiar faded graffiti along the walls and the half-pipe Brad broke his arm on trying to stick a landing two summers ago. I crouch down, gripping my board with one hand and filming Tristan skateboarding next to me with the other.

When the streetlights turn on overhead, Tristan stops and tucks the board under his arm. "I'll admit, that was a lot more fun than I thought it'd be. You're actually pretty good."

I scoff, placing a hand over my heart. "Were you expecting me to be bad?"

He shakes his head furiously. "Not at all. It's just—when you did that thing with your foot—"

"Relax, Tristan. I already know I'm kickass!" I gloat,

swerving out of the way to avoid his playful kick. But I feel myself drifting over to him again the way moths gravitate toward light. I wonder if we'll kiss before saying goodbye.

We walk down to the forest behind the library where a gravel path will take us the long way back to 7-Eleven. There's a detour in the path I avoid at all costs where The Tripod usually smokes, away from the main road.

At this time of year, the forest is barren, the trees all rotting leaves and wispy branches that clatter against one another in the evening's light. We're underneath a full moon now, huddling together for warmth.

When we reach the wooden bridge at the forest's halfway point, Tristan runs over and climbs onto the railing. I follow behind him, resting our skateboards against the bridge.

"Today was perfect," Tristan breathes, flinging his feet over the side. "I didn't know skateboarding could be so challenging, but you've definitely earned my respect."

High above the frozen creek, I loop my pinkie through his, and he laughs, his voice booming through the emptiness of the night. Without speaking, we move closer, so close that our hips touch. I knock my shoe into his, wrapping my arm around his waist as he leans his head into my neck.

"What were you like as a kid?" I ask, kicking my heels against the bridge.

"Neurotic." Tristan thinks about it for a second more, then buries his face into my coat. "I was diagnosed with generalized anxiety disorder pretty early on. I hyperfixate on things I'm passionate about. And stress over things I can't control."

I toss a rock onto a patch of ice at the water's surface. I don't know how Tristan does it. How he opens up so freely like that. Like he somehow knows I won't judge him. Or he's so self-aware, so comfortable in his skin, that he doesn't care even if I did.

"Do you think it'll ever go away? The anxiety?"

Tristan raises his head from my chest. "I don't think so. It's just as much a part of me as dancing is." He twirls my skull ring around my finger. "What about you?"

I stare out into the forest. "It's hard to say. I've tried to block out as much of my childhood as I can. My dad—"

I stop myself, turning to see Tristan's reaction.

He's waiting for me to keep talking, his head tilted to the side. When I don't, he says, "You've never mentioned your dad before. Where is he now?" His breath escapes in tiny bursts, punctuating each word.

I want to tell him the truth, but what would I even say? How not even Ma and I talk about what happened? How for years after we left Louisiana, she checked over her shoulder everywhere we went to make sure he hadn't found us? The words I need to explain my past never come to me. So I don't say anything.

"I think you turned out pretty okay, Wes," Tristan eventually says, weaving his fingers through mine like he senses it's a sore subject.

That's all the reassurance I need. I lean forward then and press my lips to his. I don't think about what this could mean or how it might complicate things, I just fall into it, realizing I've wanted to kiss Tristan from the moment we met.

At first, he doesn't move, and I worry that I've made a mistake. That he only wanted to be friends. That I was right in thinking he'd never be with someone like me, like he said that night at Vincenzo's. I back away, my wet lips exposed to the cold, when Tristan grabs my arm and kisses me again. He smiles into my mouth, his lips exploring my own, as I reach for his neck. I trail the tips of my fingers through his hair, and he breathes into me, filling my core with warmth. He wraps his foot around mine in the air.

I never want this to end. Our bodies blend together, our tongues acting as one, as we teeter precariously on the bridge's railing. We could go over the edge at any moment, but the fall would be worth it.

I break away at the sound of laughter in the distance. Looking over my shoulder, my legs seize, turning into metal.

Down the path, heading toward us, are Tony and Brad.

Tristan leans back to see who it is, but I block him. "We need to hide," I announce, launching myself off the railing. I don't think they've seen us yet because Tony's leaping from one boulder to the next along the forest's edge.

"Excuse me?" Tristan asks, hopping down to grab his skateboard and bringing it to his chest. I can still feel the ghost of his lips along mine, but there's hurt in his eyes now. His expression is a combination of anger and shock. But he must sense the urgency in my tone because he lets me lead him around the bridge's side, his feet shuffling silently down to the creek.

I look back up at The Tripod. Brad's walking with a pizza box in his hands while Tony parkours against a tree stump. Thankfully, they're midconversation.

"*Fuck.* My skateboard," I whisper when I realize I've left it behind. Swallowing the lump in my throat, I race back to grab it. But I don't have enough time.

Brad and Tony step onto the bridge. I strangle the wheels behind my back to stop my hands from shaking.

"Hey guys," I say, taking a step toward them, hoping they didn't hear my voice break. "I thought you were working tonight?"

Smooth.

Tony looks around the forest, like he's not sure why I'm out here alone. "Dad called us off. The afternoon was slow, so Cooper and Juan asked to stay for the dinner rush." He pauses, looking at me. "What are you doing?"

"Some kid was looking for weed. She just left," I shrug, wondering if the lie will stick. I brush my fingers over my lips. Can you tell when someone's recently been kissed?

Brad stands a foot behind Tony, jabbing the pizza box's edge into his stomach. He's got a hoodie on with the hood up under his letterman jacket. He's not wearing his baseball hat.

I wait for him to acknowledge me, but he pulls out his phone instead and sets it on top of the pizza box. I can see even from a distance that he's scrolling through the latest football stats. He won't even look at me.

"Where are you headed?" I ask, trying to stifle the anger surfacing inside me.

Tony kicks a clump of snow through a slat in the bridge's deck. My jaw clenches as I stare down at the spot where it disappeared, praying it didn't fall on Tristan's head.

"Going to 7-Eleven for a drink," Tony says, repeating the last words I sent him over text.

I know what he's doing. He's getting back at me for ditching him the other day. And I realize what he's saying between the lines too. That I'm not invited. That they've made these plans without me. Without saying it directly, they've shut me out.

Brad watches a squirrel as it scurries up the side of a tree, and Tony stands his ground. He meets my eye.

But I don't take the bait. They're to blame for our falling out just as much as I am.

"Cool. Have fun." I nod my head as I straighten my back against my board to appear taller. To pretend I'm not affected by any of this.

They both shrug and continue over the bridge. No one says they're sorry. No one explains why we haven't been talking. I lock eyes with Brad when he passes. I half expect him to be angry at me, to mutter something under his breath. Is he disappointed that I didn't chase after him that night? Does he hate me now with a burning passion? But there's nothing behind his eyes. No rage. No remorse. No love. Nothing.

The Tripod disappears over the hill.

"You can come out now," I whisper, my eyes still glued to the trail of their footprints left in the snow.

After a moment's pause, Tristan reappears and stomps up the creek's side.

"Here." He shoves his skateboard into my chest and storms off in the opposite direction.

I juggle the two boards in my hands and race after him. "I'm sorry, okay?" I exhale loudly, stepping haphazardly through the snow. "I still haven't told them about you yet. I thought you said you were okay with that?"

"*Don't* twist my words, Wes," Tristan huffs, looking everywhere but at me. "What are you so afraid of? That they'll judge you for being seen with me? The boy from the party with the *nail polish* on?"

I run my fingers through my hair. "You're angry," I breathe, deflating into myself. "If I can just—"

"I'm allowed to be pissed off, Wes!" Tristan cuts me off. "You kissed me and then made me hide under a bridge! Like I'm some kind of troll!"

"I know, I know. I didn't mean for that to happen. I—" I look down, rearranging the skateboards under my right arm. "I don't want to say the wrong thing here."

Tristan stomps through the snow, apparently not caring if his shoes get ruined. "Then don't."

"It's just . . . you wouldn't understand."

"Of course I wouldn't! How am I supposed to unless you talk to me?" Tristan walks off.

But how can I explain this? I can't exactly bring up all the times The Tripod's said something homophobic. Even if they were jokes, they were at the expense of people like Tristan. People like me. We might be fighting, but I still have this lingering feeling of wanting to protect them. I know I should tell all this to him, but I can't. What if it only makes him more upset? Either way, it's a lose-lose situation.

"I'm not good with words," I yell, punching the tree next to me. A murder of crows scatters from the branches overhead, and pain ripples through me as droplets of blood fall from a cut along my knuckle. I watch them fall, turning the snow at my feet red.

I look up to see that Tristan's stopped walking ahead.

"Forget it, Wes. We can end whatever this is between us right now. Because I've had a lifetime of people making fun of me for being gay, and I don't need that coming from the guy I like too."

"Wait," I say, trailing behind him. "You just said you like me."

He clenches his fists beneath his armpits. "'Tolerate' would have been a better word choice," he says. "And just so you know, I scratched myself back there when you forced me to hide." He spins around and lifts the sleeve of his jacket to where a piece of skin hangs from his wrist.

"I said I'm sorry, all right?" I huff, angrier now than I was before. "I panicked. I didn't know what else to do. Maybe you've always been out, but I'm not, and I'm scared, okay?"

For a brief moment, the hardness in Tristan's eyes dissolves, and I feel myself recoil. What does he see when he looks at me? A wounded dog? A soldier with no fight left in him? Weakness?

"Coming out isn't just a onetime thing, Wes," he says, sighing. "You don't think I get scared every time I meet someone new? I'm a Black gay man, for fuck's sake! I was terrified when I realized who you were! Your reputation isn't exactly a secret. But I gave you a chance, even though Emily told me not to. And I'm sorry that I did."

The skateboards fall from my arm as he speaks, each word like a dagger being shoved through my heart. I've never thought about that before. Am I an idiot for believing I only had to do it once? For thinking I'd come out to Ma and The Tripod and that would be enough? I can't imagine spending the rest of my life not knowing whether people will accept or shun me. The thought alone makes me want to stay in the closet forever.

I think back to when we met in the lobby at Walter Prescott Theater, at Tristan holding out his hand to greet me. He didn't seem scared. In fact, he looked as calm and collected as ever. Was I so wrapped up in my own fears that I didn't recognize how he might have felt meeting me?

"What can I do to make it up to you?" My voice is desperate. Even after everything he's said, our kiss has to count for something. Doesn't it?

Tristan tugs his sleeve down, his expression closed off. "For starters, you can leave me alone."

14.

I CAN'T BE PERFECT (I'M SORRY)

I spend the next week in a haze.

Tristan won't talk to me. He's posting daily on Instagram like nothing's happened. Brad and Tony continue to ignore me in the halls. Even Ma's noticed my mood change and has stopped bringing up Tad's proposal. She's resorted to leaving slices of white chocolate raspberry cheesecake on the counter before school with corny *Golden Girls* quotes she finds on the internet. But not even a sugar high can fix the emptiness I feel inside.

I try paying attention in class, but nothing the teachers say seems to stick. Most of the time I'm just sitting there, staring out the window, picking away at the scab forming along my knuckle.

My life is in shambles.

I skip first period and return to the forest where Tristan and I fought. As if being here will somehow change the past. The snow's started to melt, but there's a somberness that lingers in the tree line like fog, like even the forest is mourning.

I wander through the network of trails, letting my feet lead the way. Aside from Walter Prescott Theater, this used to be one of the only places in Valentine I truly loved. I'd run here to avoid punishment when the secretary called my name over the PA system, and would sit for hours until I was certain Principal Cohen had gone home for the night.

I follow the creek through the trees until it opens up to a frozen lake. Who needs therapy when I can come here for free and listen to the wind as it blows through the branches, as clumps of snow thud to the ground?

"What happens now?" I ask, tapping my toe on the thick layer of ice that's formed over the lake. I don't expect an answer, but I'm still annoyed when it doesn't come to me.

I gave up last weekend's shifts because I couldn't bear the thought of standing next to Brad and Tony, swirling sauce while we all worked awkwardly around each other. I never thought it would come to this. In my head, I pictured myself eventually figuring out how to tell them. I'd bring Tristan home and introduce him to Ma and the guys, and everything would turn out okay. But during world history class on Friday, I caught The Tripod through the window as they goofed around on the football field, clearly ditching class without me.

I pull out my phone and take a picture of the lake, zooming in on a duck as it pecks the ice with its beak. My first instinct is to send the picture to Tristan, but I know he won't respond. I doubt he'd even click the message. He'd opened himself up to me, but like always, I had to go and screw everything up.

Three times one is three.

Three times two is six.

I lean into photography to calm down and spend the next hour walking aimlessly around, taking pictures of my surroundings—of the pair of gloves someone left behind on a bench, of the gay couple holding hands across the lake. I lower my phone as I watch them kiss, feeling my pulse race. I hate them for showing their affection so publicly, without fear of judgment. A pang of jealousy runs through me because it's not fair. I had that with Tristan, but I was stupid enough to jeopardize it for The Tripod. And look where that got me.

By the time I return to school, the lunch bell rings.

I've taken to eating alone in the cafeteria and set my tray down on the only empty table left in the corner. And since everyone at Stonebridge has always avoided me, you could draw a perfect circle around my table and label it a quarantine zone like we're still in the middle of the pandemic and I'm patient zero. I should have never let Tony pick on kids who sit by themselves. It's awful enough without having someone point it out to the entire cafeteria.

As I pull back the wrapper on my sandwich, the girl with the eyebrow piercing from photography club takes the seat in front of me. I learn her name is Velvet Rivera, after a one-hit wonder from the eighties. My hunch was right; the guy that was sitting next to Skye during last week's meeting is Velvet's twin brother, Hayden.

Velvet takes an earphone out of her ear. It reminds me so much of Tony that my heart aches. "We were wondering if you'd like to come sit with us," she says, waving over to where her brother and Skye are sitting across the room. They're at a table near the art department, which, speaking from experience, is the closest table to the exit in the event of a run-in with The Tripod.

I take a bite out of my dry ham sandwich. Stonebridge's cafeteria food sucks. It's either week-old deli meat or chicken nuggets sitting in grease. "Why would I want to do that?"

"Well," Velvet says, resting her elbows on the table, "I noticed you've been sitting by yourself the past couple days, and no offense, but you're not very good at talking to people, so I wanted to see if you'd like company."

I set my lunch aside. "So what you're saying is that your friends don't really want to be part of this. You've just decided to take pity on me." My voice cuts across the table at her, sounding angrier than I'd intended. But I don't care. I've been in a constant state of aggravation since Tristan left me alone in the woods.

"What? That's not at all what I said," Velvet insists, fidgeting with her piercing. "I see right through you, kid."

I tilt my head, taking in her bright yellow bucket hat, the black choker around her neck. While I'm thankful she helped me out last week, I'm not some lost soul she needs to save. "Somehow, I don't think you do."

Velvet returns the earphone to her ear. "Suit yourself." She gets up to leave, the legs on her chair screeching against the cafeteria floor.

Without thinking twice, I jump up, flipping my lunch tray into my lap. "No, wait."

The whole cafeteria watches as I scramble to upright a bottle of Gatorade.

Velvet looks down at me with a huge grin. "Thank you for proving my hypothesis," she says, taking her phone out from her back pocket and writing something down in her notes.

"Your what?"

Velvet sits back down across from me. "My hypothesis. I read an article in *Psychology Today* that if you want someone to do something, you should walk away and pretend like you're unaffected by their indecision. Eighty-five percent of the time, they'll call you back." She knocks her fist along the table, leaning back in triumph.

"I didn't know this was a social experiment."

Velvet lets out a whistle. "Life is a social experiment, darling. You joining us or what?"

Some kids next to us laugh, and it takes everything in me not to react.

Actually, screw that. "What are you looking at?" I bark. They return their attention to their lunches with a startle.

Velvet leans over and takes one of the carrot sticks off my tray. No one has ever stolen food from me, and I think she knows it. She watches me, pushing her cheek out with her tongue, waiting for a response.

I glance around the room, knowing if I don't accept, I'll have to finish lunch alone. "Fine," I reply quietly.

"Excellent," Velvet says as she skips over to rejoin Skye and Hayden.

I grab my things, tucking my skateboard beneath my arm in defeat, and try my best to ignore the hundreds of eyes tracking my journey across the cafeteria.

I drop my tray down in front of Hayden.

"Hey, I'm—"

"We know who you are, Wesley Mackenzie." Hayden snickers into his food as Velvet reaches over and tousles his hair. His eyes crinkle at me from behind his glasses.

"Right," I say, taking the seat next to Velvet. "Look, I'm sorry for ganging up on you before the holidays. I was—in a different place then."

Hayden holds out his hand. "It's all good. My dad says it builds character."

I cross my legs under the table and avert my eyes. I wonder if Hayden told his dad exactly what happened that day. That I only confronted him so he'd delete the image that could get me into trouble. I glance over at Skye and wonder what they've said about me to their parents. Until now, it's never occurred to me how many people's stories I'm probably the villain in. If given the chance, who would they compare me to? Freddy? Jason? Probably Chucky because of the hair, only five feet taller.

We shake hands, and I peer down at Hayden's open notebook on the table. He's laid out an assortment of green pencils that make me think of Tristan. Would he be proud of me for sitting with the photography kids? If it wasn't for him, I wouldn't have even stayed for their meeting. My stomach turns at the thought of him walking away in the forest.

Hayden gets to work shading in what looks like a trampoline, his pencil scratching the page.

"What's that?" I ask, taking a bite out of a carrot.

"Our act." Hayden turns the notebook around, gesturing for me to flip through. I turn the pages, and everywhere I look, he's filled in the space with little cartoon drawings.

"Your what?" I ask again. The scene in front of me looks like something straight out of a circus, with blasts of flames and a clown on a unicycle.

Hayden reaches into his backpack and pulls out a giant blue elephant. At first, I think it's a stuffed animal, until he shoves his hand inside and moves the mouth. "Meet Mr. Dinglefletcher."

He leans forward over the table so the elephant puppet bites down on my fingers. Its fur is made from wool, and its eyes, pieces of leftover fabric.

"Oh, dear God." I feel my face turn red as I shove the puppet into Hayden's lap. "Put that thing away."

Velvet laughs, pulling her own puppet out of her backpack. Hers is a purple hippo wearing a tuxedo.

"Not you too," I groan, covering my face.

"If you only care about what other people think, Wes, we're not going to get along," Velvet says, throwing her voice so it's like the puppet's talking.

The brother-sister duo starts putting on a show as I slide down my chair. Velvet introduces her puppet as Miss Bond. I peek through my fingers at the other kids in the cafeteria. Why couldn't the football team have invited me to sit with them? I search the faces closest to me, wondering if The Tripod's seen me with the photography club yet. I sink down further in my seat.

But I stay.

Velvet grabs Skye's photography book with Miss Bond's mouth and tosses it to the floor.

"Mark my words," Hayden says, pulling his hand out of his puppet's ass. "Velvet and I are going to be the first Puerto Rican duo to win *America's Got Talent*."

"I thought you were photography ner—" I stop midsentence when they look over at me. "I mean, photography *enthusiasts*."

Velvet rolls her eyes. "We can be more than one thing."

Skye and Hayden nod in agreement, and I feel stupid for having mentioned it. Of course they can like both photography and ventriloquisting. Ventriloquism? Ventriolo—you know what, never mind.

I've never spent much time with anyone other than The Tripod, so I don't know how to act. Do I offer them weed? Something tells me they wouldn't like that. Though, Velvet might.

We sit in silence, chowing down on our lunches, as the twins make these little incoherent Muppet sounds like Mr. Dinglefletcher and Miss Bond are having a conversation between themselves.

"So, Wesley, what makes you tick?"

I turn and watch as Velvet steals another carrot from my tray. "It's just Wes," I say, correcting her. "What makes me tick?"

Velvet smirks. "Yeah. What makes you excited to get out of bed every morning?"

I pinch my eyebrow. "I've never really thought about it."

That's a lie. Of course I've thought about it. It's all I've thought about lately. It's Tristan and skateboarding and photography. It's Ma and The Tripod. Hell, it's even Tad.

Velvet exchanges a look with Skye, the same look everyone has when they talk to me. The arch of the eyebrow, the subtle way their shoulders droop. Like they're not sure if I'm taking the question seriously.

"Well, think about it now," she says, stuffing the hippo back into her bag.

I tilt my skateboard up under the table. "I enjoy skateboarding. I didn't take photography seriously until someone pointed out that they liked my work, and now, it's like it's the only thing I want to do." I feel cold all over again at the thought of Tristan. At how I ruined things between us.

Hayden snorts. "I tried skateboarding once. Ended up breaking my radius bone. If you look close enough, you can still see the scar." He reaches across the table, pointing at an invisible mark on his arm with pride.

Velvet flicks the side of his head. "You didn't break anything, dumbass. You just cut out a piece of Styrofoam, put it on your arm, and pretended it was a cast for an entire month."

Everyone laughs, though Hayden says, "It was a preemptive measure."

"Have you ever broken any bones, Wes?" Skye asks, focusing not on my eyes, but my chin.

Pfft. I lean back in my chair. "I've broken so many I can't even remember them all."

They stare at me with fascination, as if my injuries are something to be proud of. Hayden makes me run through each one. Most of them are from when I was a kid, first learning how to skateboard.

Velvet considers this for a moment before saying, "You aren't half bad, Mackenzie." She takes the last of my carrots as the bell rings, and Hayden and Skye nod their heads, agreeing.

My shoulders hunch beneath their stares. I never thought I was good at making friends. I started hanging out with Tony when we were little and talking to other kids meant playing with them on the playground. When you're that age, friendship comes so naturally. Tony's the one that brought Brad into the mix. But the people sitting across from me now, the ones who actually seem interested in learning about me, are *not* Tony and Brad. I try letting that sink in.

Skye nudges me as we walk to class. "Sit with us tomorrow?"

I search the halls. Brad and Tony must have skipped today, because I haven't seen any sign of them.

"Yeah, sure. Okay," I say indifferently. Like I'm asked that all the time. Then I stop myself and look Skye in the eye. "Thanks for asking."

15.

THE BOY IN THE BACKWARD HAT

During my next shift at Vincenzo's, I pull Mr. Pecorino into the office and ask to be moved into the dining room. He agrees right away, saying that he's been meaning to promote me for months, though I suspect Tony begged him to do it.

I'm only a busser, but it gives me a chance to interact with some of the servers, something I wouldn't have cared to do even three weeks ago. I go around the dining room interviewing them and taking their portraits for a new employee spotlight series I want to try out for our Instagram page. After only one evening together, I don't get why we hated them so much in the kitchen.

When the tips roll in—something that doesn't happen when you're in the back slinging pizzas—I hand in my apron and tell Mr. Pecorino I'll never work in the kitchen again. I even start slotting a few extra dollars away to save up for a camera of my own.

At some point, Brad and Tony must have found out I abandoned them, because when they saw me ringing in an order to help a server out, they put onions on a custom order, and I got into major trouble.

After a week of putting up with their BS, I removed myself entirely from The Tripod's group chat. And since Tristan still wants nothing to do with me, hanging out with the photography kids has become my new normal. We usually spend lunch wandering through the school, taking pictures of things we come across. Hayden's even shown me some tricks on my phone to help me edit my growing portfolio of local architecture. Since then, I've taken every chance I can get to fine-tune my skills, though I'm nowhere near his level of talent.

Skye's pretty cool too. They carry a different Funko Pop figurine in their backpack every day for "good luck" (my favorite is Maleficent) and swear George Ezra is the most underrated artist of the century. We've gotten into the habit of trading lunches every Tuesday because Skye loves Ma's tuna pickle sandwiches and I can't get enough of their dad's bánh gối.

Hayden and Velvet bring out their puppets more. Maybe it's because I'm here to stand up for them now, or because I'm one less threat to worry about, but we see Mr. Dinglefletcher and Miss Bond on a regular basis. They've even gained a decent following of juniors who sit at the tables around us, waiting for the show. Someone even created a TikTok account for them that's gained over a hundred followers.

For once, it feels good laughing with people instead of at their expense. So why can't I stop myself from constantly searching for The Tripod in the halls?

ON WEDNESDAY AFTERNOON, as I'm walking to the photography club's weekly meeting, I catch Brad heading to the bathroom alone. Knowing I can't confront him in front of

Tony, I take the only chance I've had in weeks and follow him inside.

Brad's standing at the urinal, his back turned toward me, wearing a red Nirvana band tee and khakis. His shirt is so wrinkled it looks like he just picked it up off the ground and threw it on. I step over to the sink and lean against the porcelain.

Brad's blue water bottle sits on the ledge.

Quickly, I reach down and give the bottle a squeeze, and it wheezes beneath my grip. The smell of spiced rum wafts through the air.

I wasn't expecting that. Brad's drink of choice is beer. It always has been.

He turns at the sound and, when he sees me standing there, zips up his fly. "Get lost, man," he says, staggering over to the sink to wash his hands.

I scrutinize him in the bathroom mirror as he flicks the tap on. I haven't seen him this up close in days. He's got dark circles under his eyes like he hasn't slept at all. His skin is ashen gray.

I'd prepared to go off on him—to tell him that it wasn't okay to kiss me at the party like that—but seeing Brad now, seeing the toll the alcohol has taken, I'm at a loss for words.

"We need to talk," I say, my heart racing as fast as my words. I think back to all the times at work where he's paid more attention to his water bottle than his duties on the kitchen line. He always said they were energy drinks, but has he been lying this whole time? This is so much worse than I thought.

I catch his gaze in the reflection. Brad studies me through milky eyes.

"Wait, are you drunk right now?"

Brad snorts, reaching over to dry his hands. "So what if I am?" The sound of the hand dryer muffles his response, but I think he's slurring.

I take a step closer so he can hear me. "Brad, you're at school."

His shoulders lift as he snarls. "So?" There's a delay in his movements, in the way he waves his hands in front of the sensor, making the dryer hum back to life.

"You can't avoid me forever." I grab Brad's arm and spin him around, and he pushes me. I lose my balance, stumbling into the restroom's only stall. I reach around to stop the pink metal door from falling open behind me.

"Forget it, okay?" Brad snaps, tugging the bottom of his shirt. "Nothing happened. I was drunk. It was a mistake. I don't want to talk about it."

I take another step toward him, emboldened by the fact that he mentioned the kiss without me having to bring it up first. Is this his small way of opening the door? Of letting me in? "I don't think that's true. That it was a mistake," I stammer, suddenly struggling with what to say next. "This isn't you."

My hands drop to my sides. I feel sorry for him. And worse, I feel powerless to help. Brad's my best friend. We're the same. Now more than ever. Coming out should've brought us closer together, but it's only pushed us apart. If I'd known we were both questioning our sexuality—that he was someone I could've confided in this whole time—what would our friendship have looked like all these years?

I can't ask him that, though. Not when he can barely stand on his own two feet. I take a closer look at him: his eyes dart around like he can't concentrate, his body sways as if the ground's coming out from beneath him.

I want to scream. Tell him how worried I am. How it only takes one moment of weakness to get behind a wheel and kill someone. But none of that comes out of my mouth because we've sat through those lectures in school before. If it didn't get through to him then, why would it now?

I look at him and say, "Brad, you have a problem." It's so

quiet, the thing I've been meaning to tell him since New Year's, that I don't think he hears me. I say it again, this time with conviction. "You have a problem."

Brad rolls his eyes, drying the leftover water from his hands over his pants. "Like you care."

"Of course I do." I hide my hands behind my back, not letting him see as I clench them together.

Three times one is three.

He tilts his head, dropping it lower than he should. "I saw the way you were looking at that guy. You ditched us for *him*." He finishes his sentence with a guttural growl, dragging the last word out like metal over pavement. "And now you don't even want to work with us anymore."

I flinch. "You haven't talked to me since Stacy's party. What was I supposed to do? But you're right. I shouldn't have lied. I wasn't ready to tell you. But this isn't about The Tripod. This is about your life. We can't just ignore the way you kissed me—"

Brad grabs me by my collar and throws me into the stall. He's got at least fifty pounds on me. If he wanted to, he could beat me up right here and now, and none would be the wiser.

"I said forget it," he shouts into my ear, the dog tags around his neck clanging together. He holds me against the stall, searches my face, before letting me go. "I've got somewhere to be."

Brad shoves past the bathroom door, out into the hall. I take a moment, see my terrified expression looking back at me from the mirror. Afraid he's going to get into his Jeep and drive off, I chase after him.

We step out onto the sidewalk, and I race in front of him to block his path.

"Brad, stop!"

Brad looks down at me, watching as I fight to catch my

breath. The smell of alcohol is so strong on him, like it's leaking from his pores. Was he like this at Christmas when Ma first asked about his drinking? How could I have missed that?

"I don't take orders from you," Brad grumbles, pushing past me and thumping down the stairs.

"Come on, Bud. You can talk to me."

At the mention of his nickname, Brad stops on the last step. For a moment, I think he might take me up on the offer.

But he looks over his shoulder and says, "No, I really can't."

I want to argue with him, but I get it. I really do. We've never allowed ourselves to talk about anything. The closest we've ever got is the time Brad mentioned his dad's own drinking problem while playing video games at Tony's. He shut down before it got too intense, turning over in his sleeping bag and pretending to fall asleep. I remember how Tony waved him off like it didn't matter. But it did then, and it does now.

We've never allowed ourselves to talk about anything, but that doesn't mean we can't start. I want to save this friendship. I need to for his sake as much as my own.

"Does Tony know?" My voice comes out even quieter than before. Am I asking about his drinking or his sexuality?

Brad's eyes narrow. I think he might cry, but he blows out a breath and runs his hand through his hair. For some reason, I can't stop focusing on the fact that he's not wearing his hat lately. "Does he know about you?"

I've mulled the scene over in my head since Brad stormed out on New Year's. We could sit Tony down, get everything out in the open once and for all. I know he's proud, but Tony would never allow himself to lose both of his only friends. Family is everything to him.

"I thought—if we told him together . . ."

Brad turns his back toward me. "I said get lost, Wes."

And he leaves me standing there like that. I feel the energy drain from my body—all the anger, all the sadness—escape through the soles of my shoes.

I watch him walk away.

"Okay." I swallow down my fear as he turns the corner of the gymnasium and disappears.

I have no choice but to go back inside.

16.

DON'T WRITE YOURSELF
OFF JUST YET

Unbeknownst to me, Ma stays home from her Saturday morning shift with the flu. Had I known she was in bed, juggling consciousness between episodes of *The Golden Girls* and a fever, I'd have never started crying in the kitchen.

Somewhere between getting out of bed and eating breakfast, it finally hits me. The Tripod and I are never going to recover from this. I can feel the gaping hole left by their absence like a weight sitting over my heart. Adding insult to injury, Tony sends me a text with a screenshot of his Instagram feed.

WTF?

It's the first time he's reached out in over a week. For a minute, the picture he attaches doesn't even register, and I think I've imagined the whole thing. But I didn't. Because staring up at me is a photo of the photography club from Stacy's Instagram page. As we counted down from three, Velvet had made some pun about f-stops that I actually understood for once.

And though my eyes are red in the picture, if you zoom in close enough, my smile is genuine.

I don't reply to Tony. Instead, I click away from his message and open the last conversation I had with Tristan. I don't know why I torture myself like this.

We were in the middle of debating the hottest male celebrities—pitting Michael B. Jordan against Henry Cavill (respectfully)—when one of us must've fallen asleep. If only I knew then what was about to happen. Maybe I would've kept the conversation going. Stayed up just a little bit longer. To savor the before.

I've spent all week writing and rewriting an apology text, to put down in words how awful I was to him in the forest that night. Even now, I fight the urge to send him a Snap of the tiny paper Kremlin in my hand. But I have to respect his space. If nothing else, I owe him that.

At noon, Ma emerges from her room in the same satin pink and white laced robe as Rose Nylund, her nose bright red and runny. She finds me sitting at the kitchen table, gluing down important dates for my world history project and trying my best not to let teardrops fall on the poster paper.

"Joseph Stalin, eh?" Ma swipes my hair back and kisses my forehead. "'It doesn't matter how many people vote. Only who counts them.' That man was batshit, though I'm afraid he was right about that one."

I slam my phone face down on the table, hoping she didn't see Tristan's name on the screen.

Do you ever feel like if you stood still and held your breath, time would stop?

I did that a lot when we first moved to Valentine. I'm not sure why. Maybe all I wanted was to rewind the clock and go back to my childhood. I know it's not what I really wanted. I sure as hell didn't want my abusive asshole of a father back in the picture.

But sitting here now, I hold my breath again, hoping to turn back enough time for Ma to reverse walk into her room. For me to scrub my eyes and keep it together long enough for them to dry.

But that's not how time works, apparently.

"Stevia, is everything okay?" Ma's voice is tender, like she knows anything more will overwhelm me.

"Why wouldn't it be?" I sniffle when I ask, screwing up any chance I had of her believing me.

Ma leans over my shoulder and gives me a hug. Her hair is done up in a fountain ponytail so that when she holds me, it tickles my nose and I sneeze, sending loose pieces from my project to scatter in the air.

I could tell her right now. That I'm gay. That I've met a guy I really like. That I've pushed my friends away in the process by keeping it all a secret.

As if reading my mind, Ma shuffles in her bunny slippers and flattens her back to the fridge. She waits for me to look over before speaking. "I regret not being a good enough parent and having to spell this out, but I hope you know we can talk about anything."

This is it. Ma's laying the bait out in front of me. All I have to do is bite.

But I see Tristan's face in my mind, see the way Tony shot me down in the forest, how Brad snubbed me as he turned the corner. I've already lost everyone close to me. I can't risk losing Ma too.

"I'm fine," I grumble, not looking up from my homework. This isn't a Hallmark movie. I'm not going to come home from college during Thanksgiving and surprise her with a boy I met during orientation week. Ma won't embrace me and tell me how much she loves him. Because life isn't like that. It's not like the movies at all. "Maybe I'm getting sick too. Germs travel fast in small spaces." I cough, patting my chest and pretending to clear my lungs.

Ma doesn't buy it. Not even for a second. She reaches over and grabs my neck, pushing her thumbs below my hairline like she used to when I'd get migraines as a kid. "Is this about The Tripod? I haven't seen them around lately."

I close my eyes, shrugging her hands away. "I've been busy."

Ma picks up a cutout picture of the Soviet Union flag, flipping it over to read the number on the back that corresponds with where I need to place it on the poster. "Right. Because you're doing homework."

"Yes?" I ask as she drops the flag into my hand.

"Which is something you never do . . ."

I look up as Ma grabs a Kleenex and blows her nose. "Wait. Are you judging me for getting an education?"

"Not at all," she says. "I just don't get the reason behind it."

I shrug, returning my attention to the table. I can't tell her that the conversation I had with Mr. Hamilton about colleges, and the subsequent one with Emily and Tristan, has been weighing down on me now that it's the New Year. If I admit one thing, I'll have to admit everything.

But what I do say is, "I figured I'd better take school seriously if I want to graduate in May."

Ma smiles out of the corner of her mouth. "Very good. Carry on, then," she says in her terrible British accent.

"Do you need anything?" I ask, hoping it'll be enough to change the subject. "Soup? Cough medicine? Cheesecake?"

Ma chuckles, then nearly coughs up a lung. "You know I'm the adult here, right? You don't have to look after me all the time."

"Maybe not, but that doesn't mean I don't want to. You're not just my ma."

Her eyes grow big at that. "I wish Tad were here."

I run the side of my foot along the kitchen table's leg. I know Tad is probably keeping his distance to protect Hannah from any germs, but he'd be here in a second if Ma asked him to. He'd drop anything to be with her. That's the kind of person he is.

"Don't make me say it." I sigh, glancing up at the ceiling. There's a large, yellowed spot in the stucco, right above Ma's head, where the ceiling leaks in heavy rainstorms.

"Wes? What is it?"

"You should say yes to Tad."

Ma freezes. "Where is this coming from? Are you sure?"

I grab her hands, her palms clammy in mine. "He makes you happy. I don't want to stand in the way of that."

I look Ma in the eye as she covers her mouth and weeps. I've held this over her for too long. I was selfish. I put my own feelings before hers, not caring how much it might hurt. But she deserves to be happy. I'm the asshole for not realizing that until now.

Ma squeezes me into a hug, smooshing my ear against her chest as she takes in a ragged breath.

"God, Ma!" I say, pushing her back.

She apologizes but pulls me in again, this time for a proper hug. "That means a lot, Stevia. Thank you for being a friend."

After we let go, I allow myself to imagine what the next few months could look like. I want Ma to have a big summer wedding, with baby's breath everywhere and a midnight taco bar, like the one I overhead her mentioning to Tad when they thought I was asleep in my room.

"For the record, Tad's very fond of you."

I take a deep breath, and we head into the family room.

I can do this. I can pick up the pieces of my life and glue them back together. It may start with Ma, but it doesn't have to end there. Like Tristan learning how to skateboard, all I have to do is bend my knees and lift.

As Ma begins an episode of *The Golden Girls*, I pull my phone out and text Emily.

> I really need to talk to Tristan.

> I want him to know how sorry I am.

> Please, Emily.

By the time my phone pings in my lap, I've watched Dorothy and Sophia bicker for thirty whole minutes.

Emily doesn't say anything.

She just sends me an address.

17.

WELCOME TO THE APOLOGY PARADE

After talking to Ma, I formed a plan to stand up to the guys at school on Monday. I decided I'm not going to let The Tripod crumble without them hearing me out first. Even though I've told my fair share of lies the last few weeks, they've been shitty friends to me too.

But before I can do that, I have to do right by Tristan.

Ma lets me take the car with the promise that I'll pick up something for dinner. I plug the address Emily sent into Google Maps and follow the directions through Valentine, up the winding roads toward Stacy Evans's house. When I think I'm going to turn into her gated community, my phone instructs me to take a sharp left and drive along the same wall The Tripod hopped over on the way to Stacy's party. My stomach lurches at the thought of us together. Back before everything changed.

I run my hands over the steering wheel as I get closer to seeing Tristan. I haven't rehearsed what I'll say when I get there. I know I should because my words will get all jumbled like they usually do at the sight of him, but how will he react when I walk through the door? Will he be upset at the sight of me?

I don't have time to worry though when Google Maps announces that I've arrived at my destination. I step out of the car and into an elementary school's parking lot packed with silver mom vans and expensive baby strollers.

I stomp the snow off my boots in the lobby, surrounded by screaming toddlers wiggling in their parents' arms as they fight to get them into their shoes. I forgot how much I hate kids who aren't Hannah.

Following the pitter-patter of feet, I find Tristan in the middle of the school's gymnasium teaching ballet exercises to a group of restless children. He talks to them calmly, in a voice much higher than I'm used to hearing. I watch him lead the class as he stands over his arched left foot, extending his right leg out behind him. The kids seem to hang on to his every word as they dance around in black unitards and leg warmers, mimicking how Tristan points his foot in the air (though with 75 percent less accuracy).

After a few minutes of twirling with barely enough rhythm to call it ballet-adjacent, Tristan blows the whistle hanging around his neck.

The kids go wild and run into their parents' arms. You can tell which ones want to become dancers when they're older from those who do it because mommy needed an hour to herself. I swerve out of the way before they can crush me.

As the gym empties out, I walk toward the center, where Tristan's talking with one of the only dads in the group. I hang back, clearing my throat behind him when their conversation ends.

"Is there anything you can't do?" I ask, and he turns. "I need to know now because a Westgate Academy, electric car-driving, dancing humanitarian I can handle. But a Westgate Academy, electric car-driving, dancing humanitarian who can't pat his stomach and tap his head at the same time might be an issue."

Tristan blinks like he can't believe I'm standing there and takes in my clothes. Under my leather jacket, I'm in a mint green collared shirt and acid-washed black jeans. I even scrubbed the dirt off my white skate shoes before leaving the house.

"What do you want, Wes?" Tristan coughs, turning to make sure there are no stragglers in need of his attention. He's dressed in a baggy gray sweatshirt with Westgate's falcon mascot on the front over his black leotard. It's the most casual outfit I've ever seen him in.

I look around the gym at the blue floor mats and volleyball net resting along the far wall. There's an underlying hint of sweat in the air, the smell of dirty socks.

"I liked what you did back there," I say pointing, lifting my foot out behind me.

"It's called an arabesque."

Tristan steps around me then to gather the orange pylons littered around the gymnasium floor. "Answer the question," he says sternly.

I head in the opposite direction to help. "I needed to see you," I reply, sticking my hand in one of the pylons so that it covers my forearm.

Tristan puts his hands on his hips. "Didn't I tell you to leave me alone?"

I lower my arm, dropping my eyes to my shoes. "You did. I know. And I tried." I walk over and hand him the rest of the pylons. "Honestly, I did. But you deserve an apology in person, and I wanted to show you all the pictures I've taken during photography club, and Ma's sick so I knew if I stayed home, I'd keep thinking about you and debating whether or not to text you, which is basically what I've been doing all week, and—"

Tristan reaches out his hand to stop me. "So you told your friends about me?"

"Have I told my friends about you?" I repeat what he's asked, looking down at his open palm. I think back to my admission to Brad in the restroom. While I didn't outright say it, I did apologize for ditching them for Tristan. I know that's not at all what he's asking now, but it's at least a step in the right direction. Isn't it? I scrunch my nose. "Kind of."

Tristan huffs and pinches the skin between his eyebrows. "Look, Wes, I respect you needing time to process everything. And I would never pressure anyone to come out when they don't feel ready. But you shouldn't be friends with people you can't be yourself around. And I can't be with someone who's embarrassed to be seen with me. This is my life too, and I won't put myself through that."

I smooth down my shirt to occupy my hands, feeling like a damn idiot.

Tristan is out and proud. It's the first thing I learned about him. Why would he ever want to be with someone like me, who can't even look their friends in the eyes and tell them the truth?

"I'm going to talk to them on Monday."

Tristan opens his mouth like he's about to speak.

"Not because of what you've just said," I throw in, carrying on before I lose the nerve. "But because I've realized how broken our friendship really is. To be honest, I think it's been that way for a long time now. And I don't want to keep things from them anymore. I think I'm ready."

I watch for his reaction, hoping he can see that I'm telling the truth.

Tristan checks the time. "My car is in the shop, and I actually have to catch the bus." He goes to grab his bag, leaving me standing among the drawn-in lines of the gym's basketball court. He's about to open the door when he turns to me and says, "You coming?"

"Yes," I say, a little too earnestly. "But I can drive you if you want?"

OUTSIDE, THE SNOW has turned to rain.

Tristan places his hands over the car's air vents. He's sitting rigidly in the passenger seat, his shoulders turned toward the door. He's not ready to forgive me. I can see that just by looking at him.

I keep my eyes facing forward, tracking a raindrop as it makes its way down the windshield.

Neither of us say a word.

I don't know where to start. Tristan did agree to let me give him a ride, so maybe it's not only me. Maybe he wants to make amends as much as I do. That, or he forgot an umbrella.

When the windows finish defrosting, I crank the steering wheel and guide Ma's blue Pontiac down the street.

I've never been to Tristan's house, so he has to direct me where to go as we drive through an unfamiliar neighborhood. All the houses on this side of Valentine are red stone brick with wraparound patios. Weeping black willows line the sidewalks. If I didn't know any better, I would think we were driving through the British countryside. The city's kept the main roads clear since the first major snowfall back in December, but the side streets leading to Tristan's house are still blocked.

I take a detour and climb the side of Mt. Rockwell. I apologize to Tristan for taking the scenic route, thinking he might laugh at my lame attempt to make a joke. He doesn't, though I take it as a win when I catch the hint of a smile in the side mirror.

Ma's car heaves up the hill as I push down on the gas. It's getting dark—the kind of darkness I try to avoid when driving.

I start breathing heavily.

I don't mean to.

The last thing I want is for Tristan to see me like this. I'd meant to stay in control, to look him in the eye and say I was sorry. But it seems the night has other plans.

We're the only ones on the road now. There aren't any streetlights to light our path ahead. I flick the high beams on as a semitruck comes out of nowhere, rocking us back and forth.

"Wes, are you okay?" Tristan asks, looking at my hands as I readjust them over the wheel.

I turn down the music on the dash. It's getting difficult to swallow.

I don't tell Tristan my heart is pounding inside my chest or that there's a sharp pain just below my right knee. We're only *maybe* making up, so I need to keep calm. I can't afford to blow this. Not again.

Tristan launches into a story suddenly about something that happened this week at school. Maybe it's to distract me, I don't know. I'm not listening anymore. I can hardly hear him. All I can focus on is the sharp drop-off up ahead, the road as it disappears over the crest.

I press down on the brake when I should speed up.

Tristan laughs nervously. "Are you purposefully going slow because you missed me and want to spend more time together?"

I can tell he's getting worried. I want to explain, to tell him that I get like this when I drive in the dark. How the past has a way of resurfacing when I do. But my body won't let me turn to reassure him. My limbs are frozen in fear.

Tristan asks me something again, but the thread of pain

shooting up my leg drowns him out. Ma's voice—whispering that she loves me—is a million miles, a million memories away.

My heart leaps out of my throat as I accelerate the car just enough to get us over to the shoulder.

I blow out the breath I'd been holding, dropping my head to the steering wheel. Tristan gives my forearm a squeeze.

"What just happened?"

I take a deep breath, holding on to a lifetime of heartache.

Three times one is three.

Three times two is six.

Three times three is nine.

"It's my knee," I breathe into the wheel's leather, pulling up the emergency brake. "It locked up. It . . . does that sometimes."

Tristan leans over to see my face. "You told me you pulled a muscle," he says, running his hand down my arm. His fingers trace over my skin.

I turn to stare out into the cold winter night. Beyond the road ahead, the hill drops off into a snowy abyss below. "I try so hard to hide it."

"Hide what?" Tristan pleads into the silence. "Let me in, Wes."

The car suddenly feels too cold, like it'll freeze over and trap us inside forever. Tristan watches me. In the dark, I can't make out his irises from his pupils.

I clutch my jacket. "It happened on a Thursday night. We hadn't even made it past Mississippi . . ." I fiddle with my hands in my lap. I've never told anyone this.

Tristan doesn't react; he looks over at me, his eyes imploring me to go on.

"My dad found us outside of Jackson. He used to drive this beat-up truck . . ."

I can still see its rusted red frame in the back of my mind.

Still smell the gas that leaked from the pipes below. He always let me sit in the front seat without a seat belt. I used to think that was the coolest thing in the world, but I know better now. Every time we left the house, he was putting me in danger.

"I knew in my gut it was him," I continue, trying my best to steady my voice. "He flashed his headlights for Ma to pull over, but she wouldn't. She knew we couldn't go back to the life we'd been living." I shake my head, tears falling over the seat's black cloth. "Ma sped up the first time he hit our bumper. She thought she could protect us. She thought we could get away. But he came around the side of the car. He didn't even look over at us. He didn't roll down his window and beg for us to come home like he used to." I point ahead, and Tristan follows my finger to where the road swerves to the right and disappears behind the trees. "He drove us straight off the cliff."

Through the darkness, I can picture the interior of Ma's car rolling around, the loose change from the cupholder flying past my head like darts. When you're suspended between your seat belt and death, the inevitable landing feels so much longer than it should. Like it'll never happen. But when the impact of the ground finally does come, it rattles you to the core. When I opened my eyes, I was upside down in the backseat, watching my dad drive away.

Tristan gasps, covering his mouth, his own eyes welling up now with tears. "Wes, I'm so sorry. I didn't know—"

I don't let him finish what he's about to say. "How could you? I've never talked about it. I guess it's kind of a recurring problem," I say, remembering his words to me in the woods. I shake my head to rid the image of me and Ma falling. "I couldn't feel my legs. I remember turning to Ma in the driver's seat. She'd lost consciousness. There was blood everywhere."

Ma's hair touched the ceiling like we were on a rollercoaster at Six Flags. The front window had shattered into a million pieces of glass. They were like little rainbow bows in her hair.

"I tried screaming for help, but everyone must have already gone home for the night. It was dark out. I don't know how long we were hanging there, but someone must have driven past eventually and saw the barrier missing from the road. I thought maybe I'd dreamt the whole thing, but the sky turned from gray to white and then there I was, in a hospital room. Ma was nowhere to be found. You can't imagine the pain a kid feels when he wakes up and thinks his ma has died. I was hysterical. The doctors had to sedate me so I'd stop crying."

I grind my teeth. When I touch my lips, my fingers come back red. "I screwed my leg up pretty badly in the accident. The doctors couldn't find anything physically wrong with it when they ran their tests, but it's like there's this unbearable weight below my kneecap I can never quite shake." I run my fingers along both sides of my right knee, where it's hard to distinguish muscle from bone. "It hasn't been the same since."

Tristan grabs my hand. I try snaking out of his grasp, but he holds on tighter.

I fidget with a loose stitch on my jeans. "I think I've always blamed myself for what my dad did. Like if he couldn't have Ma, no one could. Not even me."

"How old were you?" Tristan says, swiping at his nose with his sleeve.

"Seven. I managed to keep it a secret for a while, but after my teachers found out what happened, they let me skate around on the school grounds even though you're not supposed to. I'd always been terrible to them, but I guess they felt bad for me."

Tristan stifles a cry. "What about your ma?"

"She had a concussion for a few months, a couple of broken ribs. The doctors said she shouldn't have made it out alive, but she did. She was holding my hand when they found us."

Tristan grabs my neck and pulls me into a hug. I've never let anyone see me like this. My body shakes against his, but he doesn't tell me to stop. He just pulls me closer.

"I'm all she's got, Tristan," I murmur into his sweatshirt, choking on the words. "I can't follow you to New York. I can't leave her." I can see Ma in my head the way she had been, how frail she was when we were finally discharged from the hospital. We had to make multiple stops on our way to Valentine so she could rest. When we found the apartment above the laundromat, I did everything I could to help out.

Tristan's breath runs over my ear. He begins to lean away, but I pull him back in.

"What about Tad?"

The question catches me off guard. I run my tongue along the roof of my mouth. "What about him?"

"Won't he always be here to look after her?"

I suck a breath between my teeth. Now that they're getting married, we'll most likely move into Tad and Hannah's townhouse since they have three bedrooms and an extra bathroom we wouldn't have to share. I should be relieved that Ma has found someone to be with. I meant what I said to her about marrying Tad, but right now, I can't shake the feeling that it's only temporary. "You don't know that for sure."

There it is again. The shadow of my dad leaving us to fend for ourselves.

I feel Tristan nod his head in the crook of my neck. I can smell the aftershave on his skin, just like on New Year's. I grab at his sweatshirt, bundling the extra fabric in my hands.

"Is that why you don't want to go to college? Are you afraid she'll move on without you?" Tristan speaks slowly when he asks, contemplating each word carefully like they have the power to break me. Maybe they do. "You haven't applied because something's holding you back."

I wipe my tears on the cuff of my jacket. "Ma's not holding me back. I'm helping her out. We're still paying off medical debt."

Tristan shrugs, thinking over what to say next. "She's not going anywhere, Wes. You know that, right?"

"You're wrong."

"Am I?"

I pull away from him then, letting my head rest against my seat. "No, probably not."

Aside from The Tripod, Ma's been the only constant in my life. Once she gets married, where does that leave me? Am I the one who's afraid of being alone?

I start the car—not realizing I'd turned it off—and Tristan lets me drive the rest of the way without saying anything.

"Thank you for being vulnerable with me, Wes," he says as I pull up to the curb. Turns out, Tristan only lives a few blocks away from Stacy, in another gated community called Serpentine Hill.

The Monroe household could fit my entire apartment, Mr. Fong's Laundromat, and half of the playground across the street, inside. The driveway winds in an S shape up to the front of the house, past a copper mailbox designed to look like a tree and flower beds lying dormant for the season. Even leaves leftover from autumn look like they've been placed there on purpose.

"Just telling it like it is." I return my eyes to the road, letting the trauma and the embarrassment of the drive recede into the night.

"Sometimes, there's vulnerability in telling the truth." Tristan gives me another hug before reaching to unbuckle his seat belt. "My birthday's Monday night. My parents are making dinner, and I'd really like it if you came. Emily will be there too."

He waits for me to reply. I glance over at his lap.

"Okay."

I barely manage to get the word out before Tristan leans over and kisses me, softer this time than in the forest. I don't move as his lips skim lightly across mine. I breathe him in, letting his soft scent intoxicate me. His fingers are delicate when they touch my cheek to swipe away a tear.

"I didn't mean to derail our conversation back there," I whisper into his mouth, laughing weakly when I do. "But I am sorry for making you hide that day in the forest. That wasn't cool." I feel my knee seize up again. "I-I want to be your boyfriend . . . if you'll have me."

Tristan peels back. He stares into my eyes, searching for something, and I'm afraid he's going to reject me. Tell me he doesn't want to be with me. I look down at his hand on the door handle next to him, wondering if he'll bolt. But Tristan turns to me then, a smile creeping over his face. "I want you to be my boyfriend too."

I lean back on the driver's door, and I think Tristan's about to kiss me again when he punches my arm and jumps out of the car.

I roll down the window as he heads up the front stairs to his house.

"That hurt, you know!" I shout after him, rubbing my arm.

He turns and looks at me. "Sorry," he teases, "I've been spending too much time around you."

I watch as he steps inside, and I can't help the smile from forming on my face.

I have a boyfriend.

18.

STEVIA, WE'RE GOIN DOWN

We become official on Instagram just after midnight. Tristan made sure I was okay with it before posting one of the pictures I took of him in Walter Prescott Theater and tagging me as the photographer.

I'm not usually someone who cares about that kind of crap, but the minute I see my name next to the red lips emoji on Tristan's profile, it's as if our relationship is an e-transfer between AI robots, and my heart skips a beat. I guess it's a love thing, because that shit is totally real in an "I almost died from emotional overload" sort of way.

Wait, did I just say love?

We spend all of Sunday afternoon together, drinking peppermint mochas in Mariner's Park, having lunch in the food court at the mall. It's not how I imagined my coming out being, but maybe that's a good thing? Come tomorrow morning, for the first time ever, I'll be showing up at school as my whole self. Which is kind of terrifying if I give it too much thought.

I know Tony and Brad have probably already seen the news, but it doesn't matter. I'm going to find them at lunch and explain everything. I'll sit them down, apologize for the way I've acted over the last few weeks, and give them a chance to do the same. Despite what Tristan said about not needing them, they are my best friends.

When I arrive at school, I half expect my entire world history class to message me when the teacher isn't looking, asking if what they heard was true. But the messages never come. In fact, no one acknowledges the monumental change that's occurred in my life in the last forty-eight hours. When I pass them in the halls, no one even looks at me. It's like nothing ever happened.

I guess the perk of being me is that nobody cares enough to ask questions about my life, let alone my relationship status. Maybe they're afraid I'll lash out at them and cause a scene. Or they already knew I was gay and just couldn't care less.

Though I was prepared to fight over any homophobic comments, I'm kind of relieved I don't have to.

At the end of first period, I walk out of class with my first ever B- for the project I busted my ass on over the weekend. I swear I've never sweat so much in my life when Ms. Dillion handed back our marks.

I text Tristan a Happy Birthday message and tell him the news. Within seconds, my phone blows up in a storm of GIFs, all congratulating me.

> We still on for tonight?

I reply with a GIF of Marge Simpson throwing her arms in the air with the caption *Well, duh.* I just got a B- on a project I actually managed to finish, and I'm texting my boyfriend about it on his birthday. I can't contain my smile.

I'm so damn proud of you. Xoxo

When I open my locker, a stack of college brochures is waiting for me inside, held together by ribbon. I roll my eyes as I flip through several community colleges I've never heard of. While I've managed to avoid Mr. Hamilton for over a month, I guess this was bound to happen. But I won't let him get to me. Not today.

Walking through the halls, I hold my chin high—feeling taller than I ever have before—but the smile melts off my face as I round the corner. Because at the end of the hall, as if expecting me, Tony and Brad are standing there. And they're not alone.

Oh, hell no.

"Oh, hell no."

Any confidence I felt evaporates, leaving my body with the release of my breath. I want to crumble to the ground, curl my knees into the fetal position, but I can't. Because Hayden is standing next to them with his back against the lockers. He looks between Tony and Brad, holding the straps of his bag with closed fists, nodding furiously.

I don't have time to ask questions. Before The Tripod can lift a finger, I race over and grab Tony's backpack from behind.

Tony swings his arms out like he's lost his balance. He tries to clip me, but I'm too quick, twisting out of the way so his hands come back empty. He should know better. I invented that move junior year.

"What the hell are you doing?" Tony snaps when he sees that it's me. His voice sounds hollow, devoid of any emotion.

I take in The Tripod's appearance then: the disheveled look of Brad's hair, the way Tony's silver chain necklace sits off-center on his chest. Their brown eyes scan the hall like they're hunting for their next victim.

This is all my fault. They know I joined the photography club, know that Hayden is my friend. They're upset and targeting him on purpose to get back at me. I feel ashamed suddenly, both of myself for thinking belittling people made me happy and of them for still believing it.

"Did they hurt you?" I ask Hayden, watching Tony from the corner of my eye.

Hayden's eyebrows crease. He shakes his head. "Wes, no—"

Brad cuts him off. "Are you joking right now? We weren't doing anything!"

"I don't believe you." I flinch at the guys' laughter but keep my eyes trained on Hayden. "Get out of here. *Now*."

I don't have to tell him twice. Hayden looks up at me—as if to say he's sorry—before running out of sight.

Brad takes a step in Hayden's direction, no doubt to chase after him, but I clutch his arm. "Let him go, Bud."

"Stop calling me that," Brad huffs through gritted teeth.

"What the hell has gotten into you, Wes?" Tony asks as the final bell for second period rings.

All down the hall, doors close. No one comes to help. No teachers peek their heads out of their classrooms to check for stragglers. If they did, they'd see us standing here. See the fight about to break out.

Because that's exactly what's going to happen. I can feel it in the air like a warning.

I turn to Tony, then back to Brad. They're both scowling at me like I'm Principal Cohen confiscating their ziplock bag full of weed.

"Me? What's gotten into the two of *you*? Does this not mean anything anymore?" To prove my allegiance, I lift my pant leg and show off the three interlocking triangles tattooed on my right calf. They've faded a bit since we got them, the surrounding hairs have long since grown back, but the symbol's still there, permanently marking our friendship.

They both laugh.

"Please. You haven't been a part of the crew since you went off and got yourself a *boyfriend*," Tony hisses, the corner of his mouth lifting at the word "boyfriend." Like it disgusts him.

Tony goes to turn his back, like he's decided I'm not worthy of his time, and I tackle him to the floor. He thrashes under my weight, throwing fists at the air between us. The only thing he's got against me is his height, but lying on the floor, that advantage is useless. It's not like this is the first time we've fought. Growing up, we used to wrestle on the trampoline in Brad's backyard. But this is different. Tony claws at my jacket now with a fevered determination, his nails nicking the side of my neck.

I push back and punch him square in the face, the bones in my knuckles buckling under his jaw. I let out a cry, cupping my hand to my chest. The skin hasn't even properly healed since punching the tree in the forest.

I never wanted it to end up like this. I'd meant to apologize today. But seeing them about to harm Hayden, I couldn't take it. When I look between them now, there's no mercy in their eyes. It's like they don't even care we're fighting.

"Fuck you, Wes," Tony yells as he wipes spit from his mouth.

I go to shout back, hurl an insult that'll cut just as deep, when I'm lifted off of him and thrown down the hall. Even through my jeans, the skin on my knee splits open as I skid across the linoleum floor. I bite back a scream.

I turn around, ready to charge, but Brad's hovering over me.

"Can we at least talk about this?" I choke out.

"Why should we listen to you?" Brad asks, tilting his jaw back and forth like he's only warming up.

I gulp down a sour taste in my mouth, feeling utterly help-less. Tony squints his eyes, fury written plainly across his face.

"Because we're supposed to be best friends," I say, trying my best to stand. The side of my face feels like it's starting to bruise from the fall.

Tony snorts, pulling an AirPod out of his ear. "That's rich coming from you. All you care about is your new boyfriend. Which, by the way, thanks for telling us about. You think you'd have shared something like that with your *best friends*. But you're embarrassed by us."

I look to Brad for backup, but he shakes his head, the muscles in his neck convulsing.

"I get that you're mad at me," I say, reaching a hand out to show I mean no harm. "I just want to talk. Clear the air."

Tony contemplates my hand as it hangs between us before taking it and twisting it behind my back in one swift motion. "Who even are you right now?" he growls, his breath hot against my ear.

"Yeah! Stop pretending to be someone you're not," Brad says, coming over and punching me in the stomach.

"You're one to talk," I cough out as Tony pulls my arm back farther. The tendons in my shoulder tear from the strain.

My eyes dart between them, and I know there's nothing I can do to stop this. I remember the high of being in their shoes. The rush of excitement that courses through your veins. But don't they realize that when they've thrown kids into dumpsters, when they've shoved them back and forth like human ping-pong balls, I've always been in the background?

"What's that supposed to mean?"

I glance up at Brad, seething from the shooting pain beneath my ribs. "Want to tell Tony what I'm talking about, or should I?"

I don't actually want to out Brad—I'm not that kind of

person—so I search the hall, desperately looking for another way out of this.

Brad cracks his knuckles. Instead of retaliating like I'd feared, he reaches into his backpack on the floor and grabs his water bottle. He wipes his forehead with the back of his arm and unscrews the cap to take a swig.

Of course.

"Sure, yeah. Keep drinking your feelings away. Just like your dad."

Brad homes in on me, his eyes suddenly feral. And when I look further, I see the same glazed-over look he had in the bathroom. He's as drunk now as he was then.

"What did you say to me?" Brad comes up so close to my face that his eyes morph into one. I can smell cheap bourbon on his breath.

"You're acting just like him."

Brad slams his fist into my eye, and air escapes my lips. Except instead of air, I think it might be blood. Tony lets go of me as I keel over in pain. Before I can get up, Brad's pinning my chest down with his knees.

The room begins to spin. I can't tell the ground from the ceiling.

Three times one is three.

Three times two is six.

Three times three is nine.

I lose track after fifty-four, but I know I can reach 486 on memory alone. I've been doing it since I was a kid.

I remember the way Ma would fall to the floor as my dad reached for an empty bottle. She used to shield her face automatically, as if her body knew to take cover. To move into survival mode. I watched everything from under the kitchen table, my body small and tucked into itself (like Ma had taught me). But I never once took my eyes off of her. I kept counting in my head because I didn't know what else to do. I was only a child.

Despite being my dad's coworkers, the police used to show up at the house once a week because the neighbors would complain about the noise. But no one ever truly offered to help. They just listened through the walls and gossiped with each other during Sunday service.

In the back of my mind, I can still picture Ma crying on the kitchen floor, and it's like I'm that little, defenseless kid all over again. But this time, I'm the one trembling in the corner, my body being used as a punching bag instead of hers.

I yell for The Tripod to stop, for everything to go away, but they don't hear me.

I'm not sure I've spoken at all.

My lungs fight for air. My heart hammers inside my rib cage. The hallway falls away from me, like it's come undone from the light fixtures on the ceiling. Tony and Brad's faces disappear until all I know is agony. All I see is darkness, like I've lost my vision completely or been swallowed into the pits of hell. After all, there must be a reason why I remind Tristan of Lucifer.

When I come to, there's a crowd of students forming a circle around us. Some are whispering among themselves. Some are shouting for us to keep fighting. Others have whipped out their phones to record us.

I look down at my hands, shaking and pale, like I'm seeing them for the first time.

I blink back the thick layer of fog that's shrouded my brain. Brad's clutching his jaw like it'd fall off if he didn't. Tony's sprawled out on the floor, cursing through his teeth. The skin on his face has turned a deep, midnight blue.

What have I done?

"I'm sorry. I'm so sorry—" The words get lodged in my

throat. I look over and see Skye in the crowd, their hand covering their mouth in shock.

"Mr. Mackenzie!" I crane my neck to where Principal Cohen is standing with her arms crossed. She's glowering down at me. "My office. *This instant*," she commands, pointing down the hall.

I don't stick up for myself. I don't tell her how Tony and Brad started it. I don't even recall hobbling across the school to her office—either on my own two feet or with help. I just cram inside as she slams the door behind her.

19.

FAT LIP / BRUISED EGO

My fingers tremble as I scrub them in the bathroom sink, tearing the loose skin around my knuckles. I laugh bitterly at the thought of putting up a good fight when even my reflection is judging me through the mirror.

Principal Cohen expelled me. She didn't wait for me to tell my side of the story. As far as she was concerned, I was the one who threw the first punch. I deserved the punishment. Tony and Brad got away with only a week's suspension while I had to sit silently in her office and wait for Ma to come pick me up. I've never felt more ashamed as she sat down in the chair next to me with a thud, squeezing her purse to her chest. She didn't look at me once.

After my expulsion, Ma hurried down the hall, and I had to hobble behind her to keep up. She grounded me for life before I could get into the car. It's not like I didn't have it coming. I know I did. But I didn't have the energy to argue with her. It was bad enough that Principal Cohen told her who I'd been fighting with. I could practically hear her heart breaking.

Ma dropped me off on the curb outside our building, her tires screeching as she raced back to work. I'd made her miss three hours of her shift, which she'd have to make up for by staying late tonight.

When I got home, I sent Mr. Pecorino a text telling him I quit. I'll need to find a new job ASAP, but I have enough money in my bank account to fall back on in an emergency.

I step into the shower now, and hot water scorches my skin. But I let it. I let it run over the open cuts and wounds on my face. Down my throbbing legs. I don't feel anything.

What the hell just happened? I've never had time slip away from me like that. It was like something took me over completely, something I had no control over. I clench and unclench my fists, turning my hands over like I don't recognize them.

I lean against the mint-green tiles and moan. My right kneecap feels like it's been dislodged. I try slamming it into the wall to pop it back in place, but that only makes it worse. Suddenly, I'm lying over the drain, curling into myself as the busted showerhead above rains down on me in spurts.

When the water turns cold, I step out of the shower and wrap a towel around my waist. I force myself to look in the mirror.

My lower lip is swollen and red. My left eyebrow is inflamed, drooping slightly over my eye. There are finger marks over my neck from either Brad or Tony.

I light a joint, though I'm not supposed to in the house, and try to recall everything, from pulling Tony off Hayden to Brad hovering over me and punching my face. It took the whole car ride home for the rage inside of me to fade. Not fade completely, but enough to bring me back to the moment. To Ma shouting at me from the driver's seat, to feeling the disappointment radiating off her. Tristan said she'd never leave, but after today, I'm not so sure.

I thought you wanted to change, Wesley. I thought I saw some-thing different in you lately.

Ma's voice echoes around me.

"I did! I do!"

I can't take it anymore. I slam my fist into the mirror, and the glass whimpers before giving way around my knuckles. My reflection crumbles inward as it shatters over the counter.

I step back, watching as slivers of broken glass cascade to the floor.

Blood seeps between the tiles from a gash on my palm, carving tiny rivers across the bathroom. I have to stand on my tiptoes to avoid stepping on them like a ballet dancer moving through a valley of death. My heart aches at the thought of Tristan finding me like this.

I lean over the sink and rinse glass shards from my cuts, hissing as water sears through the reopened wounds along my knuckles. I grab a towel from the rack next to me and wrap up my hand, my fingertips throbbing as I pull the fabric tighter.

Ma's going to kill me when she gets home. We only have the one bathroom, and without the mirror, we'll have to go to our rooms or use the cameras on our phones to get ready. Well, when Ma has to get ready. I don't have anywhere to be anymore. I don't have a job. I don't have school. I don't even have a future.

I grab the broom from the pantry and spend the next hour making sure I've gotten every last piece of glass off the floor.

I'll never get into college now. How will I even finish senior year? I pull my world history project out of my backpack and unroll it on my bed. The B- grade looks up at me in red ink, and I almost laugh at the sight of my banged-up hand next to it. What was I thinking? That I'd study hard for the last few months of school and colleges would just magically ignore everything about my past? I poke the purple bruises along my skin, wincing at their tenderness.

This is who I am.

This is all I'll ever be.

Deep sobs burst from my lungs as I rip the poster into shreds and head to the kitchen to throw out the college brochures Mr. Hamilton left for me. The last one catches my eye, a picture of the Empire State Building on its cover, and I flip it over to find the college's address somewhere in New York City. I pull out the rest of them and notice a pattern: they're all located on the East Coast. Why would Mr. Hamilton give these to me? I've never once voiced any intention of moving to New York, where would he even—

My breath catches in my throat. I grab my phone to pull up my conversation with Tristan. His last message taunts me.

I'm so damn proud of you. Xoxo

What would he think if he saw me like this? I trace my swollen lip with my thumb and wince.

Any idea how these ended up in my locker?

I take a picture of the trash and send it to Tristan, watching as three blue dots appear and disappear on the screen.

Remind me, where is St. Sebastian's again?

Tristan double taps my last message, and two exclamation marks appear over it on the screen. I see him typing.

> Okay, FINE. Sue me!
> I just thought you might reconsider.

I knew it. Tristan's the only person I've ever talked about New York City with. Of course he had a hand in this.

Before I reply, I open my phone's camera and stare down at my busted-up face, recoiling at the thought of meeting his parents like this.

> I don't think I can come tonight.

A FaceTime request comes through instantly. I sigh, kicking myself for saying anything when I could've just not shown up. But I couldn't do that to him. Not on his birthday. I slide my finger over the screen to answer the call, and Tristan's face appears.

His mouth falls open at the sight of me. "Jesus Christ, what happened to you?"

I begin to explain everything when he waves a hand. "Forget it, I'll be right there."

I go to tell him no, that I don't want him seeing me like this, but he hangs up before I get the chance.

Skye, Hayden, and Velvet have all reached out, asking if I'm okay, but I don't respond. Because what good would that do? I did this to them. I was the one who put Hayden in danger. They're better off without me.

Twenty minutes later, Tristan's standing at the gate of our building. I buzz him up, and he comes storming inside with a tote bag hanging from his wrist. He's dressed in a crisp blue button-down long sleeve with a red polka-dot bow tie around his neck and brown plaid pants.

"Happy birthday. You look nice," I mumble as he grabs both of my cheeks to examine my cuts.

"You definitely do not," Tristan says with a frown. He must mistake my wincing from the cold of his hands for the pain of my injuries because he throws his things onto the couch and leads me to my room.

My sheets are slung over the side of my bed, with dirty clothes dispersed in utter chaos around the floor. You never notice how messy you are until you have company. It's like a bomb went off centuries ago and I'm only now seeing the ruin in its wake.

I realize this is the first time Tristan's been in my room, or my house, for that matter. I take the time to walk around and throw things in my hamper, flinching when I have to bend to pick something up. My room is painted a dark merlot red, with yellow caution tape I stole from a crime scene hung up where the molding should be. My gray-and-blue comforter is nothing out of the ordinary for a teenager, but the sight of it still makes me feel self-conscious. Like everything I've decorated my room with is far too immature for a seventeen-year-old. Even my bookshelf is boring; home to video games and movies I haven't watched since I was little. One of the shelves collapsed under a pile of skateboard wheels last summer and I still haven't bothered to fix it. I kick a bundle of weed into the closet and shutter the doors.

Tristan doesn't seem to mind, though, because he climbs onto my bed and gestures for me to join him. He looks down at my ruined world history project, taking a ripped piece out from under him, as I sit on the edge of the mattress. He rests his head in my lap but moves to a pillow when I cry out in pain. Tristan is already not the biggest fan of The Tripod, but he listens as I retell the story, not once interrupting. I love that about him.

There's that word again. Love.

I tell him as much as I can remember. How Tony and Brad

were picking on Hayden and how I stepped in to help. How I don't remember beating them up. If Principal Cohen hadn't intervened, who knows what would have happened? I could have seriously hurt one of them. Or worse, I could be lying in a hospital bed right now.

"Did you know Tony went around the party on New Year's insisting everyone called him 'Big Cheese'? What a loser." Tristan buries his face into my sheets and laughs, but I just sit there, staring at the lopsided Metallica poster on my wall. I don't tell him how making fun of The Tripod rubs me the wrong way. That his little jabs at them make me feel like our friendship, all of it, is something to be embarrassed about. Maybe Tony was right. Maybe I wasn't only keeping Tristan away from them because I was afraid of how they'd judge him. Maybe I was afraid of how Tristan would judge them too.

"Oh, I almost forgot." He jumps out of bed and runs down the hall. When he returns, he's carrying the tote bag in his hand. "I got you something."

"You do know today is your birthday, right?" I ask as Tristan pulls out a knitted black sweater and tosses it at me. One of the buttons catches the cut on my lip, and I grimace.

Tristan waves his hand dismissively. "I know, I know, but I saw this at the mall the other day and thought of you."

I hold out the sweater in front of me, not once taking my eyes off him.

"It's a cardigan," Tristan says, reading my thoughts. "Try it on."

I free myself from my bedsheets and stand. The cardigan's made from the prickly type of wool only rich people can afford. It makes my arms itch. I scratch at the fabric with what little fingernails I have and throw it on over my T-shirt.

"This made you think of me?" I ask, skeptical of my reflection in the mirror behind my door. My cut-up face stares back at me, and the swelling over my eyebrow makes me look con-fused. Which, fair. Though I wouldn't go so far as saying I look bad, it's definitely not my style.

"I thought your leather jacket could use a vacation tonight," Tristan says, winking. I glance over at my jacket draped over the chair at my desk and feel a twinge in my heart. I can't recall the last time I left the house without it.

I watch as Tristan walks over to my black IKEA dresser and pulls out one of my only pairs of jeans without rips in them. He makes me change out of my sweats and scours my closet before deciding on a brown polo shirt I've never worn. I step in front of the mirror, pinching my good eyebrow, and stare at my shirt underneath the cardigan. The whole outfit screams Prep School Wannabe.

"Really?" I ask, holding my hand up to block Tristan as he pulls out his phone to take a picture.

"Relax." Tristan laughs, flipping through the images he just took. "I think you look cute."

"Give me that." I grab his phone as something finishes uploading to Instagram. Tristan's captioned the photo with a red heart and some random person has already liked it.

I trace over the image. I'm not looking into the camera, instead ogling Tristan off-screen. He's applied a filter so the bruises on my face are invisible. I hardly recognize myself.

I shove one half of the cardigan across my chest, suddenly uncomfortable in my skin. Like I'm standing stark naked for the whole world to judge me. I drop Tristan's phone onto the bed next to him.

"I don't think I could ever get used to this." I bend down and adjust the legs of my jeans. They're stiff from their last wash and hugging my knees a little too tight.

Tristan takes in the sight of the new me with a big smile on his face.

A part of me wonders what this version of myself would be like. Would I ever reconcile with The Tripod? Would I transfer to Westgate, get good grades, and be elected to student council? I want to burst out laughing, but Tristan's got that look in his eye. The look of a proud parent. Does he want me to dress like this all the time? Between the new clothes and the college brochures, is this his way of sending me a message? That he wants me to change? The joke he made to Emily about me being a project pops into my mind. Suddenly, I feel exhausted.

I head to the bathroom to brush my teeth. Tristan comes in after me and closes the door. His eyes briefly wander over the barren wall where the mirror used to sit, taking in the discarded towel left on the counter. He hip checks me out of the way to wash his hands before rummaging through the drawers. When he finds what he's looking for, he makes a *whoop* noise with his lips and pulls out a lipstick container from Ma's things.

"Here, let me," he says, tilting my face toward the light as he smudges lipstick over my skin.

I grab his hand and gawk. "What do you think you're doing?"

"It's cover-up, Wes. Don't worry, your masculinity is not in jeopardy," he tells me, being careful not to push down too hard as he blends whatever cover-up is into my eyelid. "There."

I have to take my phone out of my pocket to look myself over. But when I do, it's like Brad never punched me at all. "Woah," I say, touching the skin below my eye.

"Ah ah ah," Tristan tsks, grabbing a towel to clean his hands. "You'll smudge it."

As we leave the apartment, I send Ma a quick message saying Mr. Pecorino needs me to work tonight. She doesn't know that I've quit, and she won't be home until later. That gives me at least a few hours to get away before she can do anything. I know I'm breaking the rules by sneaking out, but I can't not go to my boyfriend's birthday. What would his parents think?

I throw a wrapped box onto the backseat of Tristan's car, and he glances over at me with a grin. "Never you mind," I say before he can ask what's inside.

Most of the snow is gone now from the streets, so the drive to his house is quick. We avoid Mt. Rockwell entirely by going through town.

When we arrive, Tristan looks over the cover-up on my face and smiles. "You ready?"

I shove my hands between my legs to steady them. "Hell no."

"You'll be great. Come on."

He comes around to the passenger door and has to practically yank me out of the car. As I amble up the driveway behind him, I stare at the Monroe household—at the copper chimney at the back of the roof, at the intricate layering of bricks along its sides—and gulp.

20.

WHEN MY HEART STOPPED BEATING

Tristan's mom greets us at the door.

"Come in, come in. It's freezing out!" She pulls Tristan into eighteen birthday kisses before turning to me and smiling. "You must be Wes. Hi, I'm Cami."

Though I hold out my hand, Cami goes in for a hug, squeezing my rib cage so hard I have to hold my breath from the searing pain that shoots through me.

Cami, which I learn is short for Camisha, is a head shorter than me. She's wearing a black blouse draped off the shoulder and an orange skirt with a blue and red triangle pattern that falls to her ankles. Her hair's done up in a gray headwrap, and golden hoops hang from her ears.

Tristan's younger brother, Malik, comes charging down the stairs in a bright-yellow shirt and gym shorts, with Emily trailing close behind. I recognize Malik from pictures on Instagram with his curly black hair and brown eyes. He climbs onto Tristan's back, and together, they fly around the room.

I set Tristan's gift down to untie my shoes. "Hey, Emily."

Emily narrows her eyes as she closely examines my face. She's probably seen the TikTok videos by now. Even if Tristan did do a good job hiding the damage, Emily knows the truth. I wanted to thank her for her part in bringing me and Tristan back together, but she turns and walks away without so much as a hello.

"Are you Trissy's booooyfriend?" Malik laughs from his brother's back as they come up and orbit around me. He's missing one of his front teeth, like Hannah, so he whistles when he speaks.

"I, uh—" I stop midsentence, unsure of what to say next. I mean, the kid's not wrong. We did just get back together. But I've never met him, so I can't tell if he's joking or asking out of childhood curiosity.

"Yeah, so what if he is?" Tristan barks, grabbing Malik's ankles and flipping him upside down. Malik screams as Emily runs over and blows raspberries on his stomach.

"You have a beautiful home," I say to Cami.

It's like I've walked into a Pottery Barn catalog. A blown glass chandelier hangs in the foyer with blue spirals descending down like water trapped in a tornado. The walls are all covered in large paintings of abstract shapes and floral wallpaper. Even though Tristan's told me they've lived here for years, the house has a freshness to it, like a new-car smell.

"Thank you, Wes," Cami says, her skirt billowing out between us. "Dinner's almost ready. Jean should be down in a minute."

Tristan leads everyone to the dining room, where a large oak table is set for six. The silverware is so polished I bet I could see my reflection in the spoons. I'm about to step inside to find out when a finger jabs between my shoulder blades. I spin around and find Emily standing there, leaning over her hip with her arms folded.

"What?" I ask.

Emily grabs me by the elbow and pulls me back into the foyer. "I heard what you and your little friends got up to today. Quite the scandal."

I bite down on my lower lip to hide a cut behind my teeth. Looking over her shoulder, I see Tristan raise an eyebrow at me. "Did he tell you?"

Emily *hmphs*, pushing a stray blonde curl away from her eyes. "No, it was Stacy. But you'd think my best friend would've said something."

I feel the intensity of her glare. Does Emily regret helping me that day? Maybe she wasn't doing me a favor like I'd thought. In her mind, maybe Tristan was always going to outright reject me, and she was hoping to speed up the process.

"Whatever," Emily huffs when I don't reply. I watch her features darken as she pulls me in close and whispers in my ear, "I'd hate for Cami and Jean to know what kind of person their son is dating."

I take a step back, the blood draining from my face.

Emily leans into the wall and laughs. "What? Don't act surprised. It's my *job* to protect my best friend."

I swallow hard, my throat suddenly tight.

She's right. Tristan's parents don't know me. Anything she chooses to say to them now could influence how they see me forever.

"I'm not trying to be mean, but you and I both know you aren't good enough for him."

I lower my chin in defeat. "No, you're right," I say, thumbing the bruise over my knuckles. My eyebrows mash together as I look at her. "But that doesn't mean I won't do everything I can to be the person he deserves."

I tear up as I say it, but there's no way I'm letting Emily see that, so I turn and calmly walk away. Because it's true. While

I did my best to explain everything that had happened today, I never told Tristan I'd been expelled. I was too embarrassed. What if he breaks up with me when he finds out I have to repeat senior year at a different school? I doubt he'd want to tell his new St. Sebastian's friends he has a boyfriend who's still in high school back home.

"I'm watching you, Mackenzie," she calls after me. "Don't even think about breaking his heart."

Emily's warning rings in my ears as I join Tristan in the dining room.

There are little name tags on each of the plates done up in silver cursive. Tristan sits at the head of the table. He grabs a gold napkin out from his wine glass and lays it over his lap. "Man of the house," he says, pounding his chest, when I take the seat next to him.

I shoot him a confused look because that's a pretty bold statement when his dad's about to walk through the door. Was it "Jean" like a pair of pants, "Gene" like somebody's DNA, or "Jéan" like a French dude? I don't think I heard Cami right, but I'm too embarrassed to ask again.

Emily sits across the table from me with a smile, acting like she didn't just threaten me in the hall. She pushes her hair over her shoulder and summarizes her day to Tristan, which gives me a chance to look around.

The rug beneath the table is dark gray and freshly vacuumed. I toe at one of the tassels with my sock and wonder how much it costs. Probably more than Ma's Pontiac. There's a statue of a woman's bust without any arms in the corner of the room, sitting on a wooden hutch. I know it's supposed to be art, but it looks like it belongs in a museum rather than a random house in Ohio. A glass cabinet sits next to it, full of awards. In the middle, on its own pedestal, is a golden star with the words "Agent of the Year" inscribed at its base.

"What does Mr. Monroe do?" I ask.

Malik giggles into his sippy cup of fruit juice, and Tristan and Emily gape over at me.

"He's a realtor."

I turn around to see that Jean Monroe's snuck into the room. Except Jean Monroe isn't a man. She's a tall white woman with a purple faux-hawk. Opposite of Cami, Jean's in a white collared shirt with gray slacks and a matching vest. She takes the Bluetooth earpiece out from her ear and pockets it.

I've seen Jean—like the pants—Monroe's face on ads throughout Valentine my entire life. She may be the most recognized woman in all of Ohio.

My cheeks burn red, as I remember the time I drew a pirate patch over her eye at the bus stop.

How did I not put two and two together?

"Oh my God, I am so sorry. I didn't mean to—" I cover my mouth, my teeth clanging together like someone's opened a window.

"Wes, it's okay. I'm not offended." Jean laughs, throwing up a fist. Her eyes are bright blue as she stares at me, waiting. I leave her hanging for a moment longer before bumping her fist with my own.

Cami walks into the room, popping the cork from a bottle of red wine and waving it in the air. "Shhh, don't tell your father," she says, holding a finger to her mouth as she pours Tristan, Emily, and me a glass.

Everyone at the table laughs. Malik bangs his plastic cup over the table like it's the funniest thing he's ever heard. I sink down in my seat, laughing nervously.

Since it's Tristan's birthday, we're having chicken luwombo and chapati, which is apparently his favorite. I now understand the meaning behind the term "foodgasm," because I legit moan at the table. Malik mimics me, and we go back and forth seeing who has the biggest, loudest reaction. He reminds me so much of Hannah that for a moment, I realize how long it's been since I've seen her. Maybe I don't actually hate kids like I'd always thought.

Cami asks Tristan what he wants to do in the next twelve months now that he's a year older, and he brings up all the things he has planned for New York after graduating.

"It'll be amazing! Biking around Central Park, skating in Rockefeller Center at Christmastime. Broadway shows on the weekend!" He grabs my hand when he talks about it like he sees me in this vision of the future, and it almost makes me forget everything that happened today. That in Tristan's mind, we still could run off together and live this perfect happily ever after.

But Emily's still glaring at me from across the table—the shadow of a smile biding its time on her face—probably knowing that at any moment, she can make everything come crashing down around me.

"A full-time job between classes to pay for it all." Jean coughs over her shoulder, returning my attention to the table.

I join in laughing with the rest of them, but I cover my mouth with the napkin from my lap and see the bruises along my knuckles.

After we finish dinner, we sit around the table and watch as Tristan opens his presents. Emily bought him a pair of ballet slippers to go around his rearview mirror, and his moms hand him a card stuffed with a few hundred-dollar bills like it's nothing.

Malik climbs onto Tristan's lap, and together, they open his next gift. With some help, he made Tristan a stapled book full of "I'll do the dishes for you" and "I'll make your bed" coupons. It's super colorful, with Malik paying close attention not to draw outside the lines.

I hand him my present, and he rips it open to find a family-size box of Cheerios. Jean smiles at me, then says something snarky about fiber and low cholesterol.

Tristan frowns until he realizes the top of the box has been taped down. He pops open the flap and pulls out a smaller box, this time for saltine crackers.

"Oh, come on!" He's laughing now with the rest of the table as he tears through the cardboard and pulls out a Devil bobblehead figurine. "It's perfect."

Tristan gives me a knowing glance before leaning across the table and kissing me in front of his family. I blink rapidly, firmly rooted to my chair. I've never kissed anyone in front of other people before. Normally, I hate PDA with a burning passion, but I let our lips linger.

"Get a room!"

I shoot back in my seat, and everyone's laughing at Cami. Except for Emily. She sticks out her tongue, pretending to gag. I try to ignore it.

Jean and I get to talking about music, and soon, we're bonding over our similar tastes. She commends me when I tell her I introduced Tristan to Metallica over the winter break, something she's tried to do for years.

"Forced me to listen to, more like," he announces.

Tristan's moms tell the story of how they met at a poetry slam competition during college and how Jean proposed two years later at an Alanis Morissette concert. "It was all very gay." She laughs.

I look around the room, feeling the acceptance from Tristan's family like a wave crashing down on me. No one asks about the cuts on my face. No one shames us for being who we are. I wonder if I'll ever get to this point with Ma and The Tripod. My temples throb at the thought. But still, I absorb the joy in the room like it's a tangible thing. Other than Tony's family, I've never known any parents to stay together for as long as Jean and Cami have. You could cut the love between them with a knife.

Cami takes a group selfie as Tristan blows out the candles on his ice cream cake. He gets the biggest piece: the entirety of Garfield's head.

"So what's your wish for this year, Tristan?" Jean asks when we're done eating.

"You'll see," he says with a wink. Then he grabs me by the arm and pulls me upstairs, ignoring Emily's audible groan.

As I step inside his room, I feel like a stranger getting to know Tristan for the first time. Like his bedroom's an extension of himself I'd never know about just by talking to him. He'd mentioned the walls were blue at one point when we first met, but I always pictured them to be light blue, like the sky on a summer day. Instead, they're like the Ohio river at wintertime, opal on the surface with a dark blue undercurrent. Tristan's room is the size of Ma's and mine combined. He's got a bathroom with its own tub and a walk-in closet that could fit our kitchen in one of its corners.

I look around at the TV above the fireplace, at the rain shower in the bathroom, and realize I've never known anyone who didn't live paycheck to paycheck before. How is it that I can have all this joy leftover from dinner yet still feel so out of place? Ever since walking through the front door, those two feelings have been battling it out, fighting each other to stake their claim on me.

A picture sits on Tristan's nightstand of his family at a lake. Cami and Jean have their arms around baby Malik while preteen Tristan and another girl lie on the dock, their fists beneath their chins, smiling for the camera.

"Who's this?" I ask, pointing to the photo.

Tristan looks over from the massive bookshelf beside his

desk. "My stepsister, Carrie, from Jean's first marriage. She lives in San Francisco with her family."

Carrie's like a younger version of Jean, faux-hawk and all.

"Is she—?"

"Gay?" Tristan spits. There's an edge to his voice I wasn't prepared for. "No. Happily hetero in her perfectly average, American life."

I look over at him, and he's standing by the bookshelf, zoned out.

"Sorry." He shakes his head, as if coming out of a trance. "I get kind of mad when people insinuate I'm the way I am because my moms are gay."

I put the picture frame down. "I didn't mean to insinuate that at all."

"No, I know," he says, putting too much effort into smiling again. "It's not you. It's just a knee-jerk reaction."

He turns his attention back to the shelf.

I jump onto his bed, watching as he moves his collection of Black Panther figurines out of the way. His duvet, tucked in at the corners, is a night sky filled with constellations. A string of lights hanging from the window paints a soft yellow glow across the walls. There's a silhouette of MARY's head stenciled onto his laptop.

I could tell Tristan I've been expelled right now. We're alone again. Away from Emily's judgmental glare. Hidden from his parents' view. There's nothing in the way of the truth. But seeing how excited he was at the table . . . I don't want to ruin his birthday. To shatter his vision of our future together with the news.

"So . . . what exactly are we doing?" I ask, deflecting.

"Every year on my birthday, I get to choose what movie we watch. *Sister Act, Drumline, My Big Fat Greek Wedding.* It's kind of a hobby of mine to collect physical copies of old movies."

He sticks his head inside the bookshelf, flipping between rows of DVD cases, then shoves a pink one in front of my face. "Coming at you live, circa 2002."

I take the DVD case from him, thumbing over the words *A Walk to Remember* on the cover. "I've never even heard of this."

Tristan gawks. "It's one of my favorite movies of all time. You'll love it."

"I highly doubt that."

He sticks out his tongue, grabbing a box of Jumbo Sour Keys from his desk, and takes my hand to lead me back downstairs. I drag my feet along the floor and check my phone. Ma's sent three texts and left a voicemail.

> Do I need to go over the rules of being grounded again?

> Because I don't believe leaving the house without permission is one of them.

> But what do I know? I'm just the mother.

"Is something wrong?" Tristan's standing at the bottom of the stairs, looking up at me. Around the corner, his moms are already set up in the family room, parked in front of the TV with a bowl of freshly popped popcorn. Malik pokes his head out from the blanket between them and leans over to look at us. His Nintendo Switch sits haphazardly in his hands.

"Nope, all good." I shove my phone away and Tristan and I take a seat on the floor. From a recliner in the corner, Emily signals that she's watching me with two fingers.

The movie is, dare I say it, kind of cute. I didn't pay much attention to the beginning, and it's not something I'd ever choose to watch on my own, but being here with Tristan's family, my arm wrapped around him, feels sort of perfect. I pinch myself in the middle of Mandy Moore singing to make sure I'm not dreaming.

When the final scene fades to black, Cami passes around a box of tissues.

"I loved all the songs!" Malik says, the glow of his Switch bathing his face in white light.

Jean tickles his foot that's sticking out from under the blanket. "Me too, boobaloo."

"Can't go wrong with a good redemption story," Cami says, gazing over at her wife on the opposite end of the couch. "That's why I married you," she snickers, swerving to avoid Jean's playful swat.

The rest of the room laughs. I unbutton my cardigan and scratch at the spot between my collarbone and neck. The wool really is itchy.

"No matter how many times I watch that movie, I cannot get over how long it takes Shane West's character to realize that his friends are all pieces of shit," Tristan says quietly, not looking at me. He's scrolling through his phone, catching up on all the birthday texts. He opens Instagram to the picture he took of me this afternoon. Over his shoulder, I see a comment from someone I don't know that catches my eye.

valentinehomie106   1h   ♡
Poser
23 likes   Reply

Tristan glances up, then shoves his phone into his lap. I pretend not to have noticed and grab a tissue from Cami to wipe the tears from my cheek—ignoring the tenderness along my jawline. Even though the room is dark, I can see makeup smeared into the tissue in the dim of the TV light.

The makeup hiding my bruised eye.

The bruised eye Brad gave me.

Brad, who, until recently, was supposed to be my best friend, alongside Tony.

Tony, who accused me of ditching them for Tristan.

I swallow the lump in my throat as I go to zip up my leather jacket. Except my leather jacket is back at home. Tristan convinced me to take it off. My favorite article of clothing.

Everyone continues talking around me like normal, but the room's suddenly a million degrees.

Three times one is three.

Three times two is six.

As I begin to count, a dark thought burrows into my head. And when thoughts like that take hold, ones that consume you from the inside out, there's no way of letting them go.

I look around the room: at the paintings on the wall, the leather couches. We watched the movie on a fucking projector and I didn't even bat an eye.

Who was I trying to kid? I could never fit into this life. I live in a two-bedroom apartment above a *laundromat*. Until getting expelled, I was skateboarding through Stonebridge's halls and failing senior year. To top it off, I don't even have any friends anymore.

I never know when my anger is going to surface. Usually, I can predict it: a teacher sighs after I've answered a question wrong; a shop owner calls me a thief, though I haven't stolen anything. I can feel my skin prickle, the muscles in my hands tighten.

But sometimes, despite the warning signs, I can't see it coming until it's already too late.

And it's too late.

Without saying anything, I walk out of the room, grabbing my shoes as I head out the front door. There's a bitterness to the wind tonight, the kind that remains in your lungs long after you've gone inside. I put on my shoes, not bothering to tie the laces, and amble across the lawn. The grass is wet beneath my feet, fighting for its life after being smothered to death from the snow.

This is bullshit.

That first night at Vincenzo's, Tristan and Emily lectured me about getting into college. Was it their mission to lead me down the path of righteousness or something? The thought makes me feel sick.

The front door swings open behind me. "Wes?" I look over my shoulder, and Tristan's marching barefoot across the driveway toward me. "What's the matter?"

"I *am* some kind of project to you, aren't I?" I barely manage to say over the wind.

"What are you talking about?" Tristan's looking at me like I've lost my mind. The trees surrounding us groan.

I need to keep moving. Away from here. Away from Tristan. Away from the life he thinks I want to live.

Three times one is three.

Three times two is six.

Three times three is nine.

"How long have you been planning this? Are you trying to change me?" I shout accusations at him, one after the other.

Tristan coughs, dancing on his tiptoes. "No, not at all. Where is this coming from?"

"This isn't who I am!" I point down at myself, flicking the front of my cardigan open. I can't believe I wore this tonight. That I shrugged off my entire identity. Took on this pseudo-Westgate version of myself to appease him. In a few short weeks, I've somehow managed to cut my friends completely out of my life. I joined the photography club, something I never would have done in a million years on my own. And look how that ended up. My whole body is screaming at me from getting into a fight with two of the most important people in my life!

Tristan folds his arms over his chest to stay warm. "Why are you reacting like this? Was it the movie?"

"Just because I'm gay doesn't mean I have to be like everyone else."

I exhale as the truth of it crashes down on me.

Tristan never liked me.

He only liked the idea of me. The idea of changing me.

Tristan shakes his head. "I'm so confused right now." He raises his voice, covering his mouth to cough again. "No one said you had to be anybody but yourself. Jesus, Wes. I know you're upset, but are you really going to do this on my birthday?"

I dig my heels into the lawn, knowing I've gone and done the one thing I said I wouldn't do today. "I'm not upset!"

Tristan watches me, unflinching. "You're literally yelling at me on my lawn right now, so sorry if I don't believe you. Come back inside. Let's discuss this like adults."

I rip the cardigan off, my neck raw and exposed from all the scratching I did tonight, and curl it up into a ball. "I don't want to discuss anything! Do you think you're better than me? Is that why you dressed me up like some walking gay stereotype? So I could make a good impression on your family?"

"Wes, please, stop," Tristan pleads. He glances back at the house, and for a second, I'm afraid everyone is watching us from the windows.

"I don't belong here. Don't you get it?" I snap, throwing the cardigan to the ground at his feet.

Tristan doesn't reach down to pick it up. He lets it sit there on the wet grass. "Yes, you do. You—"

He shuts his mouth as I let out a laugh. "What were you going to say? That I belong with you? You don't want me, Tristan. Not really. Trust me."

"But I do," he whispers into the wind.

"Then you're a fool."

I want Tristan to react. To slam his fists into my bruised chest, to shout in my face. But he doesn't. He just stares at me, which is so much worse. Because everything I've done, everything I've said, is suddenly magnified under his stare.

"Tell your moms I said thanks for dinner." I cross my arms, barring myself from the cold.

"You can't always run away from your problems, Wes!"

Tristan's voice fades by the time I've walked down the street and turned the corner. Ignoring the crosswalk sign, I step out onto the road. I don't stop for cars as they speed past, their horns wailing into the stillness of the night.

21.

BOULEVARD OF BROKEN HEARTS

I sit cross-legged on my bedroom floor, my back against the door.

The cover art of Metallica's *Hardwired . . . to Self-Destruct* album hangs next to the light switch. I consider each of the band members' screaming faces, amalgamated into a single display of suffering.

I try not to think about any of it. About Tristan or The Tripod or getting expelled. About the eventual wrath I'll face from Ma. My phone sits face down on the ground next to me as I rock back and forth. I can see the screen lighting up against the carpet, but I don't reach for it.

At some point, Ma bangs on the door. "Wesley, open up."

I didn't even hear her come in. The glow from Mr. Fong's Laundromat sign outside bathes me in red and blue light. Like the cop car when it arrived at our accident. And again when The Tripod set the car ablaze.

My nails dig into my palms. "I don't want to be like this anymore."

I pin my shaking knees to my chest, resting my forehead on my wrist. I didn't mean to run out on Tristan on his birthday. I didn't mean to hurt him with my words. I didn't mean anything I said. Because I wasn't the one in control. The anger was.

Ma wiggles the doorknob. "Stevia, please."

I don't reach up to unlock it. I don't want to explain how I left the house when I wasn't supposed to. How I shattered the bathroom mirror earlier because I couldn't bear the thought of looking at myself anymore.

My nose won't stop leaking, but I don't bother to grab a tissue. I stay put until Ma disappears down the hall and the lights go out from under her bedroom door.

I lay out on the floor, my arms firmly at my sides, as I lower my cheek to the ground.

Eventually, darkness consumes me.

AROUND SIX THE next night, the intercom buzzes.

I haven't left the house all day.

Ma's already been to work and returned, but I haven't been able to get myself out of bed. I felt bad for making her get ready this morning without a bathroom mirror, but I couldn't face her. I didn't have the energy to.

My stomach rumbles as I walk down the hall and crack open the front door.

Hannah comes into the apartment in her tutu, rolling a purple plastic suitcase behind her. She gives Ma a quick peck on the cheek, and together, they lay out her dolls in the family room. Ma looks up at me with a sad smile as Tad taps my shoulder.

"Hey, Big Mac."

"It's Wes." I sigh, not bothering to look at him. I don't have it in me to fight tonight.

"Right." Tad takes off his leather jacket and hangs it in the closet.

I stare down at my wrinkled shirt and jeans from last night. I probably stink. "Actually, Tad, you can call me Big Mac if you want."

Tad turns to me, his forehead creased. "Really?"

I nod my head.

Hannah slides in next to me at the kitchen table, climbing onto a cushion she grabbed from the couch for extra height, so she can show off her fully grown front tooth. She pulls up a picture on her iPad of Punxsutawney Phil, the groundhog who's about to decide if spring will come early this year.

I pick away at my dinner plate, moving a meatball around with the prongs on my fork.

When my phone buzzes in my pocket, I slide it into my lap. Even though I was the one who blew up, I hope it's a text from Tristan, but an email for an upcoming clothing store sale pops up instead. I don't even remember signing up for their notifications.

I open the last message Tristan sent, time-stamped around midnight last night.

> I guess this is it then.

There's a lump in my throat as I read it over. Why did I expect Tristan to fight for us? I've given him no reason to think I want anything to do with him. I stormed out on his birthday and threw the cardigan in his face. I sent the message loud and clear. I start typing.

> I guess it is.

I don't click Send. I know I should to put him out of his misery, but I can't bring myself to do it.

When we finish dinner, the table draws straws, and Tad and I head to the kitchen while the girls resume playing house in front of the TV.

Tad hands me a towel. "Amira used to hate helping with the dishes. She'd make every excuse not to be in the kitchen after dinner. Her bibi was calling from India. She forgot her phone upstairs. She only had one more chapter to read."

I rinse the soapsuds from the plates, rotating them beneath the cold stream of water from the tap, before toweling them dry. "You really miss her, don't you?"

Tad watches me through the reflection of the kitchen window. "Every day." He grabs a piece of steel wool and gets to work on some baked-on tomato sauce in the pan sitting on the counter. He seems nervous. "Big Mac, I was hoping we'd have the chance to talk."

"About?" I turn the same dish over in my hands, drying it for the second time.

Tad leans back on the counter, sweeping his bangs to the side with the back of his hand and smudging a wad of soap into his eyebrow. He fiddles with the tap. "I wanted to thank you."

"For what?"

"I know how hard it must have been for you to give your blessing. Your ma really is a wonderful woman. If I were in your shoes, I'd protect her any way that I could too."

"It's fine, Tad," I say, tossing the towel back onto its rack. "Really."

Sometimes, there's vulnerability in telling the truth.

Tad shakes his head. "No, I need to say this."

I remember when he picked Ma up for their first date. They'd met the week prior at a singles event at the bowling alley, and Ma's team had crushed his. Tad had insisted on coming up and meeting me. Back then, he had this horrendous mustache. It was the first thing I commented on when he came through the door. By their second date, he'd shaved it off. Has he always been looking for my approval?

He gazes down at the floor. "You'll always be the main man in your mother's life, Wes. I can't compete with that, nor do I want to. But I hope you know I love you too, kid."

I tense up. Tad's never told me he loves me before. Even though I've been a total jerk over the years, he's always been there with some corny dad joke and a smile. Like a father should be.

"I love you too, Tadpole," I say, punching him in the arm.

While I might hate to admit it—and a part of me does die a little when I say it—I realize I'm telling the truth. But I don't say it just for myself. I say it for Ma. Sometimes, someone else's happiness means stepping outside of your own.

Tad smiles, dunking his hands into the soapy water. "I've always loved that nickname."

He hands me a bowl, and I take it. "Really? Because I secretly wanted you to hate it."

"I know, kiddo. I know."

Hannah comes dancing into the kitchen then and shoves us into the family room. She's decided to turn on a movie and insists we all sit down and watch it with her. With a wince, I remember being in Tristan's living room last night. Right before I screwed it all up.

Halfway through the opening credits, Hannah falls asleep in Ma's lap. Tad dozes off shortly after that too, leaving Ma and I to finish the movie on our own. I don't think either of us is paying any attention by the time Lightning McQueen and Cruz drive off into the sunset.

"Good movie," Ma says absentmindedly, like she wasn't pinning wedding inspiration photos to her Pinterest dream board the whole time.

"Yeah." I couldn't summarize the movie's plot even if you paid me, but Ma doesn't seem interested in discussing it either way.

She puts her phone down. "I don't like seeing you like this," she whispers.

"Like what?"

Ma watches me as she runs her fingers through Hannah's hair. I used to love it when she did that to me as a kid. Her lips purse while she thinks. "Lost."

I couldn't fool her. Ma always knows when I'm upset. She reaches her hand out, and I take it in mine. A tear rolls down my cheek.

And we sit like that. Listening to the stillness in the room. After a while, our silence opens up into conversation.

The words tumble out of my mouth, but I don't stop them. I tell her how I quit my job, how I screwed up with The Tripod when Tristan came onto the scene. I tell her that I kept my sexuality a secret because I didn't know how she'd react. I talk about how all I want to do now is to go to Tristan.

It's like I've spent my whole life carrying this weight around me, this shame. In my knee. In my heart. All because I was too afraid of—of what? Ma walking out on me? But she doesn't flinch. She sits there, listening intently, without interrupting. Just like Tristan.

When she's sure I've finished, Ma opens up too: about how she's failed as a mother for not making me feel comfortable enough to be who I always was, how she never got back on her feet to provide for us the way she wanted to after we left Louisiana. I tell her that's impossible, that she's the best ma I've ever had, but she looks away.

We talk about it all, filling in the gaps of all the things we've been too ashamed to share.

Finally, Ma asks, "Do you love him?"

I close my eyes.

In fourth grade, we used to do this reflective activity every time we talked about big life subjects. Ms. Higginbottom would tell us to close our eyes, to shut out the rest of the world, then she'd say a single word and we would all blurt out the first thing that came to mind. Things like "fear" elicited spiders and clowns, "joy," ice cream and summer vacation. I contemplate the word "love" now, and all I see is Tristan.

"Yeah, I think I do," I say, opening my eyes.

Ma squeezes my hand. "I'd really like to meet him."

I glance up from my lap, blinking back tears. "You already have, remember? At the ballet."

Ma looks at me, her lip quivering. "I know. But now that I know he's important to you, I want to meet him again so he can be important to me too." She leans over and kisses my forehead.

I take a deep breath and hold it. Sometime last night, Tristan unfriended me on everything. I can't tell Ma I've already chased him away. I can't put into words how much I've hurt him. Because if I do, I'll shatter what little hope I have left of fixing this.

I guess this is it then.

"He wants me to follow him to New York, but I can't," I say, rushing the words out with the release of my breath.

Ma tries to read me, searching for an answer behind what I'm saying. "Why not?"

A teardrop falls into my palm. "You need me."

Ma's eyes go wide, and she jumps to her feet. Hannah's head falls to the couch with a thud.

We cover our mouths, waiting for Hannah to wake up. But she just turns over on her side, taking one of her dolls under the crook of her arm.

Ma sits down to face me. "Stevia, you are my son. I will

always need you. But you listen to me, and you listen well." She crosses her legs and leans forward, taking both of my hands. "You cannot live your life tiptoeing around me like you're scared of upsetting me. I will not allow it. Do you understand?"

She waits for my response.

"I'd be so far away . . . What. About. You?" My bottom lip trembles so the question comes out in three separate parts.

"What *about* me? When I was your age, I traveled the world. I jumped out of *planes*, for God's sake. I met your father at a Full Moon Party in Thailand. And if it wasn't for him, that asshole, I never would have had you." Ma grabs my head and kisses my forehead again. "You are my most beautiful miracle, Wesley," she says, resting my head on her lap. "You gave me the strength to put myself first. I think it's about time you do the same."

I tuck my feet into the cushion between us like I did when I was young. I see my leather jacket behind Tad's head, my skateboard resting on the wall.

"I'm so tired of being someone I'm not."

It comes out as a whisper, like if I spoke any louder, I'd shatter.

Ma runs her fingers through my hair, the same way she did with Hannah. "What do you mean?"

"With The Tripod, I always had to pretend to be tough."

In the back of my mind, Brad tosses some junior's bag into the trash, their homework flying everywhere. Who knows how long it took them to get everything back? I used to watch Tony throw kids into their lockers, patting their pockets down for anything to take. But I never stopped them. Not once. Even if deep down I knew it was wrong, I let it happen every time.

"And with Tristan, I always felt like I had to be on my best behavior because if I wasn't, if I let my guard slip, I was afraid I'd end up getting hurt. So, I did it first."

Saying the words out loud, it's like I've spoken the truth

into existence. I didn't know it at the time, but that was exactly what I was doing. I think about all the things I did to make him like me. I pretended to know what he was talking about when he compared me to Lucifer in *Paradise Lost* because I thought it would make me seem smarter. I traded my leather jacket for a black cardigan because I wanted to impress him. The only thing I did for myself was join the photography club, even if he pushed me to do it in the first place.

Ma gets up, resting my head on a pillow first, and walks over to the hall closet. She takes out her phone, turning on its flashlight to see in the dark. After some searching, she pulls down a small black box from the top shelf.

When she returns to the couch, shimmying back into her place under my head, Ma hands me a four-by-six photo, the ones we used to print at Walmart.

"Do you remember this?"

I tilt the picture toward the TV's light. A younger version of Ma stares blankly into a mirror, her makeup smeared from crying.

"No."

There are yellow daisies on the wallpaper behind her. Her favorite.

I scan the image again. Ma's standing in the bathroom in our old house in Louisiana. I remember sitting on the floor, coloring, while she painted the flowers on the wall.

"You used to love taking pictures. You'd steal the camera when no one was watching, and I wouldn't find out until months later when I printed them." She laughs at the memory. "I found this one the day before we left."

She points down at the corner, and I can't believe I hadn't noticed it before. In the image, I'm visible in the mirror, sitting behind her on the toilet and holding the camera upside down.

"Maybe finding yourself means meeting somewhere in

the middle of who you were and who you want to be." I see her reflection staring back at me through the TV. "My sweet, sweet boy, you have to learn to love you for you. Faults and all. No one else is going to do that for you."

Ma wraps her arm around my stomach and lets me cry. I squeeze my eyelids together, tears splashing over the hairs on her arm.

"I know I was never the world's greatest mom," she continues, swatting my hand away when I go to protest again. She plucks the picture from my fingers. "But I take this photo out every now and then to remind myself I'm so much more than my past." Her hand trembles as she looks at me. "I'm sorry, Stevia. I should have gotten us out of there sooner. But I was so scared. And then the accident happened—"

I pinch my eyebrow, shaking my head at the floor. "Ma, no. That wasn't your fault."

I remember hiding under the covers as my dad tore through our old house. How I'd cry myself to sleep in bed to drown out his shouting. I rub my forehead, feeling nauseous, as a realization washes over me. "I turned out just like him."

I know it's the truth when I say it. I can't stand the thought of looking at Ma right now, at seeing the terror in her eyes confirming what I've always feared most. I've let anger control my entire life. When teachers talked down to me. When kids ran away from me in the halls. I resorted to lashing out because if I hurt the people around me, at least I could cover up what I've always felt in my gut. That they were right. That I would never be good enough.

Ma slides off the couch and kneels in front of me. "No, Stevia. That's not true. I know your heart." She rests her hand on my chest. "There's so much good in you. You deserve happiness, even if you don't believe it yourself."

I stare down at my hands, tracing the lines along my palm.

How many people have I driven away because of my outbursts over the years? How many hearts have I scarred?

Is Ma right? Looking past everything I've said and done, am I more than my anger? Even when I felt like I was getting my life together, I ended up ruining everything. I chased Tristan away. I fought The Tripod. But is there still time to fix this? Would they ever forgive me if I tried?

"I think you should talk about these things to someone, Stevia. A professional."

Normally, I would laugh off her suggestion. We've been down that road before, and it didn't turn out according to plan. But when I look at Ma, see the worry on her face, I know she's right. There's too much I've kept bottled inside of me to deal with alone.

"Yeah, maybe. But a good one this time."

She turns toward Tad then, whose chest rises and falls with soft snores. Like me, she's never believed in her own self-worth.

"You deserve happiness too, Ma," I whisper, squeezing her hand.

She doesn't respond. And that's okay. Maybe life isn't always perfect. Maybe things need to fall apart before they get better.

I close my eyes, a smile forming on my face, as I curl up in Ma's arms and listen to her humming. I can't be sure, because she's a little tone-deaf, but I think it's "Songbird" by Fleetwood Mac.

She finishes the song in a hushed whisper, the last note suspended in the air. "Thank you for being a friend."

I fall asleep in her arms, and when I do, I dream of New York City.

22.

IN TOO DEEP, BUT DIGGING MY WAY OUT

I spend the next week going down the TikTok rabbit hole. It starts off innocent enough, but when I come across a conspiracy theory on the whereabouts of Walt Disney's frozen head, I've had all I can take. By Monday afternoon, I've resorted to deep cleaning my room: dusting, vacuuming, the whole nine yards. Ma would be so proud of me if I hadn't gotten expelled.

I pull my phone out and scroll to my last conversation with Mr. Pecorino. He didn't reply to my last text, but that doesn't matter. I swallow my pride and ask for my job back.

Tristan was right. I can't keep running away from my problems.

I'm emptying my backpack over my freshly made bed when the Picture PIC-tacular flyer Stacy handed out the first day I joined the photography club falls to the floor.

I sink down the side of my bed and skim the details on the paper. I check my phone's calendar. Submissions are due today.

Sighing, I pull up the group conversation Skye added me to last week and send a picture of the flyer.

 for you all

The twins reply at once.

Hayden
Don't tell me you forgot 😫
Send in a photo this instant!

Velvet
DO IT! I'm not above forcing Stacy's
hand ☠

I check the time. If I book it, I could theoretically make it to school before the last bell.

But when I open my camera roll, my stomach plummets. All my photos are either blurry or out of focus. Of the select few that aren't, none are of the caliber where I'd be confident enough to submit them to the contest. I wouldn't stand a chance next to any of the photography club members, anyway.

One by one, I delete the poor quality images until all that's left are pictures of pizza and of Tristan dancing. I can't bring myself to get rid of those. My mind wanders to our photo shoot at the theater. It seems like a lifetime ago now. Tristan wanted so badly to get to know me then. And now . . .

After scrolling for a while, I notice a pattern.

From that first day at the ballet, almost every photo I took is of Tristan. Ignoring our breakup, his face fills every thumbnail in my phone, recapping the days together like a visual tapestry of our relationship. There's the one of him leaping on stage dressed as the Nutcracker, another where he's standing in the snow on New Year's Eve. Photo after photo, he's there.

A message from Skye pops up on my screen.

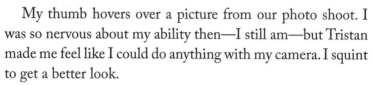

Skye
There's still time

My thumb hovers over a picture from our photo shoot. I was so nervous about my ability then—I still am—but Tristan made me feel like I could do anything with my camera. I squint to get a better look.

Half of the photo hides in darkness. I didn't do it on purpose, but the effect the darkness has ends up setting the mood for the rest of the image. In the top right corner, an industrial light emits a soft glow onto the stage. Tristan's on his hands and knees, head turned toward the sky. His face is painted in sorrow; brows together, eyes focused, yet he's somehow full of joy too. Just like he was on stage as the Nutcracker. Sweat glistens on his forehead as dust motes catch the light, surrounding him like fireflies.

I send the image in the group chat, and my phone lights up instantly with their replies.

Velvet
HELL TO THE YES!!!

Skye
It's beyond perfect, Wes

Hayden
GO GO GO

Hayden drops the location to a print shop nearby. Before leaving the house, I throw on a baggy hoodie and a hat, making sure my face is well-hidden. I'm not supposed to be on school grounds, but if I don't go now, it'll be too late. I grab my skateboard and race out of the apartment.

When the image finishes printing, I borrow a Sharpie from the shop clerk and, after a quick Google search, title it *Terpsichore* for the Greek goddess of dance. Because that's what Tristan is to me when he dances. A deity from another world.

I slip my submission into an envelope and stuff it into my backpack.

The wind is cold on my face as I skateboard along the side of the interstate. What I'm doing is technically illegal, and I could get myself killed, but it's the most direct way to school without wasting any more time.

I manage to make it to Stonebridge right as the last bell rings through the PA system.

"No, no no no!" I take the stairs three at a time, shoving past other students and booking it down the hall.

Stacy steps out of the photography club room in a pink blazer and heels, holding a binder bursting with paper.

"Stacy!" I yell, waving my envelope in the air to get her attention. I have to stand on tiptoes to see her over the crowd.

Stacy glances up as she closes the door behind her, and her mouth falls open at the sight of me. Like she can't believe her eyes. She storms over then, a scowl painted across her face.

"You shouldn't be here," she hisses, looking over both shoulders to make sure no one's seen me. She grabs my arm and pulls me into the janitor's closet. "Cohen could call the cops on you for being on school property."

My shoulders sag as I collapse into a metal shelving unit lined with toilet paper. "I know. I know. But I had to give you this. My submission for the contest." I hand her the envelope, the paper creased down the middle from the ride over.

Stacy smashes her lips together as she takes out the photo. I didn't think it was possible to be this nervous, but it feels like she holds my fate in her hands. I wipe my forehead with the sleeve of my hoodie.

"I could get you into a lot of trouble for this, y'know," she says, scrutinizing the image.

"You definitely could." All Stacy has to do is turn the corner right now and find the nearest teacher to rat me out. But what's the worst that could happen? I've already been expelled. "But I don't think you will."

Stacy pauses, sizing me up, as I try to catch my breath. My lungs are heaving from the ride over. I have to throw my hand up and rest against the wall to stop the room from spinning. I wonder if we'll ever be on good terms or if Stacy will always hate me for the whole "gum in the braids"/"metamorphosis" thing.

"What makes you so sure?" She curls a piece of hair behind her ear like she remembers. With a 4.0 GPA and the photography club presidency under her belt, Stacy's a shoo-in for valedictorian. If anyone could get me into trouble on merit alone, it'd be her.

"Because you're not like that." I lower my head. "You're not like me."

Stacy doesn't say a word, but her face goes soft with a slight relaxing of the skin at the corner of her eyes. "This is important to you."

It's not a question, but the weight of her words feels like one.

"Yeah," I say, fidgeting with my hoodie strings. "It's the only chance I've got to make something of myself."

Stacy glances down at my photo again and sighs. "Fine. But only because it's good."

I grab her free hand, about to thank her, but she holds up a finger to silence me. "Do not think for a second that I'm doing this because I like you."

"I know," I say, encasing her finger in my fist. "That's what makes you a good person."

I back into the hallway without another word, lowering my head so I won't be seen.

Stacy walks in the opposite direction. She doesn't bother looking back.

When I've made it outside, I jump in the air, fist pumping at the sky.

23.

WHO I AM HATES EVERYTHING I'VE BEEN

To pass the time, I pick up a lunch shift at Vincenzo's. Mr. Pecorino agreed to give me my job back on the condition that I never quit over text again. He said it was a cop-out, which is totally fair. I need to work on dealing with my problems head-on. I make sure to run it by Ma first, but she gives me the all clear, so I skateboard through town and arrive just before opening.

I have to admit, being at work is a nice break from the stale apartment air. There's only so much TikTok a person can consume before restless leg syndrome kicks in.

Tony shows up just after eleven. I pause midstep between the dining room and the kitchen at the sight of him. Maybe it was Vincenzo's way of divine intervention, because other than Tracy and another server, we're the only other staff in the building.

We keep our distance from each other. Tony passes it off like it's nothing by jamming out to his music, but I catch him watching me bus tables through the kitchen window. I know he's checking in on me.

Around four, I'm shoving glassware through the dishwasher when Tracy comes into the back and whistles at me. "Some kid's looking for you at the host stand," she says, pointing to the door. "Says he wants to talk."

He?

My heart hammers away inside my chest. I pull off one of my rubber gloves to check my phone. Tristan left a voicemail ten minutes ago.

I press my back against the dishwasher, its latest cycle rumbling beneath me. My ears perk up at the sound of Tristan's voice. What is he doing here?

I creep through the kitchen on bent knees, popping my head into the order window like a Whac-A-Mole in one of those carnival games. Tony stops kneading the dough in front of him as I pass by.

Tristan's in the lobby, scrolling through his phone. He must be heading to the theater straight from school because he's got his gym bag swung over his shoulder. I know I said I needed to deal with my problems head-on, but I'm not ready to talk to him yet.

"Shit," I groan, crouching to a squat behind a stack of flour. Sooner or later, I'll have to go out to the restaurant to wipe a table or prep cutlery for dinner.

Tony peers under the counter, one eyebrow raised. "Uh, you okay, bro?"

It's the first time we've spoken since our fight. I think I catch him taking in the bruises on my cheek, but I can't be sure. I hadn't noticed earlier, but his lower lip is drooping, still slightly swollen. The skin below his right eye is purplish blue but beginning to fade.

"Tristan's out there," I say, exhaling. I reach up onto the counter and grab a napkin to hide my face. "We broke up the other night."

My voice catches in my throat when I realize I hadn't actually admitted it out loud until now. That we're no longer a thing.

I expect Tony to laugh or say some off-the-cuff comment, but he nods his head like he understands. The song blaring from his AirPods ends. He shakes his hands out on his apron before untying it and setting it on the counter above me.

I watch as he goes through the swinging door and it shuts behind him. Beads of sweat break out along my forehead as I jump out of my squatting position.

In quick flashes, I imagine what might happen next. Upon seeing Tony, Tristan runs up and punches him in the nose, adding insult to his already banged-up face. Tony stands there stunned, unable to comprehend that a ballet dancer managed to punch him. He'll grab his nose, grumble something about it "not being over" and waltz back into the kitchen. The half-empty restaurant will cheer.

But that doesn't happen. When I peer out the kitchen door's circular window, ready to run out and stop him, Tony's in the lobby, opposite Tristan. Talking. Calmly. There isn't a standoff in the middle of the dining room like some old Western movie.

I rest my ear against the door to listen.

"I know he's here," Tristan says, raising his voice. "I saw him through the window."

I duck down when he throws a finger over his shoulder, pointing at the kitchen. For a second, I'm convinced he'll storm right in and see me crouching behind the door. How would I explain myself?

But then, I hear the bell above the front door as it slams shut.

I wait a few seconds, my legs shaking from having squatted for too long, until I'm sure the coast is clear.

Tony walks back into the kitchen and silently reties his apron around his waist. I watch him pick up the dough he was working on earlier and roll out a new pizza order like it's nothing.

"So?"

Tony glances up, continuing to fold the edges of the dough without looking. He takes the AirPods out of his ears and drops them into the pouch on his apron. "I told him you left."

I tilt my head toward the sky, letting go of my breath.

"I don't think he believed me, but he knew he couldn't come back here, so he dipped."

I rub the back of my neck. "You didn't have to do that."

Tony shrugs, grabbing a new tray of dough from the fridge.

"Well, thanks," I say, walking over to the sink to wash my hands. I grab a wad of paper towels and push the door open with my knee. "And Big Cheese?"

Tony looks up. His eyes are red.

"I'm sorry for . . ." I make a circle with my finger around my mouth.

Tony lets out a snort. "I know."

"No, really," I say, nodding my head. "What I've been going through was never about you guys." I look down at my hands, at the scabs still healing along my knuckles. "Well, maybe it was a little. But I—" I pause, unsure if I should continue. It feels weird talking to him like this. Tony usually shuts down before we can ever get into it. "I have a lot of unreconciled anger toward my dad that I still need to figure out."

Tony stays silent. I can tell he wants to ask a question, but his jaw moves up and down like he's not quite sure he knows how.

Maybe we're not there yet. Maybe when the dust has settled, and we get used to openly talking about these things, we will be. But for now, I won't push.

I head back into the dining room to begin setting tables for the dinner rush when Tony appears in the kitchen window.

"What happened between the two of you anyway?" he asks, pointing at the ghost of Tristan in the foyer.

I cross my arms, hesitant to say anything, but Tony's looking at me like he genuinely cares for the first time since we fought. Maybe this is him trying to make amends.

So without thinking about it, I start talking. And for once in his life, Tony is quiet as I explain how Tristan and I met. How at first, I didn't think he wanted anything to do with me until realizing he actually wanted to get to know me for me. I open up about feeling insecure, about never really needing to acknowledge my sexuality until Tristan came into the picture. How I kept that part of myself hidden from The Tripod because of our image at school.

The whole time, I can't tell what Tony's thinking. When I talk about Tristan's birthday and the fight that happened on his lawn, he flinches and closes his eyes. "Sounds like you overreacted."

I stop midthought, opening and closing my mouth. "What? What do you mean?"

Tony claps flour between his hands as he goes to spin another pizza. He takes a minute to think. "I've known you practically my whole life, Big Mac. You assume the worst in everyone. You always have," he says, pointedly. It's not an accusation, though. He says it like it's a fact.

"That day at school, when we—" Tony stumbles his words then, his bottom lip trembling. "Brad and I were asking that Hayden kid to look out for you. We just wanted to make sure you were okay."

I jerk my head back, my mind reeling in shock, as Tony continues. "And the same thing happened with Tristan. He busted down your walls, you got scared, and you lashed out because you didn't want him to see the real you and leave. But by doing that, you *did* show him the real you, and he still didn't walk away."

I knock on the counter, so taken aback by how completely Tony's managed to sum me up. Because I *do* jump to conclusions. I did it with The Tripod when I saw them that day and thought they were about to beat up Hayden. I did it with Tad—thinking he'd eventually leave Ma—when it's obvious he loves her more than anything. And I did it by walking out on Tristan on his birthday when I thought he and his family were judging me. But in every situation, I couldn't have been more wrong. I couldn't have been further from the truth.

I run my tongue along my teeth and pinch my eyebrow. "So you're not weirded out?"

Tony shoots his head back and looks over at me. "By what?"

"By me being, you know." I flick my wrist, which feels oddly offensive. "Gay."

I roll the word around in my mouth like gravel pebbles between my tongue. Saying it out loud is going to take some getting used to.

Tony snorts again and puts the freshly formed pizza onto a stone slab. He grabs a ladle and drops a dollop of sauce in its center. "Dude, my favorite musician is YUNGBLUD. That guy is pansexual AF."

"Right," I say, smiling, as I go to fill the empty salt and pepper shakers sitting on the shelf. We work side by side in silence, and it feels good to return to this. This part of my life I thought I'd lost.

Tony walks over to the pizza oven and shoves the stone slab to the back with a large metal rod. "Look, I don't want to get in the middle of anything here, but you really should talk to Bud." He looks over his shoulder at me, adjusting the hairnet on his head. "That kid is so far in the closet he might as well be searching for Aslan."

"I already tried to. He doesn't want anything to do with me." Then, I shake my head in shock. "Wait, you knew this whole time? About both of us?"

Tony laughs. "No, I really didn't." He pokes at the burning coals in the oven. "It just never mattered to me."

"It should have, though," I say, grabbing another pepper shaker. "Mattered."

Tony looks me dead in the eye. "I know that now. What happened between us is as much my fault as it is yours or Brad's."

I huff out a breath, sniffling back tears. "Why didn't you say anything then?"

Tony watches as I spill peppercorns over the counter. "Because I've never been good at opening up. You know that. And your coming out journey is your own. You didn't need me influencing how you did it."

"Huh," I say, impressed. I always thought Tony was a one-track mind kind of guy. He only ever showed interest in the girls at school. But like Skye, I never noticed all the little pieces that made him, him. "That's actually really sweet, Tony."

Tony switches the timer off next to the oven and pulls out the pizza. He looks around the kitchen before taking a piece of pepperoni and shoveling it into his mouth. "Believe it or not, your boy's not all bad."

At the mention of being my boy again, the tension in my muscles releases. Is it that easy? Are we friends again?

Tony licks his fingers and turns over his phone on the shelf to read a text. I don't think he sees me watching him, because his shoulders drop as he sighs.

"Who are you texting?"

He looks up, pocketing his phone. "No one."

I tilt my ear to my shoulder and purse my lips. "Really? I come out to you and tell you my life story and you can't let me in on what's bothering you right now? Who was it?"

Tony shakes his head, his bangs escaping from behind his hair net. "It doesn't matter."

"Big Cheese."

He turns and rolls his eyes when he sees I haven't moved. "All right. All right," he huffs, muttering in Italian and taking his phone out again. He rereads the text on his screen and sucks in a breath. "Girls only talk to me to say they've hooked up with a bad boy. By the next morning, they want nothing to do with me. Don't get me wrong, it's great in the moment, but it gets old real fast. I'd like to think I'm more than that."

I sidestep over to bump his hip and smile. I know Tony has a reputation as a player at school, but I always thought he took pride in that. That he reveled in the number of girls he's hooked up with. But seeing the sadness on his face, I know he's been pretending like the rest of us.

"You are, Tony, trust me," I say, walking over to one of the computers and ringing in a slice of pizza. "And someday, you're going to find someone who'll love you for you."

"Dude." Tony covers his mouth to stop himself from laughing. "You're better than that."

The rest of the afternoon drones on. I'm not used to working lunches, but after a while, I fall into a rhythm of clearing dirty dishes and wiping down tables.

Fifteen minutes before the end of my shift, I hear Tony yell "Order up" from the kitchen.

I grab my to-go box from the window and head to the back door. I lift the lid, and the pepperoni is all clumped together in the middle of the pizza, spelling out I'M SORRY 2.

24.

SMELLS LIKE STONEBRIDGE SPIRIT

The Picture PIC-tacular starts at 7 P.M. sharp. After ignoring Tristan at work on Monday, I forwarded him tonight's details, hoping it might be enough. That we could hash things out here, now that I've figured out what to say.

Ma and I race through the empty halls of Stonebridge, stuffing pizza crusts into our mouths and dusting the crumbs from clothes. Under my leather jacket, I settled on a white collared shirt and a pair of dress pants I borrowed from Tad. Ma trails behind me in a denim dress, cinched at the waist with a brown belt. Her lime-green heels click over the linoleum as she cusses. Ma hates getting dressed up almost as much as I do.

We burst through the gymnasium doors right as Stacy steps up to the podium. I pinch my eyebrow, eyeing the exit as the audience turns to frown at us.

I try searching for the photography club, but the gym is swarming with people. There isn't a single seat left. The PIC-tacular is open to anyone in Valentine who wants to apply; I guess I just didn't expect it to be this popular. Seeing how intense the competition really is makes me want to turn around and leave behind any hope I had of winning. Which wasn't even that big to begin with, but still.

Ma grabs my elbow, probably sensing my hesitation, and weaves us through the crowd. The perimeter of the gym is lined with easels, each displaying a framed contest entry under black draping so that no one can spoil the surprise. I find my name in the back corner crammed between the bleachers and the exterior cement wall. If that isn't a metaphor for my life, I don't know what is.

As with any contest, there were rules to the PIC-tacular. The use of professional cameras was strictly prohibited. The same went for any editing software. The contest is meant to showcase photography for what it is, capturing the beauty of the natural world, just as Regina Hale had done in the seventies. Looking around the gym, maybe I am in my element. I don't have to compete with anyone's expectations or high-tech equipment. For once, it's a level playing field.

On stage, Stacy introduces the panel of judges sitting behind her. They're mostly teachers and local business owners who've sponsored the event since its inception. When their names are called, the judges stand and acknowledge the audience, holding clipboards in their hands. Mr. Pecorino sees me by the bleachers but doesn't wave, which I appreciate. I don't want anyone thinking he's playing favorites before the contest has even begun. Especially because I know he won't.

Tad and Hannah find us in the crowd. Hannah hands me a picture, drawn in orange crayon, of myself holding a gigantic trophy over my head. The words YOU'RE NUMBER 1 are spelled out in glitter. The B in NUMBER is backward.

I ruffle her hair and say thank you, looking around the gym for any sign of Tristan. I can't blame him for not showing up.

Not after the way I treated him. Still, a part of me hoped he would come.

When Stacy finishes her speech, I pull back the draping on my easel to reveal the picture of Tristan blown up to be almost life-size. Tears form in Ma's eyes as she instructs me to take my place next to it and snaps a picture.

Hannah tugs at my jacket, laughing with glee, and Tad lets out a long whistle. He claps a hand down on my shoulder. "It's beautiful, Big Mac. I'm so proud of you."

"Thanks, Tad."

The next hour flies by in a blur of people coming and going. Some loiter, tilting their heads to contemplate my image like its abstract art hanging in the Guggenheim. A few strangers hug me as if we're long-lost friends. Others grumble with disappointment and walk right on by. This is the Midwest after all. Not everyone has to like it.

Skye texts around the halfway mark, asking where to find me. When they arrive with the twins in tow, I give them all hugs and introduce them to Ma and Tad. Hannah's hiding under the bleachers but sticks her head out to fawn over Skye's cobalt-blue áo dài, a traditional Vietnamese silk tunic with matching pants.

Velvet already seems to know Ma, which is something I'll have to remember to ask about later. She's probably a frequent shopper at Quilts & Things. She seems like the kind of person that crafts on weekends, based on the homemade red plaid miniskirt and black halter top she's wearing now. Or she's been to one of Ma's *Golden Girls* drag shows, which is just as likely.

Hayden is in a three-piece suit like we're at the Met Gala instead of our high school gymnasium. When I ask about his photo, he describes it so perfectly I can already picture it in my head.

Ma offers to watch my station so I can see the other entries with my friends.

I can't believe the talent in the room.

There's an image a few easels down from mine of a sun rising over a lake. The photographer is a woman in her forties with cat-eyed glasses and a tie-dyed blouse. I tell her how beautiful her work is, and she shares that she took it up in Canada over the holidays.

Hayden's entry is on the opposite end of the gym, where a crowd of people are gathered. In the picture, the twins are sitting back-to-back, their arms intertwined behind them. Hayden's crying in the photo, black mascara traveling down his face, while Velvet's been captured in a laughing fit. I bend down and read the title: *Agony & Mirth*.

"Wow," I say, taking out my phone to take a picture of a picture. Hayden shakes his head and tells us about how difficult it was to get the right angle using the self-timer on his phone.

We continue around the gym, admiring all the entries. And as we walk around, people actually come up to congratulate me on my work. I discuss my thoughts of each image with Skye, Velvet, and Hayden, and they nod their heads like I've made a good point. Like I actually know what I'm talking about. Maybe the nerves I was feeling at the thought of everyone judging my photo weren't really nerves. Maybe I do belong here after all.

At the five-minute mark, Stacy blows her whistle.

"May the best person win," Hayden says. Velvet and Skye say their goodbyes too and head back to their seats.

When I arrive at my station, Ma's finishing up a conversation with one of the judges. The lady's name tag says she's from the Valentine school board. My natural instinct is to think I'm in trouble, but the woman shakes my hand and commends me on a job well done. I shuffle next to my easel, painfully aware of how big my smile is.

"This evening has been full of so much talent," Stacy's voice booms over the speakers. "From cherry blossoms blowing in the wind to a duckling searching for its mother. But like everything in life's gentle grasp, there can only be one champion."

I find Velvet in the audience, and we roll our eyes.

Stacy thanks the evening's sponsors and rambles on about the importance of the arts in our community. She has a point, no doubt, but the way she's dragging on, avoiding announcing the winners, is making me nervous.

I look across the gym and see Hayden crack his neck, annoyed.

My heart pounds inside my chest. I didn't think I'd cared this much about the contest, but now that I'm here, I really do want to win. It's not even about the prize money. I just want to be able to say that I did it.

Okay, $1,000 sounds pretty nice too.

Ma holds my hand. She can tell I'm anxious.

One of the judges gives Stacy an envelope, and she reads out the name for third place. I don't even hear the winner's name she announces, but a woman with gray hair walks up the stairs to the stage. Her photograph appears on a projector screen above the basketball hoop on the wall. It's of what I assume to be one of her grandchildren, his face smooshed against the glass of an aquarium. A dolphin stares back at him. It's titled *Reciprocal Intrigue*.

Mr. Pecorino gets up next and hands Stacy another sealed envelope. His eyes meet mine, and I gulp.

"In second place."

Someone claps their hands into their lap, mimicking a drumroll.

Stacy peals the envelope open and her shoulders fall. "Wesley Mackenzie?"

Skye and Velvet jump to their feet, shouting over the crowd's raucous applause. Ma and Hannah squeal next to me as Tad tousles my hair.

I can't move.

Stacy holds the card out with my name on it and shows it to the crowd like she can't believe it either.

This can't be real.

I won.

It may only be second place, but I've never won anything in my entire life. My picture of Tristan flashes on the screen overhead, and the cheers grow even louder until they match the unsteady beating of my heart. Hannah nudges the back of my leg, forcing me to stumble toward the stage.

"Yeah, WES!"

I turn around, searching the crowd for whoever shouted my name, but I can't make out anyone's face. Too many people are cheering. The overhead lights are blinding.

On stage, Stacy rolls her eyes as she hands me a gift bag with a Canon camera inside. I take it—thanking her as I do—and I think I see her smile.

I sit down next to the elderly woman and thump my hands against my legs as the drumroll starts up again. This time, the whole room joins in.

Stacy walks over to a giant blank check that's propped up next to the judges. "And now, the moment you've all been waiting for." Grinning, she pulls back a strip of paper covering the name of the grand prize winner.

The audience stands.

I'm sitting behind Stacy at this point, so I can't actually see who's won. Everyone's turned, their backs toward us, as the winner makes their way to the front.

I lean over in my chair as Hayden jumps on stage, clearing the stairs completely. He holds the check up to the crowd.

Agony & Mirth flashes on the screen above.

A newspaper photographer from the *Valentine Reporter* herds the winners together to take a photo for tomorrow's front page. I throw my arm over Hayden's shoulder as the camera shutters.

Once the gym clears, my family races over to congratulate me. Ma's makeup is smeared over her cheeks. She tells me to stand still, timing the taking of her photo with Tristan's image in the background.

I watch as Velvet and Skye tussle Hayden to the ground. "Watch the suit!" He grins into his sister's hair, laughing.

The three of them are sprawled out on the floor, not caring when people have to step over them to leave. They're more similar to The Tripod than I ever realized. Skye's the quiet, reserved one, like Bud. Velvet's loud and in your face, like Tony. And Hayden's artsy . . . like me.

Artsy.

That's a strange thought.

Someone punches me in the arm, breaking my train of thought, and I turn around to see both Tony and Brad. Brad has his Cleveland Browns letterman jacket on. He rocks back on his heels as Tony hands me a bouquet of candied bacon.

"Bro, what?" I shout, bringing them into a hug.

In the moment, I forget everything that's happened. I forget the anger and the hurt and the distance between us. The guys must do the same, because we're all laughing together, just like we used to.

"How'd you know about this?" I ask, waving my bacon flowers around the gym.

Brad smiles, fixing his hair with his fingers. "Hayden messaged us. He knew today was important to you."

I take a step back, speechless. Hayden messaged Tony and Brad? I look over at the photography kids. They're a few feet away, talking among themselves. I nod my head at Hayden in thanks, and he reacts with a shy smile when he sees The Tripod back together.

"Who knew you had it in you?" Tony says, pointing to Tristan's photo on the screen. "I always knew you liked taking pictures of pizza, but now I know it had more to do with the pepperoni."

He starts to close his fist in a lewd gesture, but Brad threatens to smack him.

"It's cool, though," Tony laughs. He glances back up at my photo on the wall. "I'm not going to lie, that tutu guy is pretty cute."

"Yeah?" I elbow him in the side, staring up at Tristan and ignoring the sharp spasm that ripples through my chest.

"Hey, bro, I am very comfortable with my sexuality." Tony blushes. "I can appreciate when a man is attractive. You've got good taste."

"Thanks, Big Cheese."

Brad scratches his neck. "We never cared that you were gay, Wes, or that you were even hanging out with other people. We just didn't get why you shut us out like that."

"But we are sorry for how we acted. Really," Tony adds, puffing out his chest like it'll make him more macho. "Bros before . . . wait. What's the gay version of bros before hoes?"

"It's fine," Brad says, clamping his hand down on the back of Tony's neck. "We get it." He looks back over at me, his eyes damp. "Listen . . ."

I shake my head. "I'm sorry for what I said to you, Bud. I should never have brought your dad up like that. It was wrong of me."

"No, you were right. I hadn't realized my drinking had gotten that bad until New Year's Eve. And when you cornered me in the bathroom, I'd already called Dez because I'd slipped up again." He motions toward a guy in a red Ohio State pullover standing beside the bleachers. I hadn't noticed him, but the skin around his eyes crinkles when he looks up from his phone and waves. He looks kind.

I go to raise an eyebrow, but Brad's shoulders lift, and he snorts. "Dez is my sponsor."

"Your sponsor?"

Brad nods. "I've started going to Alcoholics Anonymous meetings. It was pretty rough at first, but I'm getting the hang of it. My dad kicked me out after I came out. I've been living with Dez the past few weeks."

I cover my mouth with my hand. "Brad, I'm so sorry."

"I should be the one apologizing for kissing you. That wasn't right. I don't even like you like that, but I felt you pulling away, and then your friends showed up at the party, and I got scared. We've always been a team, and it freaked me out to think you were abandoning us. Dez has really helped me identify my triggers. He's queer too. He left his life back in Mexico after his family disowned him."

I nod my head slowly, the puzzle pieces falling into place. Even before I got expelled, Brad had been missing for weeks. I figured he was skipping school, but I see the subtle changes in him now. The return of color to his face. The way he stands without slouching.

"I'm really happy for you, Brad." I smile. Though I was afraid of coming out, I never once thought Ma would kick me out of the house. That didn't ever cross my mind. But knowing that still happens, that people are disowned and even killed for being who they are, I realize my coming out story could have been so much worse.

Tony comes up behind us. "My two GBFs. Reunited at last."

I tilt my head at Brad.

"Don't think that just because he knows everything now, he isn't still a douche," he says, throwing Tony into a headlock.

Tony tries kicking Brad from behind, to no avail, and we all laugh.

I'm helping Tad take down my easel when Skye comes up behind me and reaches into my gift bag.

"No way, is this the EOS M50 model?"

I shrug because I honestly have no idea what they're talking about. It's like they're speaking in tongues.

"Okay, *king*!" Skye says, turning the box over in their hands. I see the joy in their eyes when they take the camera out.

"Keep it."

Skye's eyes pop like they're ready to fall out. "What? Are you kidding?"

"Nope. It's yours."

"I can't accept this." They take a step back into Velvet, their voice cracking.

"Think of it as repayment for all the lunches I stole from you."

They kiss me on the cheek. "Oh my God. Thank you, thank you thank you thank you." Skye turns to Velvet, and they both scream into each other's faces.

Hayden bumps into me, holding the oversized check against his stomach. "You know, I never thought I'd live to see the day, but you're a good guy, Wes."

I watch as Velvet and Skye leap around the gym before staring up at Tristan's photo again. "I'm trying to be."

25.

I WRITE SINS, NOT ESSAYS

I'm not one to sit down and write an essay on purpose. But when I get home from the PIC-tacular, I open up my laptop and get to work.

Maybe I'm still riding the high of coming in second place, or maybe it's because Principal Cohen found me at the showcase and reversed my expulsion after Brad and Tony sat her down and explained what happened the day of the fight, but I'm feeling inspired.

An online application for the Sierra Institute of Liberal Arts sits in front of me on the screen. I'd never even heard of the school before tonight, but when I started researching photography programs in the US, theirs piqued my interest the most.

I've already filled out the important details, like my full name and address. I even curated a selection of photos to send as my portfolio. All that's left to do is provide a copy of my transcript and write an admissions essay. The transcript's the easy part; I can get it from Mr. Hamilton when I return to school on Monday.

My hope was that the essay would write itself, but it turns out that's not how it's done.

I drag my mouse across the essay topic, highlighting it back and forth.

Share an interesting fact about yourself.

I mull it over all weekend. And again between classes. I've even thought about it at work, trying to form sentences in my head while picking gum off the underside of tables, but nothing ever comes up.

I'm back to believing there's nothing interesting about me.

I search my room for inspiration. There are clothes all over the floor again. My skateboard's sitting at the base of my dresser, so I start there, writing down what it's like to be a skater. I press delete when I realize how dull it is, watching an hour's worth of words disappear.

A week goes by, but I haven't made any progress.

Ma comes home around six and asks me what I want for dinner. I oblige with a fan favorite in our house, grilled cheese and tomato soup, even though I'm not hungry.

The application window for the essay closes at midnight.

"Come on, come on."

I tap my foot, holding down the U key, hoping for inspiration to strike.

The Sierra Institute is located just outside New York City. If I get in, if the admissions board looks past my horrible grades and gives me a chance, I'll only be an hour away from Tristan. If he was able to show up the way he did at Vincenzo's, maybe there is hope for us.

I hear Ma turn off the TV and head to her room for the night. It's quarter to ten. There's only two hours left, and all I've done is copy and paste the essay question into my document.

I dig my palms into my eyes, and my mind turns back to Tristan again. We haven't spoken in weeks, but I see us outside on New Year's Eve, snow falling in buckets around us.

Don't you ever feel like that? That anyone watching would be completely and utterly bored?

I remember the way he looked at me when I had asked, like he couldn't tell if I was being serious or not.

The next chapter in your life is for you to define, Wes.

I didn't believe him then, but thinking about it now, seeing a future where I'm unafraid to be myself, taking pictures and selling them for people to hang in their homes, I feel an electricity that wasn't there before.

I tilt my head back. Every night since Ma and I had our talk, I've seen New York City in my dreams. And Tristan's always been right beside me.

I start writing.

When you're a kid, you can be whatever you want. There are no limits to what is possible—it's just you and your imagination against the world. No one ever sits you down and tells you you can't walk on the moon or be the first person to discover a cure for cancer. Your dreams are a tangible thing you can reach out and grab.

No one ever told me I couldn't be myself, but for some reason, I internalized the thought that I wasn't good enough . . .

I have to use the bathroom by the third paragraph, but I don't stop.

I barely move.

Words flow through me and onto the blank page. I hammer away at the keyboard, pumping out sentences faster than I ever have before.

I talk about The Tripod and my love of skateboarding, of

leaving Louisiana and my abusive father behind for good. I mention Metallica and finding myself in four old ladies and midnight slices of cheesecake.

I don't hold back.

I write about meeting Tristan and letting him walk away because I was too afraid to show him the real me. I talk about Ma and how I took on the role of her caretaker, even though she never ask me to.

I check the clock. It's ten minutes to midnight as I finish writing the last paragraph.

> *I've learned more about myself in the past few months, about love and friendship, about hard work and following your dreams, than I ever thought I would. Maybe there isn't anything interesting about me, and that's okay. I might not be what you're looking for at the Sierra Institute, but I am trying to be a better person—and to me, that is greater than any grade I could show you on a transcript.*

At 11:59 P.M., I hit submit.

At 12:07 A.M., I send it to Tristan.

26.

IF I COULD FIND HIM NOW

I've stayed up every night this week, wondering if Tristan's read my essay. I should've told him I was sorry at Vincenzo's when I had the chance, that I didn't mean to walk out on his birthday. But I hid like a coward and let Tony do the talking for me.

It doesn't matter anyway because he never replies.

Which is why I'm lying face down on the floor at Tony's house, painfully aware of how tired I am, while the guys play *Tony Hawk's Pro Skater*. Brad heads into the kitchen to grab chips from the pantry as Tony smashes the buttons on his controller. He does a series of pop shove-its with his avatar, raising his score by four hundred points.

"Suck it!" Tony shouts at the TV. He steals a quick glance at me from the couch, though his attention never quite leaves the game. "Shit, am I allowed to say that?"

I reach over and swat at his leg unenthusiastically. "Shut up, man."

The Tripod's been hanging out every day after school, and we quickly fall back into a rhythm of wrestling and making fun of each other. Only this time, we're not vandalizing the skate park or stealing stuff from 7-Eleven. We usually rotate between my house and Tony's since Brad is still crashing at Dez's cramped basement suite outside of town. Brad's parents haven't made any contact since kicking him out, but he's doing okay given the circumstances. He's been attending weekly AA meetings to keep himself accountable and has picked up extra shifts at Vincenzo's to help Dez pay rent.

It feels good to shoot the shit with them again, like old times. Even if something's changed between us since the last time we hung out. We all sit a little closer to one another and listen more intently when one of us is talking. Maybe we've all realized how good we have it. That after senior year, we won't find friendships like this again.

Brad comes back into the room, licking sour cream and onion seasoning from his fingers. He grabs the controller sitting next to me on the floor, landing the perfect Indy backflip while "Euro-Barge" by The Vandals plays in the background.

I side-eye my phone, waiting for the screen to light up.

"BRO . . ."

I snap my neck up to return my attention to the game. "What?"

"Go after him already," Tony moans, sticking his tongue out as he fires off a combination move.

"Go after who?"

Brad lets out a dramatic huff and pauses the game. "Don't pretend like you're here right now. You've barely looked at the TV since we sat down."

I glance over at Tony, and he nods his head. He's been shadowing his dad all week at work, learning the ropes to become assistant manager. Our time together is the only chance he gets to unwind.

"Okay, fine," I admit, unplugging my phone from the

charger on the wall. "It's just . . . what if he doesn't want to see me?"

I pull up Tristan's contact picture. It was one of the last photos I took of him before we broke up. He's sitting on a park bench in beige chinos and a jean jacket, his hand covering his face. I hadn't thought about what I'd do if he actually replied to my last message, but even asking the question now, I know it'll never happen. The damage has already been done. He's probably just trying to move on.

"That's a possibility for sure," Brad says. "But what if he does want to see you?"

The Tripod was never good at talking about our feelings before, but the guys are looking over at me now with such concern I can't believe it took us this long to open up. There's a real stigma around men sharing their emotions, and we became a walking endorsement of that. Brad took up drinking to cope, Tony used hooking up with girls as a defense mechanism, and I let my anger get the best of me. Because "boys will be boys," isn't that what we're taught?

But that's the problem. Saying shit like that doesn't teach us anything. It only gives permission for inexcusable behavior.

"You're absolutely right," I say, getting up slowly to throw my leather jacket on. "There's somewhere I've got to be."

"Go get 'em, Prince Charming!" Tony chirps, body slamming Brad into the couch.

I take back what I said.

They'll never change.

AS I COAST down the street toward Tristan's house, I finally gain enough courage to call him. It's pouring rain, and the trek on my tires is so worn out I swerve on the road, riding waves as they crash along the curbside like I'm a surfer in Malibu.

On the third ring, the FaceTime request connects, and Tristan's face appears. He's wearing his over-the-ear headphones and a Sullivan-Richards zip-up sweater. The background blurs behind him like he's rushing to get somewhere.

"Hey." Tristan coughs, looking from me to something off-screen and back again. He's fidgeting with his zipper, running it up and down the track along his chest.

"Hey." I pull up onto the sidewalk, dipping under a hawthorn tree to take cover. The bark is rough against my back, but I use it to steady myself at the sight of him. I pinch my eyebrow while he talks to someone I can't see. He must've put his mic on mute because his lips are moving, but I can't hear what he's saying. "Is this a bad time?"

Tristan laughs at something the other person says, and my heart falters. Is he with another guy? Have I missed my chance? Maybe I was stupid to think he might be missing me too. Though his eyebrows are creased like he's squinting to read something, he looks genuinely happy.

He takes himself off mute and looks down at me, almost like he'd forgotten I was there. "Sorry, yeah. I can't really talk right now." His words come out curt. "Can you call back tomorrow?"

Tomorrow. I scratch my back along the tree, leaning into a sharp branch sticking out on its side. "Okay, sure, yeah."

Tristan hangs up while I'm midsentence. I guess I should take it as a good thing that he's asked me to call back, but a small voice tells me he only did it to be kind. I look down at my screen, at the thirty-two seconds our call lasted for. The wind picks up, beating raindrops at my face.

I pocket my phone.

WHEN I ARRIVE at Tristan's house, I walk up the driveway, not wanting to leave scratch marks on the tiles with my skateboard. I pull my beanie further down my forehead to hide my face. Why did I come here? Tristan seemed annoyed that I'd called. Is he even home?

Peeking through a window to the right of the door, I ring the bell. He may have been heading to the theater for all I know, but I at least have to try.

There aren't any shoes on the mat inside, but something tells me the Monroes aren't the type of people to leave them lying around even if they were home.

I try the doorbell again, and a single metallic note echoes through the house. After a few minutes, I hear footsteps on the other side of the door.

Cami's face appears in the window as she fumbles with the lock. "Wesley," she says, waving me inside. She gives me a huge hug like I hadn't just met her the one time and walked out without saying goodbye.

I like that Cami's a hugger, but I feel bad as she squishes me into her arms. She went through all that effort to make Tristan's birthday dinner special, and I didn't even thank her for it. I did ask Tristan to tell her for me, but I doubt he did. I wouldn't have if my boyfriend broke up with me and stormed off like I did. I want to tell her I'm sorry for the way I acted, but how do I bring it up without acknowledging the fact that I dumped her son on his birthday?

"Would you like anything to drink?" Cami asks as we walk into the kitchen. She's wearing a furry bathrobe and slippers like she'd stepped out of the bath to answer the door.

"No thanks," I decline. I take my wet jacket off and drape it over a barstool.

When I ask if Tristan's home, Cami looks over at me like she's confused. She shakes her head. "Didn't he tell you he's in New York with Jean? His audition for St. Sebastian's is this weekend."

Of course.

I knew his audition was coming up. It's all he ever talked about in the weeks leading up to our breakup. He was so excited. I was too. Even though the thought of us going our separate ways after high school terrified me, I knew how much St. Sebastian's meant to him. He was probably heading through the airport when I called. I'd been so caught up in everything—the PIC-tacular, the Sierra Institute essay, The Tripod—that I forgot the single most important trip of his future career as a dancer.

I look around the kitchen. Someone's pinned the selfie we took on Tristan's birthday to the fridge, and I feel my arm begin to lift as if it's yearning to reach out and touch it. It suddenly occurs to me that Tristan may not have told his family what happened between us. But why would he keep that from them? I haven't been around for weeks.

Cami continues talking about Tristan's trip, and there isn't any malice behind her eyes. She doesn't seem mad that I showed up on her front step unannounced. In her mind, Tristan and I might still be together.

My lips part slightly in a smile. Maybe Tristan is hoping it'll work out between us too. Maybe, like me, he still wants to try.

I turn toward the family room. "Can you remind me when his audition is exactly? I've been so busy lately; it completely slipped my mind, and I want to make sure I wish him good luck."

Cami walks over to the fridge to check the chalkboard cal-endar on its door. She has to pull reading glasses from a drawer to see what she's scribbled down. "It's tomorrow," she says, tapping the fridge. "At four-thirty."

I pull out my phone and add it to my calendar. "Is the audition actually at St. Sebastian's?"

Cami smiles conspiratorially, her glasses sliding down her nose. "Yes." Her voice is low, deliberate. "In the Jefferson Theater."

"Jefferson. Theater. Got it," I repeat, starring its location when it pops up on Google Maps.

Cami laughs. "Now don't you go getting any crazy ideas, young man—"

I don't wait to hear the end of her sentence. I grab my jacket off the back of the barstool and tell her to say hi to Malik for me as I fly out the front door.

Cursing against my better judgment, I skateboard down the driveway, wheels clunking over the tiles.

I've only met Tristan's mom twice, but both times I've stormed out of her house without so much as a thank you.

With any luck, I'll make it a habit.

27.

ANARCHY IN NEW YORK CITY

The lady at the airport check-in hands me a boarding pass with my seat number on it. She must notice how lost I look because before I can ask for directions, she tells me to take the second staircase to the right and head straight on until the moving sidewalk. It's too early to laugh at her mediocre joke.

This is ridiculous.

This is *beyond* ridiculous.

I know it is.

Ma is going to kill me when she finds out.

It's 11 A.M. on Friday morning, and I'm about to board a three-hour direct flight to New York City. I paid for the ticket with the money I'd been saving for a new camera. It wasn't that expensive, but it was enough to set me back. I'll have to work double shifts during spring break to make up for it.

I've never been on a plane before. It never occurred to me that I might be afraid of flying, though I should've remembered how scared I was of the Goliath roller coaster at Six Flags Great America. And how much I puked after riding it.

I wish Tristan were here to tell me it'll be okay. He'd only need to give me a look to calm me down. To say I'm being dramatic. Though he's expecting me to call him later today, how will he react when I show up in person? Will he be happy to see me? Or will he tell me that it's over—forever? That it was stupid of me to travel all that way for nothing?

On the plane, I sit down next to a little girl wearing the same pink tutu Hannah has at home and take it as a sign that I'm doing the right thing. That flying across the country to see my ex-boyfriend audition for the most prestigious performing arts school in North America is not at all irrational. But I don't care. It's about time I proved to Tristan what he means to me.

"I like your hair," the little girl says.

I go to thank her when she stands up in her seat, ignoring the fasten seat belt sign, and yanks my head back.

"What the hell?"

Across the aisle, the girl's dad lifts his eye mask and tells her ("Lucy!") to sit down. He doesn't wait for her to comply, though. He just turns back around and pulls down his mask.

Despite popular opinion, I hate Lucy.

When we're thirty thousand feet above, I ask a flight attendant if it's illegal to sell alcohol to minors in international skies. She sizes me up with one look and offers a ginger ale. I take it without a fight, fiddling with the pull tab between my teeth.

Lucy pinches my forearm. "Why are your teeth so pointy?"

I spin my head around like I'm that girl from *The Exorcist* and grab the armrest between us. "So I can eat kids like you for breakfast."

She falls silent after that, electing to sit in her dad's lap the rest of the flight.

Okay, so I snapped. We can't be good *all* the time.

SKYSCRAPERS TOWER OVER me, unlike anything I've ever seen.

The air in the city is wet, but it's not raining. I wouldn't say the sky is full of clouds, though I wouldn't say it's clear either. It's just gray everywhere I look.

I start skateboarding down Tenth Avenue, but the streets are so busy for this time of day, with yellow taxis speeding past and horns constantly honking, I give up and walk the rest of the way.

New York City is chaotic. Not "Avengers destroying the entire city in a ten-minute battle sequence" chaotic, but there's something going on around every corner. A man shouts at me from the other side of the road. I can't hear what he's saying, but he looks angry, so I put my head down and keep moving.

Google Maps tells me I've arrived at St. Sebastian's Conservatory of Performing Arts as I stop in front of a large, rectangular building with floor-to-ceiling windows and a beige brick exterior that looks like the sandcrawler fortress in *A New Hope*.

I walk into the school through glass doors, and a group of students part like the Red Sea to avoid me. It's not like back home at Stonebridge, where they move out of the way in fear; it's more like they don't even bother looking up from the scripts in their hands as they pass.

I check my phone. It's 4:23 P.M.

I wave down a student carrying a trombone and ask him how to get to Jefferson Theater. He pulls me over to the directory on the wall to show me the way, and I thank him before heading in the theater's general direction.

A row of dancers line up along the wall leading to the auditorium. Some stretch their legs out on the floor. I try to find Tristan among them, but he's not there.

Inside the theater, auditions are already underway. I find a seat in the back, behind a family taking up the entire row in front of me.

A girl is on stage dancing to what sounds like Beethoven. I've never had a good ear for classical music, so it could be Mozart. Or Bach. It's irrelevant. She points the toes of her right foot into the air, high above her head. The number fifty-three is pinned to her leotard.

In the middle of the audience, three people are sitting behind a table. Everyone keeps looking over at them for their reactions, so they must be important.

The dancer on stage bends into a low squat and kicks her leg behind her, and the people at the table shake their heads. I can't see their faces, but the backs of their heads seem disappointed. Why, though? The girl is good. She's twirling around so fast I have to spin my head to keep up. But who am I to tell? I know nothing about ballet. Maybe she sucks. Maybe the others auditioning today are off to the side, laughing at her expense. I can't imagine what it must be like to be her, being judged like that.

At least at the PIC-tacular, I could hide behind Tristan's photo. Sure, I was being judged too, but this is different. This is in real time. Anything that goes wrong today could jeopardize the girl's future. Tristan always made it look so easy, but watching the dancer on stage now, I can see how technical ballet is. How every move has to be calculated, precise.

The girl takes a bow as the music ends and the row in front of me stands up to cheer. They must be her family, which would explain why they think she aced it. Poor girl.

One of the judges leans forward and says a quick thank you into a small microphone, and the dancer dances offstage. Before she disappears, I see her wipe a tear from her face.

The lights overhead fade.

In the dark, a silhouette walks over to a mark at center stage and takes position. Two crewmembers follow behind, carrying a wooden bar. They place it at the dancer's left.

When the lights turn back on, my pulse quickens. Tristan is standing there, posing in a black leotard with heavy mascara lining his eyes and the number fifty-four on his chest. He's shaved the sides of his head so the curls on top are more pronounced. His hair has grown longer since I last saw him in person. There's a sparkle in his eye as he scans the audience, smiling at no one in particular.

He looks good.

Confident.

Like he was born for this.

Music plays over the sound system. It starts off quiet at first, like someone's dragging the soundbar up. I tap my foot against the back of the chair in front of me, and the woman sitting in it turns around to scold me.

I raise my hands to say I'm sorry and hum along to the melody.

Wait.

I know this song.

"There's no way," I whisper.

Tristan is dancing to "Nothing Else Matters," from Metallica's self-titled 1992 album. I know it without a shadow of a doubt because it's the same song I introduced him to as he drove me home on New Year's.

The judges turn to each other, puzzled, but Tristan ignores them. He sets off around the stage, his face contorted like he's angry. He's the perfect image of concentration, his arms and legs extending out with flawless execution.

As the music dies, I start clapping, but Tristan keeps dancing, and the instrumental outro morphs into another song entirely. This time, it's "For Whom the Bell Tolls."

Tristan rocks out on stage, thrashing his head with the music, and I can't stop smiling. Unlike the first time I saw him as the Nutcracker, Tristan has transformed into something else entirely. He moves freely now, like nothing is holding him back. Not the stiff sergeant costume he wore that night or the rigid technicalities of the ballet. He's free, and he's amazing. More than amazing. Tristan's managed to mix ballet seamlessly with heavy metal. The audience knows it too because they lean forward, enthralled by his performance.

Everyone watches as he lifts off the floor on one leg and lands perfectly on the other. He uses the wooden bar to his advantage, grabbing on and dipping low. He runs and turns in the air and lets the music completely take him over. I've never seen anything like it. Tristan is twirling and pirouetting, hitting each move in time with the music. He sets himself spinning toward the audience and slams down on his knees at the exact moment the song ends.

Down in the second row, Jean calls out his name. She's bouncing up and down in her seat, and the whole crowd joins in, cheering.

I blow a whistle between two fingers, feeling breathless and energized as an adrenaline rush courses through me.

I can't believe Tristan did that. It was a risky move choosing Metallica for an art usually reserved for classical music, but his performance was so graceful it was like the two were meant for each other. The whole room pulses with an electricity that he alone created with his routine. One by one, the judges rise and clap their hands. The third judge, a tall regal-looking woman with a pointed jawline and a mink coat, even bows.

Tristan bends forward, sweat flying from his forehead. He breathes into his hands, laughing.

I know how much this moment means to him. He's

worked his whole life for it, and I'm so glad I got to be here to witness it.

I let out a cheer from the back of the theater and watch as Tristan brings his hand up to shield his face from the light. His eyes find me in the crowd, among the theater's rows, and my hands freeze midclap.

At first, I don't think he realizes what he's seeing because I can't actually be in New York. It's a school day back in Valentine. Besides, we're broken up. I wouldn't do something wild like this.

Then, tears fill his eyes.

Anyone watching would think he's overcome with joy from his performance, but I know him better than that.

I clutch my throat, deflating back in my seat as Tristan takes his final bow. He thanks the judges for their time before scampering off stage.

The whole world fades away. What did I think would happen? That he'd see me, and all would be forgiven? That he'd climb over the seats, and we'd fall into an embrace on the theater floor? I'm such an idiot.

I grab my backpack and skateboard and race out into the rain.

Three times one is three.
Three times two is six.

28.

HEY THERE, TRISTAN

I don't stop running until I'm out of breath and heaving in front of a gigantic statue of Alice sitting on a mushroom in Wonderland.

My lungs are on fire. My kneecap is throbbing. All I want to do is go home.

Why did I come here?

I had no right barging in on Tristan's dream like that. Maybe it was a romantic gesture in my head, but I didn't consider his feelings. I only did what I wanted to do. Like always.

The rain's coming down diagonally now, striking like tiny needles against my face. I hear it dripping off the sides of the Mad Hatter's hat, softly pinging as it falls to the ground. People along the path to my right run beneath the surrounding elms to wait out the storm, their shoes the only sound for miles as they tap over the concrete.

I should be on the next flight out. A one-way ticket back to Valentine, to a time before Tristan pirouetted into my life. I don't even know what to do now. I hadn't planned this far. In my mind, I figured Tristan and I would make up and we'd go from there. Maybe spend the night exploring the city.

I guess this is it then.

"Wes?" A voice asks behind me.

I turn around, and Tristan's standing in the rain beneath a yellow umbrella. He's still wearing his leotard under his jacket, his neck exposed to the cold. The shoelaces on his runners are untied.

"Holy shit, it is you."

Tristan clutches his umbrella, observing me quietly through the onslaught of rain like he's trying to determine if I'm real or not. I wasn't smart enough to pack an extra outfit, so raindrops fall over my shoulders, soaking through the only clothes I have.

"How'd you find me?" I ask.

Tristan exhales, his breath rising in a cloud of smoke. Even though he must have chased after me, he isn't even slightly winded. "I followed you from the theater. I couldn't believe my—Why are you here, Wes?"

I shrug and pinch my eyebrow. "I wanted to surprise you."

"You certainly did that."

I force out a nervous laugh, picking at a smudge of dirt on my elbow. I know what he must be thinking. Who in their right mind travels across the country to surprise the boyfriend they dumped and ignored for weeks?

"I shouldn't have showed up like this. I'm sorry."

Tristan holds up his hand, urging me to stop. "What are you apologizing for, exactly?" He takes a step back, keeping me at arm's length. Though we're only standing on a small hill, the distance between us feels monumental. He looks out at me from under the rim of his umbrella, the fabric bobbing over his eyes.

"For everything," I huff, feeling relief as it starts to pour because tears and rain look the same. "For running out on your birthday like that, for ignoring your messages. For hiding from you at work."

At the mention of that day, Tristan leans in closer. He stands at the bottom of the hill, his umbrella swaying in the wind.

"I pushed you away because that's what I do when I think someone's about to leave me. I did this to us. Not you. Not The Tripod. Not my dad." I take a step toward him over the grass so I'm within his reach. Tristan motions for me to come under his umbrella, and I do. "But I couldn't stand the thought of not being there for you on the biggest day of your life. Not after you made me realize how important it is to fight for the life you want to live."

Tristan considers the grass beneath his shoe.

"The thought of you moving to New York City without telling you how I feel, I couldn't live with that. I need you to know how sorry I am. How much I want to be with you. And I hate that I can't even enjoy being here right now, in Central fucking Park, because all I can think about is how I screwed up. And I'm going to screw up, Tristan! It's who I am. But I'm going to keep trying until you know how much I love you. Because when I'm with you, I can be myself. My whole self."

"Hold up." Tristan laughs, placing his hand on my chest. "Did you just say you love me?"

I nod. "Yeah, I did. I do. I was afraid of what you being in my life meant. I thought you were trying to change me. First with my friends, then the college applications. And the cardigan. I never felt like I was good enough the way I was. So . . ." I let my gaze fall to my shoes. "I get it if you want to end things. For good."

Tristan frowns. "Why would you think that?"

I shrug. "Because I've been a total asshole to you . . ."

He's staring at me intently now, his hand still resting over my jacket. "Yes, you have."

The rain bangs over our heads. It's so loud I almost don't hear him exhale. "After what you said outside my house, I wanted to hate you. I really did. I plucked a page from your notebook and set that stupid cardigan on fire in the backyard when no one was home." He waits for me to laugh, but I don't. "After a while, though, I got where you were coming from. I would never have made you do or say or wear anything if I knew it'd upset you. You know that, right?"

I drop my chin to my chest. But Tristan raises his hand, looping his finger under it so we're looking into each other's eyes.

He takes my hand for a moment before letting it fall. "I don't want to change you."

"I know."

"And if it's worth anything"—Tristan smiles—"you're not a total asshole."

I look at him, unconvinced. "Yes, I am."

"Okay, fine. But I'd say you're just *an* asshole. Not a total one."

"How many times can you say 'asshole' in a minute?"

We both laugh.

Maybe bringing up our past is his way of saying he's forgiven me. Maybe by acknowledging all the hurt I've caused, we can finally put it behind us and move on. I hope that's the case.

I turn to step out from under his umbrella, but Tristan grabs my elbow. "It doesn't matter what you are," he says, shaking his head. "You're here now. And you flew all the way to *New York City* to be there for me."

I shrug like it's not a big deal.

"That's huge," he says. He's still holding on to my elbow.

"I wanted to support you."

"Support me?" He moves in closer, sliding his fingers along my forearm and into my hand. "You did more than support me, Wes. You showed up for me."

I shrug again. "It's the least I could do."

Tristan bites his lip. "No one has ever done something like that for me."

The next thing I know, Tristan reaches behind me, his hand resting on my lower back, as he drops his head down to kiss me. His lips brush gently over mine, his breath warm as it runs across my cheek. I breathe in the familiar scent of him. Of sweat and lemongrass. Of dreams on the cusp of coming true. Of home.

When we part, we look each other in the eye and stay like that. Tristan glances over my shoulder to see if anyone's noticed, but that only makes me grab his shoulders and kiss him harder. I don't care if anyone is watching us. Let them. Their opinions don't matter. They never did.

Tristan squeezes my hand. "I never told you how proud I was of you at the PIC-tacular."

I pull back. He's smirking. "You were there?"

Tristan nods. "I was hiding in the back. I couldn't bring myself to talk to you. I was still so mad at you for refusing to speak with me at Vincenzo's."

I remember someone shouting my name when Stacy announced that I'd won, but I never placed who it was. "It's okay," I say. "I get why you didn't."

The corners of Tristan's mouth fall. "But there was no way I would have missed it. Hayden's picture was good and all, but your model was, like, *ten* times cuter. Talk about those eyes."

I swat at his stomach, and he wraps his arms around me, not caring that the rain soaks us when he drops his umbrella.

I glance up at him, my chin resting on his bare chest. "You were amazing today."

He rolls his eyes.

"I'm serious. You're getting into St. Sebastian's."

"It wasn't my best work, but I hope it'll be enough."

Like me with my college application, Tristan's unsure if he'll get in. I can see the uncertainty there, lingering behind his eyes. He's second-guessing his abilities, no doubt a side effect of his perfectionism. I think we do that to protect ourselves; if we can convince our own minds we aren't good enough, we can't really be disappointed when we don't get what we truly want.

But I want Tristan to believe in himself the way I believe in him. He didn't see the way the audience was captured by his performance. Or how one of the judges bowed like she was the damn Swan Princess.

So I recount it all as we sit on one of the park benches along the gravel path, never letting go of each other's hand. The wooden slats are wet, but we brush them off, ignoring when our pants soak through.

"Metallica, huh?"

"Shut up," he says, turning to punch me. I throw my hands in the air. I swear my body is permanently bruised from all the punching that goes on in my life.

"I actually should thank you, though," Tristan continues. "I've always been so hard on myself. I thought if I wasn't the best, I was nobody. But you taught me to not take life so seriously. I don't think I would have been able to do what I did back there without you."

"No way, that was all you," I smile. "But you're welcome."

The rain lets up for a moment then, and for the first time since arriving in New York, the sun decides to show itself by poking through the clouds. I hunch my back up to the sky, my skin prickling under the sudden warmth.

After a while, Tristan laughs.

I look over at him with an eyebrow raised to ask what's so funny, but it only makes him laugh more.

"You do realize Central Park is like three miles long and you still managed to stop at the corniest thing you could find?" He points over at Alice. "I think you've changed more than you realize."

I huff, biting back another smile. "Isn't there a Peter Pan statue here somewhere?" I ask, bending at the waist to search for the Lost Boy under the bench.

Tristan shakes his head. "That's in Hyde Park in London."

"Dammit, I really wanted to see it."

Tristan pauses, running his thumb over the back of my hand. "We will. One day."

And I hold him to that. When I think about the future, all I see is Tristan and I together, exploring New York City, cooking together in a crammed kitchen that's far too expensive for what it is. Eventually, we'll even travel the world.

Tristan pulls out his phone, not bothering to look up as he sends off a quick text. "We should head back. I told my mom to wait at the theater."

"Something tells me she wasn't impressed with that?"

"No." He laughs as he gets up to leave. "But I decided that if it really was you, it'd be worth it." He lets our hands fall apart. "I was planning to read your essay, it's just—"

"Don't worry about it," I interrupt, shielding my eyes from the sun as we pass a fountain with a bronze angel at its peak. "I don't even know if I'll get accepted anyway."

Tristan stares at me. "You applied to college, Wes. That's a pretty big deal."

"I guess you're right."

"Please. I'm always right."

As we head back in the general direction of St. Sebastian's, Tristan digs through his email and reads my essay. By the time we funnel out of Central Park, the sun is setting, turning the sky a bluish gray.

We step out onto the street right as a taxi whizzes past and shoot our arms into the air, swearing. The driver slams on their horn in response.

I think we'll fit in here just fine.

"Are we okay?" I ask when I'm sure my blood pressure has returned to normal.

For a moment, I'm afraid Tristan will tell me that we're not, that we'll never be the same again, but he leans over and kisses me on the cheek.

"We're more than okay."

Our clothes may be drenched, and my toes are definitely swimming in a pool of water in my shoes, but I don't care. I bunch his rain jacket into my hand and kiss him. I don't think I'll ever get tired of that.

Some asshole shoves into us in true New York fashion, and we part.

"Tristan," I whisper, catching my breath.

"Yeah?"

I chew my lower lip. "I hate peppermint mochas."

He laughs, pulling me back under his umbrella. "We'll make it work."

EPILOGUE.

IN THE END, IT DEFINITELY MATTERS

Five Months Later

Hannah litters the ground with flower petals as she skips down the aisle. She's in a white tutu, which she insisted on wearing, and keeps stopping so her grandparents can take her picture.

We're set up beneath the shade of an old red barn. It's the middle of summer, so guests fan themselves with the programs in their hands.

At the end of the aisle, Tad is standing under a weeping willow strung up with lights. He looks sharp in a navy-blue tux and matching bowtie.

"Are you ready?" I ask, squeezing Ma's hands. She's done up in an emerald-green silk dress with sparkling silver flats. Someone's woven baby's breath through her hair.

Ma grabs the tissue she hid in her bra and blows her nose. "Let's get this over with already. My feet are killing me."

We do one last take in the mirror before Ma loops her hand under my arm, and we make our way down the aisle. The Incisors, Tad's band from college, have reunited for the wedding and are playing "Pachelbel's Canon" softly in the back. At the sight of her, Tad lowers his head and wipes his eyes.

I catch Tristan looking at me from the third row and stick out my tongue. After a summer of punishments for flying to New York without telling her, I officially introduced Ma to Tristan. He was nervous to meet her, but Ma strangled him in a huge hug the second he walked through the door. At one point, while bonding over white chocolate raspberry cheesecake, Ma turned to me and mouthed, "Oh my God, I love him." He looks super cute in a red blazer and white button-down, with blue dress pants rolled to the ankle. Next to him, Emily waves.

When we reach the end of the aisle, I kiss Ma on the cheek and hug Tad before taking my place as Ma's man of honor.

A drag queen dressed as Betty White taps a microphone. "Dearly beloved, we are gathered here today to celebrate the love between Thaddeus Richardson III and Tamara Young."

I scoff at Tad's full name, and without turning around, Ma points a finger to silence me.

The officiant launches into a story of how Tad filled in as Blanche Devereaux when Ma took him to see the *Golden Girls* drag show on their fifth date. The audience laughs along with every punch line, and soon, Tad and Ma are exchanging their vows. There's not a single dry eye as Tad promises to always take care of Ma, to massage her feet after a long day of work. In return, Ma vows to never wear the crocheted dress he bought for her birthday last year but pledges to love him and Hannah until her dying days.

When they're pronounced husband and wife, Tad dips Ma into a kiss.

An instrumental version of the *Golden Girls* theme song plays the newlyweds out as they walk hand in hand down the aisle. Even The Tripod climbs up on their seats to cheer.

Tad looks over his shoulder to wink at me, and I can't help

myself from smiling. I can't think of anyone more suited to be Ma's life partner.

What? I do have a heart.

Somewhere.

I WAS RIGHT.

St. Sebastian's offered Tristan a full ride scholarship. The same week he got the news, the Sierra Institute granted me conditional acceptance to their photography program as long as I got my grades up to a B- average by the end of the school year. I finished senior year with straight Bs.

As Ma and Tad finish their first dance as a married couple, I catch a glimpse of Brad and Tony kneeling next to the bar, seeing who can chug a can of Dr Pepper the fastest.

Brad has to repeat senior year in the fall because of all the time he missed last semester. He wasn't mad about it when Principal Cohen told him the news, but I could tell he was upset when we walked across the stage without him. At least the school let him come to graduation to be with all of us. Next year, he's planning to move to Columbus to live with his older sister.

Tony spent most of the summer training and is already helping run Vincenzo's with his dad. He even enrolled in some part-time cooking courses at a local college. It's nice to see him looking forward to something for a change rather than only caring about what girl he takes home.

As for me? I started going to therapy in the spring. The counselor is nice enough, though I still shut down every time she mentions my father. A part of me will always wonder why he did what he did, how he so willingly put mine and Ma's lives in jeopardy, but the pain of losing someone you loved is far less than the pain of giving them another chance and having them fail all over again. He doesn't deserve to be in my life any more than I want him there. I don't know if I'll ever get over that, but I'm learning to acknowledge the part of me that's powered by anger. I think it'll always be there, smoldering in the shadows. After all, I'm only human.

Ma and I moved into Tad's townhouse in June. I'm only going to be there for a few more weeks before heading to New York City with Tristan, but Tad let me paint my room so that whenever I make it back to Valentine for the holidays, I'd feel at home.

Hayden sticks a camera in my face as he, Velvet, and Skye head over to where Ma and Tad are cutting the cake. They offered their services as the official wedding photographers when Velvet ran into Ma at Quilts & Things.

At first, I thought it might be awkward to have all my friends in one place, but once apologies were out of the way, we spent every weekend together this summer. The Tripod taught Hayden how to skateboard. Emily challenged Tony to a dance-off. We even attended one of Brad's AA meetings for moral support. As the nights grew longer and July bled into August, I think we were all latching on to any opportunity to be together because a part of us didn't want to let high school go. To venture out into the real world.

"Are you excited about MIT?" I ask Skye as I take a seat beside them. They got into the civil and environmental engineering program for the fall.

"Very. I need to get out of Valentine." Skye pauses, fiddling with the lens on their camera. "My parents don't get me at all."

"You get to be whoever you want now that Stonebridge is behind us. We all do," I say, patting them on the leg. Skye nods their head, smiling so wide I think their face might split.

Across the table, Emily sits in Tony's lap and squishes a wad of icing over his nose. They've apparently been on and off since New Year's.

When The Incisors change songs, Tristan searches the venue until his eyes land on me. He races across the dance floor, laughing.

"Can I have this dance?" he asks, waggling his finger as "(I've Had) The Time of My Life" comes on over the speakers.

I roll my eyes before he pulls me off my chair and into his arms.

"You look adorable," he says, commenting on my emerald suit as he spins on his heels to walk behind me.

"I thought my leather jacket could use a vacation tonight," I say, winking. Tristan spins me out to the side.

By the middle of the song, a crowd has gathered along the edge of the dance floor to watch as I lift Tristan off the ground and spin him slowly in the air.

Ma lets out a holler from the head table, her cheeks rosy from too much wine. She signals frantically for Hayden to race over and take a picture.

"Well done," Tristan cheers with the audience as I lower him back down.

"I've had practice," I say, shrugging.

As I look around the dance floor and see Brad and Tony laugh with the photography club, I realize they're going to figure it out eventually. We all will. It won't happen overnight, life doesn't work like that, but sooner or later, we'll think back on this moment and see it for what it was—a bunch of friends learning to be themselves, together.

I lean over and kiss Tristan.

Who would have thought?

I was a punk.

He did ballet.

But together, we discovered there's so much more to us than the labels we give ourselves.

ACKNOWLEDGMENTS

As Sophia Petrillo in *The Golden Girls* would say, Picture it! The Open Road. 2019. My fiancé and I—along with our Norwegian best friend—were driving across the continental US on a five-week road trip home to Canada after a yearlong stint working at Walt Disney World in Orlando, Florida (shout-out to the Epcot Epics and the 2018–2019 CRP cohort). Somewhere between the red rocks of Sedona and the neon lights of Las Vegas, "Sk8er Boi" by Avril Lavigne started playing on the radio, and I was transported back to a time when I was afraid to sing my truth out loud. It was on that sweltering October afternoon, in the passenger seat of my beat-up Mazda 3, that I fleshed out the plot of what became the book you now hold in your hands.

In setting out to write Wes's story, I never could've imagined where this journey would take me nor the people I'd meet along the way. To kick off my world tour of gratitude, I would like to thank my editor, Alexa Wejko, for chipping away at my original manuscript until we uncovered the beating heart of

Wes and Tristan's story. There are no words to describe what you mean to me other than you gave me the confidence I needed to believe in my dreams.

A huge thank you to everyone at Soho Teen: Janine Agro, Bronwen Hruska, Rachel Kowal, Erica Loberg, Rudy Martinez, and Steven Tran for inherently understanding this angry little gay book and for putting up with my punk-pop-loving heart. To Diberkato for creating a character art of Wes that was so arresting it literally took my breath away and to my copy editor, Adam Mongaya, for showing me how to properly use commas (lol).

I would not be here today without the invaluable feedback of my beta readers over the years. Chelsea Balbosa, Demetra Barbacuta, Kaila Butler, Claire Doubroff, Noël Keyes, Lindsay Marshall, and Amanda Schaufele, thank you for being my OG hype team and for letting me down gently when something wasn't quite right. You all gave me the courage to keep going.

A special shout-out to Becky Albertalli, Robbie Couch, Eric Geron, Jason June, Liz Lawson, Rachael Lippincott, Amber McBride, Lynn Painter, Steven Salvatore, Adam Sass, Robby Weber, and Xiran Jay Zhao for your stunning blurbs. The publishing industry can feel so far away at times that I cannot begin to tell you what it meant to have your support.

To Aaron Austin, Johnee Ayson, Greg Balentin, Meghan Caprez, Rhys Clowes, Jacob Demlow, Margo Fink, Lewis Hughes, Cait Jacobs, Eytan Kessler, Simone Richter, Rae Saint Louis, Rachel Sergeant, Rosie Talbot, and so many more for helping with my cover reveal and allowing me a moment to connect with your fans. I am eternally grateful to you all for hyping up this little debut that could.

To my friends and family, but especially the Nerada Family 5, thank you for always encouraging me even though you never quite understood how I could pump out a novel's worth of words (trust me, I still have no idea). Roxie is in the first pages of this story for a reason. And while Wes's parents are as far from my own as they come, it is in the quiet moments between Wes and his Ma that I find the beauty of our relationship lies.

None of this would have happened without Beth Phelan and the entire #DVPit team. To Morgan Rogers and Kathleen S. Allen for helping me solidify the perfect pitches and to the #writingcommunity for rallying behind me that fateful day in 2020. Please never stop sending me "Sk8er Boi" memes, they truly give me life!

A heartfelt thank you to Eileen Cook for imparting her wisdom over the years and for being the first real-life author I called a friend. Kathleen Ortiz, thank you for being the first agent I ever pitched to at the Surrey International Writers' Conference with my origin story about the Wicked Queen from Snow White. I'm so sorry I put you through that. 🫠

Writing is such a solitary act, but I would not be where I am today without the writing friends who kept me afloat; Jayme Bean, K.J. Brower, Tamara Cole, Pamela Delupio, Bryant Dill, Chad Harper, Matthew Hubbard, Nick Stine, Aaron Olátunjie, Akure Phénix, and the BC KidLit Crew, thank you for always being there when I needed a shoulder to lean on. To Bethany Hensel for workshopping my query letter in those early days while simultaneously screaming about River Phoenix in my DMs; and to Allison Mitchell for helping me go through my manuscript in a mad dash to get it ready for agents. You mean the world to me.

An extra-large soprano pizza to my fellow members of the Twitter Quartet (Diana Carolina, Elba Luz, and Amanda Woody) for always making me laugh; to Trae Hawkins for the most beautiful sensitivity reader letter when I needed it most; and to Jordan Doak for somehow capturing me at my best with my author photo. To my wonderful colleagues at Industrial Light & Magic, Lucasfilm, and Disney, thank you for supporting me on this journey. I cannot believe I get to show up to work each and every day and surround myself with the creativity and legacy of our films.

To Rena Rossner, thank you for taking a chance on me and to Maria Vicente & the P.S. Literary Agency, I cannot wait to see what we achieve together.

A huge thank you to all the teachers, librarians, and indie booksellers for getting LGBTQIA+ stories into the hands of teens who need them most, even when laws are being written to ban you from doing so. You truly are the heroes of every story.

Tim, this story and the ones that will hopefully follow, would not be possible without you. Thank you for listening to me ramble on about the hundreds of ideas swimming around in my head (and for deciphering which ones to hang on to and which ones to abandon). Thank you for always being there for me, and for not freaking out when I first told you that, before I looked for a job upon returning to Canada, I had a story to tell. You are, and forever will be, my greatest love.

And finally, to the readers, especially those belonging to the LGBTQIA+ community (however that may look like for you). Thank you for coming on this journey with me as I shined a light on a character who doesn't normally get to tell his story. I hope you didn't mind when I cranked up the volume and let my voice soar within its pages. After all, I'm making up for lost time. ♥